CHRISTOPHER BUSH
THE CASE OF THE EXTRA GRAVE

CHRISTOPHER BUSH was born Charlie Christmas Bush in Norfolk in 1885. His father was a farm labourer and his mother a milliner. In the early years of his childhood he lived with his aunt and uncle in London before returning to Norfolk aged seven, later winning a scholarship to Thetford Grammar School.

As an adult, Bush worked as a schoolmaster for 27 years, pausing only to fight in World War One, until retiring aged 46 in 1931 to be a full-time novelist. His first novel featuring the eccentric Ludovic Travers was published in 1926, and was followed by 62 additional Travers mysteries. These are all to be republished by Dean Street Press.

Christopher Bush fought again in World War Two, and was elected a member of the prestigious Detection Club.

He died in 1973.

CHRISTOPHER BUSH

THE CASE OF THE EXTRA GRAVE

With an introduction
by Curtis Evans

DEAN STREET PRESS

INTRODUCTION

Rosalind. If it be true that good wine needs no bush [i.e., advertising], 'tis true that a good play needs no epilogue. Yet to good wine, they do use good bushes, and good plays prove the better by the help of good epilogues.

–SHAKESPEARE, Epilogue, *As You Like It*

THE decade of the 1960s saw the sun finally begin to set on that storied generation which between the First and Second World Wars gave us detective fiction's Golden Age. Taking account of both deaths and retirements, by the late Sixties only a bare half-dozen pre-World War Two members of the Detection Club were still plying their deliciously deceptive craft: Agatha Christie, Anthony Gilbert (Lucy Beatrice Malleson), Gladys Mitchell, John Dickson Carr, Nicholas Blake and Christopher Bush, the subject of this introduction. Bush himself would pass away, at the age of eighty-seven, in 1973, having published, at the age of eighty-two, his sixty-third Ludovic Travers detective novel, *The Case of the Prodigal Daughter*, in the United Kingdom in the spring of 1968.

In the United States Bush's final detective novel did not appear until late November 1969, about four months after the horrific Manson murders in the tarnished Golden State of California. Implicating the triple terrors of sex, drugs and rock and roll (not to mention almost inconceivably bestial violence), the Manson slayings could not have strayed farther from the whimsically escapist "death as a game" aesthetic of Golden Age of detective fiction. Increasingly in the decade capable of producing psychedelic psychopaths like Charles Manson and his "family," the few remaining survivors of the Golden Age of detective fiction increasingly deemed themselves men and women far out of time. In his detective fiction John Dickson Carr, an incurable romantic, prudently beat a retreat from the present into the pleasanter pages of the past, setting his tales in bygone historical eras where he felt vastly more at home. With varying success Agatha Christie made a brave effort to stay abreast of the times (*Third Girl, Endless Night*), but ultimately her strivings to understand what was going on around her collapsed into the utter incoherence of *Passenger to Frankfurt* and *Postern of Fate*, by general consensus the worst mystery novels that Dame Agatha ever put down on paper.

In his detective fiction Christopher Bush, who was not quite two years older than Christie, managed rather better than the Queen of Crime to keep up with all the unsettling goings-on around him, while never forswearing the Golden Age article of faith that the primary purpose of a crime writer is pleasingly to puzzle his/her readers. And, in contrast with Christie and Carr, Bush knew when it was time to lay down his pen (or turn off his dictation machine, as the case may be), thereby allowing him to make his exit from the stage on a comparatively high note. Indeed, Christopher Bush's concluding baker's dozen of detective novels, which he published between 1957 and 1968 (and which have now been reprinted, after more than a half-century, by Dean Street Press), makes a generally fine epilogue, or coda, to the author's impressive corpus of crime fiction, which first began to see the light of day way back in the jubilant Jazz Age. These are, readers will find, "good bushes" (to punningly borrow from Shakespeare), providing them with ample intelligent detective entertainment as Bush's longtime series sleuth Ludovic Travers, in the luminous twilight of his career, makes his final forays into ingenious criminal investigation.

*

In the last thirteen Ludovic Travers mystery novels, Travers' *entrée* to his cases continues to come through his ownership of the Broad Street Detective Agency. Besides Travers we also regularly encounter his elegant wife, Bernice (although sometimes his independent-minded spouse is away on excursions of her own), his proverbially loyal secretary, Bertha Munney, his top Broad Street op, Hallows (another one named French, presumably inspired by Bush's late Detection Club colleague Freeman Wills Crofts, pops up occasionally), John Hill of the United Assurance Agency, who brings Travers many of his cases, and Scotland Yard's Inspector Jewle and Sergeant Matthews, who after the first of these final novels, *The Case of the Treble Twist* (in the U.S. *Triple Twist*), are promoted, respectively, to Superintendent and Inspector. (The Yard's ex-Superintendent George Wharton, now firmly retired from any form of investigative work whatsoever, is mentioned just once by Ludo, when, in *The Case of the Dead Man Gone,* he passingly imparts that he and Wharton recently had lunch together.)

For all practical purposes Travers, who during the Golden Age was a classic gentleman amateur snooper like Philo Vance and Lord Peter Wimsey, now functions fully as a professional private eye—although one, to be sure, who is rather posher than the rest. While some reviewers referred to Travers as England's Philip Marlowe, in fact he little resembles the general run of love and leave 'em/hate and beat 'em brand of brutish American P.I.'s, favoring a nice cup of coffee (a post-war change from tea), a good pipe and the occasional spot of sherry to the frequent snatches of liquor and cigarettes favored by most of his American brethren and remaining faithful to his spouse despite encountering a succession of sexy women, not all of them, shall we say, virtuously inclined.

This was a formula which throughout the period maintained a devoted audience on both sides of the Atlantic consisting, one surmises, of readers (including crime writers Anthony Berkeley, Nicholas Blake and the late Alan Hunter, creator of Inspector George Gently) who preferred their detectives something less than hard-boiled. Travers himself sneers at the hugely popular (and psychotically violent) postwar American private eye Mike Hammer, commenting of an American couple in *The Case of the Treble Twist*: "She was a woman of considerable culture; his ran about as far as Mickey Spillane" [a withering reference to Mike Hammer's creator]. Yet despite his manifest disdain for Mike Hammer, an ugly American if ever there were one, Christopher Bush and his wife Florence in the spring of 1957 had traveled to New York aboard the RMS *Queen Elizabeth,* and references by him to both the United States and Canada became more frequent in the books which followed this trip.

Certainly *The Case of the Treble Twist* (1957) features tough customers and an exceptionally cruel murder, yet it is also one of Bush's most ingeniously contrived cases from the Fifties, full of charm, treacherous deception and, yes, plenty of twists, including one that is a real sockaroo (to borrow, as Bush occasionally did, from American idiom). Similarly clever is *The Case of the Running Man* (1958), which draws, as several earlier Bush books had, on the author's profound love and knowledge of antiques. By this time Bush and his wife, their coffers having burgeoned from the proceeds of his successful mysteries, resided in the quaint medieval market town of Lavenham, Suffolk at the Great House, a splendidly decorated fourteenth-century structure with an elegant Georgian-era façade which he and Florence purchased in 1953 and resided in until their deaths. The dashing author, whom in 1967 *Chicago Tribune* mystery reviewer Alice Crombie swooningly dubbed "one of the handsomest mystery writers on either side of the Channel or Atlantic," also drove a Jaguar, beloved by James Bond films of late, well into his eighties.

The Case of the Running Man includes that Golden Age detective fiction staple, a family tree, but more originally the novel features as a major character a black American man, Sam, the devoted chauffeur of the wealthy murder victim. Sam, who reminds Ludovic Travers of Rochester, "Jack Benny's factotum of television and radio," is an interesting and sincerely treated individual, although as Anthony Boucher amusingly pronounced at the time in the *New York Times Book Review*, he speaks "a dialect never heard by mortal ear"—an odd compounding of "American Negro" and London cockney.

The Case of the Careless Thief (1959) takes Ludo to Sandbeach, "the Blackpool of the South Coast," as the American jacket blurb puts it, with "a dozen hotels, a race track, a dog track, a music hall and two enormous dance halls." Anthony Boucher deemed this hard-hitting, tricky tale, which draws to strong effect on contemporary events in England, "one of Ludovic Travers' best cases." Likewise hard-hitting are *The Case of the Sapphire Brooch* (1960) and *The Case of the Extra Grave* (1961), complex tales of murderous mésalliances with memorably grim conclusions. The plot of *The Case of the Dead Man Gone* (1961) topically involves refugee relief groups, while *The Case of the Heavenly Twin* (1963) opens with a case of a creative criminal couple forging American Express Travelers Checks, concerning which Americans of a certain age will recall actor Karl Malden sternly enjoining, in a long-running television advertising campaign: "Don't leave home without them." In contrast with many of his crime writing contemporaries (judging from the tone of their work), Bush actually learned to watch and enjoy television, although in *The Case of The Three-Ring Puzzle*, a tale of violently escalating intrigue, Travers dryly references Scottish philosopher Thomas Carlyle's famous observation that England's population consisted of "mostly fools" when he comments: "I guess he wasn't too far out at that. But rather remarkable an estimate perhaps, considering that in his day there were no television commercials."

Of Bush's final five Ludovic Travers detective novels, published between 1964 and 1968, when the Western World, in the eyes of many, was going from whimsically mod to utterly mad, the best are, in my estimation, the cases of *The Jumbo Sandwich* (1965), *The Good Employer* (1966) and *The Prodigal Daughter* (1968). In *Sandwich* a crisp case of a defrauded (and jilted) gentry lady friend of Ludo's metamorphoses into a smorgasbord of, as the American book jacket puts it, "blackmail, black magic, a black sheep, and murder." It all culminates in a confrontation on a lonely Riviera beach in France, setting of some of Ludovic Travers' earliest cases, between Ludo and a desperate killer, in which Bernice plays an unexpectedly active part. Ludo again travels to France in the highly classic *Employer*, which draws most engagingly on the sleuth's (and the author's) dabbling in the world of art and is dedicated to his distinguished Lavenham artist friends, the couple Reginald and Rosalie Brill, who resided next door to Bush and his wife at the fourteenth-century Little Hall, then an art student hostel for which the Brills served as guardians. In *The Guardian* Francis Iles (aka Golden Age crime writer Anthony Berkeley) pronounced that *Employer* represented Bush "at his most ingenious."

Finally, in *Daughter* Travers finds himself tasked with recovering the absconded teenage offspring of domineering Dora Marport, sober-sided head of the organization Home and Family, which is righteously devoted to "the fostering, so to speak, of family life as the stoutest bulwark against the encroachment of ever-more numerous hostile forces: sex and violence in literature, films and on television; pornography generally, and the erosion of responsibility and the capability for sacrifice by the welfare state." Can Travers, a Great War veteran who made his debut in detective fiction in 1926, bridge the generation gap in late-Sixties London? Ludo may prefer Bach to the Beatles, but in this, the last of his recorded cases, he proves more "with it" than one might have expected. All in all, *Daughter* makes a rewarding finish to one of the longest-running and most noteworthy sleuth series in British detective fiction.

Curtis Evans

1

HALLOWS CAN'T REMEMBER

LET me say at the very outset that our meeting with the man who called himself Harry Rodes would be classed by most people as a queer coincidence: in view, that is, of what was to happen later. But I'm something of a crank about coincidences. I believe with Oscar Wilde that the only queer thing about them is not that they happen, but that they don't.

In all my life, for instance, I can think back to only two coincidences that might be called queer. One was some years ago when I was walking along Shaftesbury Avenue and the sight of some theatre or other made me suddenly recall a boy who'd been something of a friend of mine at school, and who'd always asserted that he was going to be an actor. Just as I was wondering what had become of him after all those years, and at the same time paying less attention to where I was going, I bumped into a man. You're right. It was the man of whom I'd been thinking.

But look at it like this. There must have been dozens of people with whom I'd lost touch, and at any time when they happened to be in my mind I might have run into any one of them, provided, of course, that instead of turning left, shall we say. I'd turned right The whole thing is shot through and through with even more hypotheses than you'll find in the guarded predictions of a sports writer, who even then, as you've probably experienced, generally manages to be wrong. Not that I want to argue the point at more length. You're a crank about some things and I'm one when it comes to coincidences. Let's leave it like that. Let's just start at the morning of Monday the 11th of January.

Up to the previous day the weather had been wet and reasonably mild, but then the wind shifted to the north-east and later there was snow. I'd like you to think back to that change of weather, if only because it's vital to this story. It even made a difference in the matter of Harry Rodes. If there hadn't been a hard frost that Monday morning, he'd have been merely one of the scores of pedestrians whom we'd met or overtaken in Mortimer Street.

Hallows is our senior operative at the Broad Street Detective Agency. When I acquired it—and that was a long time ago—he'd been their best man for some years and it didn't take me long to find out why. His speciality is arson, and that morning I'd been with him while he inspected some premises that had been gutted during the night in Waring Street. It was an automatic check on behalf of United Assurance, by whom we're retained, and after consultation with the City expert we were absolutely sure that faulty wiring had been the cause of the whole affair. Hallows, I should add, was off duty and had had to make a special journey from his home in Croydon, and the only reason he was going back with me to the Agency instead of going back home, was that he would have to write a brief report.

Waring Street's only about ten minutes' walk from Broad Street, and we took the nearest way and that was via Mortimer Street. I don't know if you've seen those narrow City streets in the morning, but if you have, you may wonder how traffic ever manages to move at all. Single parking is bad enough, but when a van happens to be unloading on the other side, then it's just chaos. And that morning both road and pavement were slippery. The film of uncleared snow had melted the previous afternoon, and during the night it had frozen hard. I'm six foot three, which means a pretty long way to fall, so my walk was more of a shuffle. Hallows is five-nine and he was watching each step as he moved. My besetting sin is an insatiable curiosity, so I had one eye on my feet and the other on my surroundings. That's why I saw just what happened.

On the right, where we were walking, the street was jammed with parked cars. A tallish man in a dark overcoat and black bowler was thinking o(crossing to the other side and he stood tentatively for a moment in the four feet or so of space between two cars, peering both ways till the road was clear. He took a step forward and just then a car came pretty smartly round the bend and almost struck him as it passed. As he nipped back, his feet shot from under him. His head struck the rear bumper of a parked Austin, and there he lay in the narrowish space between the two cars.

I nearly fell myself as I stepped down and in. I managed to straddle him and lift his head. Blood was beginning to seep through a small cut on the back of his skull. Hallows picked up his hat and was asking me what had happened and then the man began to stir. His eyes blinked and then he looked at me. An extraordinary expression came over his face. It wasn't fear and it wasn't anger. It was something of both. I was still bending over him and his hand went suddenly out and, as he pushed me away, he was getting to bis feet.

"Take it easy," I told him. "You've had a—"

"Here, what's the game?"

His eyes were darting round and then he backed to the pavement. As Hallows inadvertently barred his way he had the look of a man who's been cornered. And then suddenly he was feeling his overcoat pockets and at once his whole expression changed. A sort of satisfied grin came over his face.

"I'm sorry, gents. I thought for a moment I'd been coshed."

"You remember?" I said. "You stepped back and slipped up and the back of your head hit that bumper. I happened to see it That's all."

He was about six feet tall, clean-shaven, sallow-faced and with deep lines running towards the mouth corners from a beak of a nose. He looked both ways along the street before he spoke. He needn't have worried. People were too busy watching their steps.

"I remember," he said. "Reckon I ought to've been a bit more careful."

Hallows brushed the hat with his handkerchief and gave it to him.

"If I were you I'd nip into a chemist's and have some plaster on that cut."

"I'm all right," he said, and felt the back of his skull. "Don't think it's anything much." He hesitated for just a moment. "Well, I'm much obliged to you two gentlemen. Think I'll be on my way."

This time he didn't try to cross. We moved to the pavement behind him.

"Queer sort of bird," I said. "Why the devil should he think we'd coshed him?"

Hallows suddenly held my arm. "No great hurry about that report, sir. Just want to try something out."

He moved off in the direction the man had gone. I waited a moment and then moved on towards Broad Street. That sudden back-tracking by Hallows was making the whole thing even more curious. I've said I've an insatiable curiosity, but maybe in my profession it's more an asset than a vice and I was wondering what Hallows had noticed that had made him suddenly stop in his tracks and decide to start tailing that man.

The pubs had just opened so I went into the Golden Pheasant and ordered a double whisky, hot, and took it over to a table by the roaring fire. I'd got chilled to my bones through that brief errand of mercy, and as soon as I felt thawed again I began thinking things over. "X", as I thought of him, was a man of about fifty. In that short, best mood of his there'd been something ingratiating: something almost patronising, too. But he'd wanted to get dear of us at the earliest possible moment. There'd been no offer of a drink, even a cup of coffee, and he hadn't even held out his hand.

I got my pipe going and began all over again. "X" had been a series of strange persons within the matter of a minute. As soon as he'd clapped eyes on me, he'd thought even in that one split second that I'd just coshed him and then came the realisation that he'd been robbed. A quick feel of his pockets and he knew that whatever he'd been carrying was still there. That had brought a quick resurgence of morale. For a second or two he'd been cock-a-hoop and then, just as suddenly, the suspicion had come back and he'd glanced apprehensively along the street.

I wondered if those quick changes of mood had been unusual after all. Suppose I'd been on my way to Hatton Garden with a parcel of diamonds in my outer overcoat pocket and that what bad happened to "X" had happened to me. Would my reactions have been the same? Maybe in those circumstances the very same. But that left out Hallows! Why should Hallows, in his own time, have decided to trail that man? What had he seen that I hadn't? And why should it be worth his time to do it? Hallows hasn't my enormous curiosity—or has he?—so why should he have let that report stand over and make a mystery out of a reasonably natural episode?

I didn't know, but there was one way to know—to let Hallows tell me about it himself. I finished my whisky and made my way back to Broad Street. I had another half-hour to wait before Hallows came in.

"What bug suddenly bit you?" I fired at him as he came through the door. "Did you know him, or something?"

"I did and I didn't," he told me. "You know how it is. I'm still dead certain I've seen him somewhere before. Probably a fair time ago, but I'm sure. It's worrying me."

I laughed. "The old curiosity bug. Well, draw up to the fire and make yourself comfortable."

He was still thinking things out as he stoked his pipe.

"It was funny, in a way," he said. "I knew him as soon as I saw his face, and for the life of me I couldn't place him or put a name to him or anything else. I just knew that I ought to know him and I had the feeling he was some kind of crook." He shook his head. "That's one of the things about getting older. You forget names. The other day I forgot the name of even my next-door neighbour."

"Older be damned!" I said. "You're only forty-five."

He shrugged his shoulders. "Maybe it's a sort of premature decay. But you know how it is. You forget a name so you start going through the alphabet Nine times out of ten it works, for me. You find out the initial letter the name has to begin with: say, a P. Every other letter strikes you as wrong. So you start from that, and before you know it the name comes back. This time it didn't. I couldn't even get an initial letter. All something kept telling me was that I ought to know him and that he was some sort of a crook. Other things helped, of course."

"Such as?"

He looked surprised. "You didn't notice his clothes?"

"I know what he was wearing. He looked at first rather like a City man of some sort—till he opened his mouth. What was it you noticed?"

"Well, that everything I saw was brand new. The hat-band was absolutely clean and the shoe soles hadn't even been scuffed. The overcoat was brand new, too. It almost had the smell of the shop."

"And you thought that was unusual?"

"Well, no," he said slowly. "Except that I was still wondering where I'd seen him. Then there was that business of thinking you'd coshed him, and how scared he was we'd taken whatever it was he had in his overcoat pocket."

"Yes," I said. "That means it was too big for an inside pocket. If it was all that valuable, he'd have had it in an inside pocket but it happened to be too big to go in. But what happened when you went after him? Did you pick him up?"

"Easy as pie. Mind you, he'd had a good look at me, so I didn't dare operate very close. And every now and again he'd have a good look round or take a look in a shop window. Then he turned into Lombard Street and you know what that's like. Couldn't get nearer than fifty yards. All the same. I did mark him down as going into the City Trust Company's place."

"That's a safe deposit company!"

"That's right," he said. "My guess is he was depositing whatever it was he had in that overcoat pocket. And I think he was a new customer or be wouldn't have been in so long. Seventeen minutes I made it."

"That's dead right. It must be. Wonder what it was."

He gave a little grunt.

"Heaven knows," he said. "My guess is that it was something he'd got hold of that someone else wanted badly. That remark of his about being coshed just slipped out. And he was taking precautions against being followed."

He paused for a moment. "That's why I lost him. He must have spotted me after all."

That was queer. When Hallows gets on a man's tail, it isn't once in fifty times that he's shaken off. I told him so.

"Maybe I wasn't taking it all that seriously," he said. "Also he'd had a real good look at me. And there was nothing I could do to change my looks. At any rate, this is bow it was. I was behind a parked car in Lombard Street and I watched him walk by and then hop one of the buses waiting for the light. He was downstairs and I went on top and that's when he may have spotted me. At any rate we went on to the foot of Ludgate Hill and got held up again and I saw him get off. I got off, too. Just a matter of half a minute, but there wasn't a sign of him. And you know what I think he did? Just moved on to the next bus in the queue and nipped aboard. Easy, wasn't it?"

"Maybe," I said. "All the same it makes him a pretty shrewd customer."

Hallows knocked out his pipe and got to his feet. "Well, it's helped to pass a morning. And my own time. Hope I run into our friend again. You never know."

"Pass the word round the staff," I said. "I'd like to know more about him myself. And you might remember his name. If he's really up to some kind of hanky-panky, we might do worse than pass a tip on to the Yard."

I rang for Bertha, our maid-of-all-work, to bring in the necessary form and Hallows got down to his report. It was a matter of only a few minutes and he'd almost finished it when Bertha buzzed through.

"Mr. Hill of United Assurance on the line."

"Right," I said. "Put him through."

John Hill is managing director. We've worked for him for years and he's become an old friend. That's why I wasn't too perturbed when I guessed that something must have gone wrong with that Waring Street fire job. I was wrong.

We wished each other a Happy New Year and had a word about the weather. It wasn't for me to mention business, but I didn't have long to wait He asked if I'd be free in the course of the next day or two.

"Absolutely free," I told him. "Anything special on your mind?"

"Yes," he said. "Something rather unusual in several ways. And personal. So could you see me here at ten-fifteen on, say, Thursday morning? That'll give us time to go into various things beforehand. And you might like to bring Hallows."

"He's with me now, making out the report on that Waring Street fire. Like to give us something to chew on beforehand?"

"Afraid I can't. What I'd like is to see you privately as I said, at ten-fifteen. I'm hoping to arrange for interested parties to be here at eleven, and what you and I work out in the interval will determine just what course of action I recommend when they join us. I'm sorry but that's all I can say."

"You're the boss," I said. "Till Thursday morning then. At a quarter-past ten."

2

THE MARRIED MAN

It was bitterly cold that Thursday morning. Snow had fallen the previous afternoon and the night had brought a hard frost To be whisked up from that morning's weather to the warm comfort of Hill's room was almost as if we'd been transported clean out of England.

Not only was that room part of the central heating system, it also had a fireplace with a real, honest-to-God fire. All that was needed, as I told John Hill, was some sprigs of holly and a couple of Yule logs.

"I thought we'd be here rather than the office," he told us, "because one of the people we'll be seeing is a great-uncle of mine who's well over eighty. I rang him a few minutes ago about the advisability of his venturing out, but he insisted." He smiled. "As a matter of fact he was quite indignant. Make yourselves comfortable. Coffee should be in almost at once."

Hill is easily the best man I know for putting you wise about a case. He's concise, lucid and, above all, patient. He can spot in a moment when you're the least bit out of touch and he'll only resume when he's sure you're with him so far. During an assignment I've never had to excuse some error of my own by saying he'd forgotten to inform me of this or that. Hill tells you what he knows you ought to know and he makes sure you know it. After that it's up to you.

"You've heard of a firm trading as C. T. Haddowe?" he asked us. We hadn't.

"There was just a chance you might," he said. "They're at 36 Walton Street, just off Old Bond Street. The business was founded well over a hundred years ago. For some years now they've dealt principally in the antique side of the jewellery trade: silver mostly. One of those unpretentious businesses you don't hear much about but which do very well indeed in their way. Stop me, Mr. Hallows, if I'm going too fast for you."

It's Hallows who always takes shorthand notes. I concentrate on general impressions.

"Now for the principals," Hill went on. "C.T. Haddowe is my great-uncle, which gives me a personal interest in the case. He's now eighty-four and retired only eight years ago. His son, who would eventually have taken his place, was killed in a plane crash ten years ago. His nephew, Julian Matching, was groomed for the job and took over when C.T.—everyone calls him C.T.—finally retired. Julian is now fifty-eight.

"Julian is the pivot. I might call it of the whole affair, so I'd like you to hear a lot more about him. His father was a feckless sort of character who never did a hard day's work in his life: he just dabbled in things: painting, poetry, that sort of thing. He died when Julian was at Winchester. The mother was the dominating influence: a matriarch with a family of one. As far as she was concerned, Julian might never have grown up, and the trouble was that he accepted all that. It was always intended, for instance, that he should go into his uncle's business, but I happen to know that he secretly wanted to go in for law. He didn't. Mother saw to that I doubt if he even dared protest. But don't mistake me. Julian always bad brains. His going into the business was rather like when you have to buy a new suit and you know you'll hate wearing the damn thing, and then time slips by and, before you know it, it's sort of part of you and finally you hate to part with the jacket even when it's getting a bit frayed. In other words. Julian got to know that business inside and out. C.T. wouldn't have retired if be hadn't been certain of that.

"Now for the business itself. Over the years it has accumulated, if I may call it that, a solid clientele. It has customers from the Americas and India, and indeed from all over the world who drop in when they're in London. It has its collectors who leave commissions for things like Cromwellian silver or Victorian jewellery which might be acquired privately or in the sale rooms. It's an unpretentious business as you'll see for yourselves. Just one display window showing very few pieces, a smallish showroom, workroom upstairs and the usual offices inside. There are two salesmen, both a bit elderly, a general man and a craftsman, and Julian, of course, has a secretary-receptionist, a very charming woman of—well, the late thirties. Her name is Lindman. Jean Lindman."

To give Hallows time, he lighted another cigarette and passed me the box. I said I'd stick to my pipe.

"Well. I think that gives you the general picture," he went on. "Now we have to look more closely at Julian. The family home—he still lives there—is a Victorian monstrosity of a house, known for heaven knows what reason as Grange House, and it's just through the village of Aldways, near Sevenoaks. I was there once or twice as a young man and it always gave me the honors. There was a sort of Victorian repression about it, let alone being cluttered up with God-knows-what. Old Aunt Maud, as I had to call her, simply venerated that ridiculous husband of hers. Rather like Victoria and Albert in a way. Everything of his had to be kept after he died. He'd frittered away most of the money, by the way, and it was Julian who had to keep the place going. There was only one family retainer, an elderly cook, and various general maids who came and went, and a part-time gardener. And then, nearly three years ago. Aunt Maud died, and there was Julian, standing far the very first time on his own two legs." He paused for a moment. "Having heard what you've heard, what effect do you think that had on him?"

I laughed. "You've got me. The obvious thing is that having lived for fifty-five years in a groove, he'd simply have to keep in that groove. The less obvious is that he'd react violently. He'd cut loose."

"What do you think, Mr. Hallows?"

"He'd definitely cut loose. He probably went haywire, as they say. Otherwise, what are we doing here?"

Hill looked positively startled.

"That's a remarkable piece of deduction. As a matter of fact you're right." He smiled wryly. "Looking back on it now it doesn't seem quite the general upheaval it was then. His marriage, for instance. He'd never looked twice at a woman in the whole of his life, and then, only about six months after his mother died, he was married. And when I say it was the last woman his mother would have picked. I'm putting it mildly. These are the facts. I've been at some pains since I first rang you to leant them. But only some of the facts. I shall probably be relying on you for the complete picture, but this is what I actually know. Her name was Mary Hyson and her professional name Moira Delane. Julian was entertaining a client, or it might have been the other way about, at Frascoli's Restaurant, and this girl—she was then only twenty-one—was a vocalist for the dance band. I gathered it was the client who was smitten with the girl and got her to come to the table for a drink. It doesn't matter. Julian married her three months later at a Registry Office. C.T. wasn't too well at the time and couldn't be there. Jean Lindman and I were the witnesses. The honeymoon was at Monte Carlo."

He stubbed out the cigarette and glanced round at the bracket clock. We still had about ten minutes.

"What I'm telling you now is not altogether factual. Some of it is general impressions, but I wasn't asked to Grange House till after the couple had got settled in. The change staggered me. It was as if an enormous vacuum cleaner had been through the place. All that clutter and frippery bad gone: in its place redecoration, new furnishings, television set, radiogram, cocktail bar—everything. Old Lucy Milford, the cook, had been retired at last, and a married couple of the name of Gambet had been installed. You might say the whole place had been streamlined. It was positively startling.

"But the wife, Moira: you'll want to know about her. A terrific looker, if I may say so, and a wonderful figure. A blonde, and if I may also say so, pretty sexy. The last time I saw her was about six months ago. I was lunching with our Glasgow man at the Cafe Royal and I caught sight of her with a youngish man at the downstair bar. I didn't speak. She was wearing a magnificent mink coat, even though it was summer, so she was probably trying to impress somebody. I did know, by the way, that Julian had bought her a Jaguar sports. And given her some pretty expensive jewellery."

"And now?" I said, slipping into the pause.

"Impressions," he said. "Just impressions. I think he's still madly infatuated with her and she's been playing him fast and loose. Spiritually, if I may put it like that, there's nothing shared between them. She's just vulgarity with an acquired veneer. And she's twenty-three to his fifty-eight Two or three times during the last six months I've had reason to ring Julian—they've always insured with us—and from what I deduced she was spending quite a lot of time with a friend with whom she used to share an apartment."

The buzzer went. I could hear the secretary's voice announce the arrival of C.T. Haddowe and Julian Matching.

"Bring them straight in, Margaret," Hill said. "Don't forget the cake and sherry, and I think we might all like some more coffee."

As soon as I clapped eyes on old Haddowe I knew I'd seen him somewhere before, and then I knew I hadn't: it was only that he was like the pictures of Little Nell's grandfather in the Dickens I'd read in my youth. The slight arthritis in a knee made him walk with a stick, but mentally he was alert enough. He was slightly bald on top but silvery hair hung over his ears and the nape of his neck. His broad shoulders were slightly stooped. Hill was obviously fond of him, and he of Hill. You could tell that by how the faces lit up and the long hand-clasp.

"You shouldn't have come," Hill said reproachfully.

"Nonsense, nonsense," Haddowe told him amusedly. "I hate being thought decrepit Took me a little longer than usual to get here, that's all."

Matching was obviously nervous. He was about five-foot ten, and very erect: almost as if he'd determined to be so. When I was closer to him I saw that the grey by his temples had been touched up with dye. There was nothing particular about his looks that would have singled him out. He might have been a reasonably prosperous lawyer, or banker, or doctor: he had just that touch of Winchester manners behind which you were aware of a certain aloofness.

Hill introduced us. He said we were all friends and what talk we had might be regarded almost as a family conference. So there wasn't any great hurry. Haddowe had a slice of the special plum cake with a glass of sherry, and the rest of us had coffee, or more coffee. Hill went out of his way to mention that I was Halstead and Cambridge, a planned bit of snobbery that definitely yanked me out of the non-U class. Hallows was described as my confidential secretary. And so at last to whatever business was really on hand.

"Now, Julian," Hill began, "I know this is going to be difficult for you, but you have to go over everything that happened last week-end, then we can decide on a line of action. Perhaps you'd better begin with what I might call actual business—that matter of the jewellery."

Julian hated it. His tone was stilted and had a hint of aggression. Before he'd got very far I knew it for a kind of protective armour. If he'd kept to the bare details it might have been better, but he kept harking back and wandering away. I'll spare you all that.

The jewellery that Hill had mentioned consisted of three pieces purchased at a Sotheby's late autumn sale—a three-stoned diamond ring insured for two thousand five hundred, a diamond necklace for seven thousand, and two especially fine drop-earrings, *en suite*, for two thousand eight hundred pounds the pair. No difficulty in reselling was anticipated when buyers began coming to London in the spring. But the firm didn't have to wait that long. On the previous Friday, January the 8th, Julian was rung by an American, a Martin

J. Hamstall, a wealthy Texan. Hamstall said he'd been recommended by a friend who'd been at that sale and, if the jewellery hadn't been sold, he'd like to acquire it. He was at the moment in Scotland but on the Monday he'd be at the Regalia, Brighton. Julian agreed to see him there at two o'clock on the Monday, with the jewellery. A price was quoted and as good as agreed.

There was nothing unusual about all that, but Julian did take one small precaution. Later that day he rang the Regalia, who confirmed that rooms had been booked for a Martin J. Hamstall, and his daughter, and that they'd be arriving at lunch time on the Monday. So Julian informed his secretary, took the jewellery from the safe, put it in his overcoat pocket and went home. On the Monday he'd go direct from there to Brighton. At Grange House he locked the jewellery in his study safe. It was at that point that Hill apparently thought that Julian was in need of a breather. I didn't know it till later, but the hard part—for Julian—was still to come. That was why he was to divulge that the jewellery was missing. That was the detonator to set the real and explosive stuff off. Not, I airily thought, that I didn't know what that story was to be. The American, of course, was a trickster, and at the Regalia, Matching had fallen clean into a trap. That's what I guessed, and never in my life had a guess been so utterly wrong.

But to get back to the moment when Hill made the interruption.

"May we leave that part of the story just there, for the moment?" was what he said. "That jewellery's missing, as we shall hear, so may I say a word about insurance liability? Or should Julian go on with the story from the more personal point of view? What do you think, uncle?"

Old Haddowe frowned for a moment in thought "I think that Mr.—I'm sorry, but I've forgotten your name."

"Travers, sir. Ludovic Travers."

"Of course, of course. What I think is that Mr. Travers should hear things as a whole. Let's deal with any insurance problems later. Is that how you see it, Julian? Doesn't matter a bit that John and I have to hear it all over again."

So that was it, I thought. That interlude had been just a bit too theatrical: probably arranged when Hill had rung Haddowe earlier that morning. What I couldn't make out was why Julian should be so chary of admitting he'd fallen into that swindling trap. What I had to be doing, as you've known, was to feel my way as that morning unfolded and duly file each piece of information, however minute, and that interruption had sent things off at rather a queer tangent. That's why I was watching Julian far more closely when he did go on with his story.

Again I have to edit it. He found it pretty tough going and it wasn't hard for old hands like Hallows and myself to know that he skidded over quite a few things and gave undue prominence to others. He flushed and he stammered and he blurted, and I doubt if he was aware of anything except the need to convince, and generally the one he was trying to convince was just himself. When I'd heard that story I was sorry for him. I even thought him a better man. A fool, perhaps, but aren't we all? No wonder that what he'd needed from us was a tranquilliser: anything to give a hope of a happy ending.

Julian Matching came home, then, on that Friday night and he put the jewellery into the study safe, but it wasn't quite the same home. A great change had taken place on the Thursday. His wife had sacked Robert and Eva Gambet, the married couple, and given them a month's wages in lieu of notice. The house had been her province and, though Julian had been pretty upset, there was little he could do. Moira Matching had given two reasons: that the couple had persistently been insolent and that they'd always spied on her. By way of a palliative she'd induced Lucy Milford, the old cook-retainer, to lend a hand till a new couple could be engaged. Julian, in other words, would have someone to cook his meals. It was a situation which, he said, he'd had to accept.

On the Saturday Moira did nothing in particular: got up very late and then made a scratch lunch. She didn't appear again till the cook arrived. By half-past six the dinner had been cooked, and Lucy Milford left when there was nothing to do but put it on the table. Her cottage was about half a mile away and Julian drove her home in his Humber. The meal was ready when he got back. After it, the table was cleared and the dirty dishes put in the kitchen sink. Julian did that last job himself and, when he came back to the dining-room, his wife had poured him a glass of port and was already having one herself. The port was apparently a regular thing. Julian drank his in an easy chair by the fire and almost at once he began to feel sleepy. It was a strange sort of drowsiness and he remembered that his eyes weren't focusing properly. Then he passed clean out.

It was an hour later when he came to. The fire was low and the house was oddly silent. He called to his wife but she wasn't there. He made his way slowly upstairs, was violently sick in the bathroom and then another shock came when he went into her bedroom. Practically everything she possessed had gone. He went out to the garage. Her Jaguar had gone, too. Although he'd suspected that she'd been on the point of leaving him, one gathered that much of his life had gone as well.

In the morning he guessed that she'd now left him for good. That was why the Gambets had been sacked—to give her the opportunity to pack her things and maybe get some of them away. He thought he knew where she had probably gone, and he hunted for the address of that friend of hers with whom she had begun to spend quite a few weekends. Her name was Hulda Bland, a mannequin, and she'd spent a couple of weekends at Grange House. Julian hadn't liked her. He'd thought her cheap and showy. In any case he couldn't find her address.

He fetched Lucy Milford, who cooked his Sunday lunch, washed up and left for the day. On the Monday she wouldn't be needed since he'd be at Brighton. And on that Monday morning he opened the safe to collect the jewellery. *It wasn't there.* His panic doesn't matter. Nor that he rang the Regalia Hotel to try to delay the American and his daughter. They hadn't turned up. It was as good as a certainty that they'd never even existed.

It was not till later that he saw Haddowe. He'd had the idea, you see, that since husband and wife were one in law, that jewellery, for insurance purposes, wasn't really missing: it was Haddowe who'd had doubts and arranged for Hill to meet him and Julian at the Haddowe house at Highgate. And so to the present moment, and the time for a few questions.

Haddowe and Hill had swivelled to face me as if throwing the ball to me. Julian Matching covered his face with his hands for a moment, then leaned back idly in his chair.

"I suppose I ought to say," I began, "that we've been listening to an extraordinary story—"

Matching literally shot forward in his chair. "You don't believe it?"

"Of course I believe it," I told him placatingly. "The word was ill-chosen, perhaps. I should have said, an unusual story. But you'll admit it has a lot of gaps. If it hadn't we'd know all the answers; so would you be prepared to answer a question or two? And let me assure you that as far as Mr. Hallows and I are concerned, nothing that's said in this room will ever go out of it."

"I'll answer anything," he said. "I want to help. I have to help."

"The jewellery, then. You showed it to your wife?"

"Yes," he said. "I never had any secrets from her." He turned to the others. "I always wanted her to be a part of everything. That's what a wife's for. That's why I showed it to her when I came home that night."

"And her reactions?"

"Well, naturally she was excited. They were very lovely things. But not more excited than when she'd seen such things before."

"Had she seen these particular things before?"

I wondered why that question should pull him up with a jerk. He had to think before he could answer.

"Yes," he said slowly. "I'm almost sure she did. I'd mentioned them just after they were bought, and some time later she saw them when she happened to come to Walton Street."

"That helps enormously," I told him. "Now I must ask you some very personal questions. If I'm to be of any help in this unfortunate matter, I must have some very frank answers. Remember what I said about confidences. Just look on me as a friend."

"Very well," he said. "Anything you ask I'll try to answer."

"Well then, your wife has almost certainly left you. If you so wish it, we'll say it's temporarily, but she's left you. So tell us. Has anything during the last few months given you the idea that she was having an affair with another man?"

He moistened his lips. He wasn't looking at me when he spoke.

"I deliberately made myself not think of such a thing."

"But?"

"Well"—he sat there thinking. He moistened his lips again. "Well, she was spending more weekends away. Then, about four or five months ago she insisted on having her own bedroom. She had moods, if you know what I mean. One day she'd be—well, just what she used to be when we were first married, and then she'd fly into rages and say the most abominable things. Once she went for nearly a week without speaking at all."

"I see." I turned to the others. "I think that's about all, except for one or two routine matters. What's your attitude, for instance, about the police?"

"No, no, no!" old Haddowe said quickly. "This is to be kept where it is now. Inside this room."

"Very well," I said. "That's how it shall be kept I want to know now if, on those conditions. I'm to try to discover the whereabouts of Mrs. Matching and recover the jewellery. You may think, as I'm inclined to, that that's one and the same thing."

Looks went round. Matching and Hill spoke at once and Hill held the field.

"That's what we ask you to do," he said. "No publicity whatever, and on no account are the police to be brought in. You know me and I know you, so we needn't start talking about a contract The usual ten per cent bonus, of course, if the jewellery's recovered. You and I won't quarrel about any of that."

"Suits me admirably," I told him. "On my side there's one condition. I promise you it shall be done with the utmost tact, but I must be given free access, so to speak, to anyone in any way connected with the affair. I'm to be the sole judge."

"Of course, of course," Haddowe said. "You can't find out things if you don't ask questions."

"Well, thank you for your confidence," I said. "The Gambets are people that'll have to be seen. They had contacts with your wife, Mr. Matching, when you were away during the day. You know where they are?"

It was the first time I'd seen him smile.

"As a matter of fact I do. When they left they went to the Grey-hound. That's the one little hold we have in Aldways. They were going to stay there till they were fixed up with another job. I saw them there last night and induced them to come back. They were already there when I left this morning."

"That's fine," I said. "What I also need is a photograph or photographs of your wife."

"I thought of that," Hill said. "You've brought them with you. Julian?"

Julian had. He gave me a largish envelope. And that virtually concluded the morning's business. There were handshakes, then Haddowe and Matching left, and Hill with them. He'd asked Hallows and me to stay. As soon as the door closed I slit open the envelope.

There were half a dozen photographs, and each a studio job. No dates were noted, but, as we agreed, Moira Matching couldn't have changed a lot, even if all six had been taken shortly after her marriage. Hill's hint that she had been a fine piece of woman was quite an understatement. A full-length one showed a superb figure: all showed a face at which Hallows gave a quiet whistle. In each the almost white hair wasn't worn long but drawn in a wavy sort of way across the head. In one she was wearing an evening gown, and the bosom and shoulders had a soft and curiously dazzling whiteness. In two the expression was so seductive as to be almost provocative.

"Might almost be a society debutante," Hallows said. "Wonder what it was like when she opened her mouth."

It was her hair that worried me. If she'd intended to disappear, then the first thing she'd probably do once she was away would be to have that hair darkened. That, and some sun glasses, and we might rub shoulders with her and never recognize her. The door opened then as Hill came back. He was smiling a bit ruefully.

"Thank God that's over! If you knew the manoeuvring it all took, you'd say the same thing. You're getting to work at once?"

I said we were. There weren't any questions I wanted to ask.

"Any rough ideas already?"

"Yes," I said. "The same as yours. I won't say any more or you might hold it against me if anything goes wrong."

He tried to look pained. "You know I'd never do that. But tell me, just as a favour. What're your general ideas?"

"Let's both listen," I said. "What do you think, at the moment. Hallows?"

Hallows smiled. "Well, if you want someone to shoot at. I'd say this. The lady had acquired a boy friend and they planned this job together. She must have known the jewellery still wasn't sold, so he was the American who rang Mr. Matching and the Brighton hold. The boy friend also provided the Mickey she slipped into that glass of port. Maybe he was outside, all ready to pop in and take the keys, unlock the safe and help with the rest of the luggage."

"Yes," Hill said. "You won't believe it but that's almost exactly the way I worked it out myself. You think you can dear the whole thing up pretty quickly, Travers?"

"Tell you that," I said, "and have you on our necks if we haven't got the job finished by the end of the week?"

"No, seriously. Knowing what we know, do you really think it'll take all that time?"

"Well, with luck it shouldn't. It'll cost money, mind you, if we have to put extra men on the job."

"The money's there," he told me. "All we want is everything to be cleared up quickly."

"Right," I said. "If quickly means a week or so, then I'm with you."

And that was that. Even now it makes me wince when I think how wrong I was.

3
WALTON STREET

As WE walked along the corridor to the lifts, I thought of something else now that I was about to venture forth, so to speak, on my own. You can't make bricks with either mud or straw, and I had precious little of either. If I could get more information quickly, particularly about Moira Matching, so much the better for all concerned. But I'd doubted if Julian Matching had seen it that way. Maybe every bit of extra information he gave would only make him look more of a fool. Haddowe and Hill had probably taken a couple of days to make him talk to me at all.

I put it to Hill. Julian was the one who knew most about his wife or, to make it less kindly, who knew what his wife had told him about herself. Now that he'd been induced to tell me the main story, mightn't he talk more freely if, say. I got him to lunch at my club? Broad Street, as I knew, would be out of the question.

"I think it might work," Hill said. "There's no doubt about it, there's a whole lot of stuff he's told nobody. Mind you. I can't altogether blame him. In his line of business he's very highly respected and if all this got out, it'd do nobody any good. And there's this behind it, too. Lots of us tried to tell him tactfully at the time of his marriage that he might be asking for all sorts of trouble, and he was absolutely furious about it. That's why it hasn't been easy to make him admit we were right and he was wrong. Still, your idea might work. Wait a minute, though."

He looked at his watch. "He and C.T. are having an early lunch in town. C.T. wants to get back to Highgate immediately afterwards. Julian'll probably be back in his office by half-past one, so why not go along there and have a word with Jean Lindman?"

"His secretary?"

"Yes. A very charming woman. I don't want to plan things for you but if you have a quick snack somewhere yourself, you could get there soon after one. That should give you a long quarter of an hour. When Julian arrives you might get him to see you in his room. That all right? If so. I'll fix it with Jean."

It sounded like a perfect set-up and I told him so. Hallows and I went down and through the swing doors to the January cold.

"You get yourself a meal," I told Hallows, "then start digging at Somerset House. I ought to be back at the office at about three and we'll compare notes."

I found an empty chair at a milk bar and had a couple of sandwiches and some coffee. Then I took the Tube to Bond Street, and Walton Street was only five minutes' walk. It was ten-past one when I reached the actual premises. Half the smallish window was grilled and half a dozen pieces of early silver were on display. I went into the shop, if that's what one should call it. A bell rang stridently the moment the door was even ajar. The room wasn't more than fifteen by ten: just an open space surrounded by show cases, except, that is, for the long counter to my right and a door with a glazed top straight ahead. A man of about sixty in a dark lounge suit was examining through his glass the various marks on a set of silver spoons, and be looked mildly up as I entered. He put the spoons aside as I came in.

"Good-morning, sir. May I help you in any way?"

No great deference. Just a quiet voice. C.T. Haddowe was obviously that kind of firm.

"My name's Travers," I said. "I'm expecting to see Mr. Julian Matching."

He smiled. "Oh yes, sir. Mr. Julian happens to be out, but Miss Lindman will see you. This way, sir."

Through the door was a lobby. It had two other doors: one ahead and the other to the left. He went left, tapped at the door and opened it.

"Mr. Travers, Miss, for Mr. Julian."

It was a smallish but comfortable office with not a lot of room between the tall filing cabinets and the desk. The desk itself was by the one window through which you could see the snow-covered backs of neighbouring premises. An old-fashioned fire-place accommodated an electric fire. A door to the right would, I guessed, lead to Matching's office.

Jean Lindman had merely turned her head as I entered, then she quickly got to her feet. She was tallish and slim. The red jumper went perfectly with the black skirt and the black of her hair, but the first thing I really noticed about her was the brown, expressive eyes.

"You must be Jean Lindman." I held out a hand. "I've been hearing quite a lot about you this morning."

I don't know why she should have flushed so violently, but she did. She was a beautiful woman. Compared with her, Moira Matching made you think of something you'd find in harems. Maybe I was getting romantic, or susceptible, in my middle age, but there she suddenly was, uniquely mature in the miraculous thirties.

"And you're Mr. Travers," she said. "I've heard about you, too." She smiled. "I've also done some research on you."

She had a delightful voice. I couldn't help smiling as well. "In connection with what?"

"Shall we say, this morning? I'm a confidential secretary, Mr. Travers. I always have been. But won't you sit down?"

I took the small office chair. I don't quite know why but for a moment I was rather out of my depth.

"You knew about this morning, then?"

"Everything," she told me calmly. "I mean everything. Everything that's happened to Julian these last few days."

"Then you definitely *are* a confidential secretary. May I say something else? I'm not a wolf and I'm not making a pass, but you're also precisely what John Hill told me—a very charming woman."

Her cheeks reddened again. "That's charming of you, too. But about confidences. My father's parish was at Highgate and Mr. Haddowe was always a friend of ours. He wanted me to come here when I left school and I've been here ever since."

"So you're a daughter of the vicarage."

She laughed. "Yes. Mr. Travers. Not always strictly Tennysonian but strictly an old maid."

"Shame!" I said. "If only I were unmarried and ten years younger. But let's talk, shall we? This, roughly, is what happened this morning. When I've finished, I'd like you to tell me everything you know about the missing Mrs. Matching."

What she could tell me was very little. She'd been only twice to Grange House since the marriage, arriving each time on the Saturday evening and leaving after tea on the Sunday. It had been ghastly. Moira's veneer was very, very thin. The more she tried, the lack of every kind of sensibility was only too clear. And Julian, she said, had always been a bit on edge, trying to show that he'd been right after all.

"You thought things couldn't go on like that?"

"They couldn't," she said. "It was all too one-sided. She was out for what she could get Nothing but giving on one side and taking on the other. Horrible forced sentimentality on her part, too. Wheedlings, cajolings: all that sort of thing when there was anything she wanted, then making his life a misery till she wanted something else. Not that he'd ever admit it."

"What about her origins?"

She frowned. "I've been trying to remember. I believe her father was owner of a chemist's shop and he and her mother were killed in a blitz when she was only about three. She had an older brother—now in Canada—and the two children went to an aunt in Fulham, said to be the widow of a doctor. She died when Moira was eighteen. The aunt was said to be musical, whatever that might mean, and Moira had singing lessons. She told me herself that her ambition had been grand opera, but she'd had to accept the fact she just didn't have the voice, and that was why she took to jazz, or rock-and-roll or whatever you call it."

"Where was she actually living at the time of the marriage?"

"She was sharing a small flat with a mannequin named Bland—Hulda Bland—at York House, Hammersmith. A rather run-down block of flats."

"You never saw this Hulda Bland?"

"Never. According to what Moira told me, she worked for some of the biggest firms. I'm afraid I was a bit cattish later on and made an enquiry or two but nobody seemed to know her."

That was about all she knew. As for impressions, she'd as good as known from Julian's edginess the last few weeks that the marriage just couldn't last. Julian never discussed his private affairs with her: only occasionally would he hint at how things were.

"Suppose something arises that I want to consult you about?" I asked her. "Where can I see you?"

"Perhaps at lunch. Or somewhere after five o'clock. There's my own flat of course. Flat 3a, Newbury Gardens, Streatham. I'm on the telephone."

I think she was about to give me her number when she was suddenly listening.

"Julian!" she said. "We really ought to be in *his* room."

We virtually scrambled through. Another bar of his electric fire was hastily switched on, I was motioned to sit, and out she went. I couldn't hear anything now through the double doors, but I must have been smiling to myself as I waited. There was something very delightful about finding oneself a fellow conspirator with Jean Lindman.

In two or three minutes Matching came in. He was all apologies. I must have had quite a wait.

"It was very good of you to come round personally," he said as he hung up the black overcoat and the Homburg. "Unhappily I had to have an early lunch with my uncle. But do sit down. May I get you a drink?"

"Thank you, no," I said. "I'm a very abstemious type. Hope I'm not being personal, but your secretary seems a very charming woman."

"Charming?" His eyebrows lifted slightly. "Yes, I suppose she is. We regard her as highly efficient. She's been with us for years, you know."

The tone was so impersonal that I must have stared and I let my eyes go quickly round the room.

"Quite a nice office you have here. I'd like to change with you."

It *was* a nice room. The carpet was really good, the chairs and desk Chippendale, and the chair that he'd taken himself was a lovely corner one with swept arms and cabriole legs. The Morland colour prints looked fine against the old gold paper of the walls and I'd have liked to own the early bracket clock on the mantelshelf. The medium-sized safe in the corner would have looked even more incongruous if its green hadn't gone so well with the mahogany.

"I hope I'm not dropping any sort of brick," he said, "but I imagine you have to receive all sorts and classes. Here we largely deal with—well, just the one type."

"True enough." I waved at the safe. "What about a burglary? You people not worrying?"

He smiled. "Not in the least. One of the first things I did some years ago was to have the latest thing in alarms installed. And, of course, we're always insured."

"That reminds me," I said. "I know you must be a very busy man but we're together here, if you know what I mean, so I wonder if you'd save any further pestering by giving me some more information. If I'm to find your wife, I ought to know every single thing about her. Family history, friends, habits—everything."

He frowned for a moment, but when he gave himself a quick nod, I let out as quick a breath of relief.

"I'll be happy to. If you can make it as brief as you can. I do happen to be rather busy."

He wasn't the same man. What had happened earlier that day—that manoeuvring him into a position where he simply had to talk—had worked a kind of miracle. I might have been a client and he the quiet, efficient executive. I whipped out my notebook.

"You have the number of your wife's Jaguar?"

It was a number easy enough to remember.

"Did she have a passport?"

"She'd be included in my own."

"And it's still in your possession?"

"I think so. I expect it's in my desk at home. Why do you ask?"

In my game you have to lie unblushingly, and keep on lying. "Well. I think it was something John Hill mentioned. About your wife having an elder brother in Canada. There's just the chance, you see, that she might be there."

"Yes," he said slowly. "She did mention him occasionally. I'll check on that passport. If it's not still there I'll let you know. Shall we leave it like that?"

Things were going so smoothly that I switched to the lady herself. I wondered how he'd react to a request for every single detail about her, but I needn't have worried, even if what I learned was very little more than what Jean Lindman had told me. Not that there wasn't a difference. In spite of what happened, he was still infatuated. He'd convinced himself and now he was convincing me. It was the good in her that he kept stressing. She hadn't had too easy a time as a child. Missing out on grand opera had been another shock. Aldways, now he'd really had time to think it over, wasn't perhaps the most desirable place for a young wife who'd had a far more glamorous time in town. If he had to do things over again, then he'd do them differently. An apartment in town, for instance. More, and longer, holidays.

"In that connection may I put a pertinent question?" I said. "If I find your wife I may have to bring certain pressures to bear: say to recover the jewellery. Am I allowed to assure her that you're prepared to take her back?"

"Yes," he said slowly. "I've thought it over. I've done very little else since she went away, but I regard it as my duty. The least I can do is give her, and myself, another chance. As a matter of fact—as an earnest, you might say—I'm making arrangements to sell Grange House."

"I see. But let me put it even more personally. What if I find she's gone to another man? That she's spent these last few days, and nights, with him?"

"No," he said. "No! She wouldn't do that. Whatever she's done, she wouldn't do that."

The sudden vehemence was a bit disturbing, not that I hadn't asked for it.

"You're the one who should know," I told him placatingly. "But about her friends. One thing rather intrigued me about something you mentioned this morning. Your wife accused the Gambets of having spied on her. Doesn't such an accusation imply that she was afraid that something she was doing might be found out?"

"No, no," he said. He smiled a bit condescendingly. "You haven't thought it over. That was the excuse she gave for dismissing them. If you remember, she had to get them out of the house before the Saturday. Any excuse was good enough."

"You're right," I said humbly. "I war forgetting it. But what did she do, as far as you know, with her time at Grange House?"

"Well, she seemed happy enough there for the first few months and then she went more and more to town. She was generally home, though, when I got in. She used to go to the cinema, or a matinée or do some shopping. You know how women are."

"And after the first few months?"

"That was when she began spending the odd weekend with Hulda Bland. In the last few months she did it more and more often."

"You haven't a photograph of Miss Bland?"

He hadn't. I asked if he could describe her and be thought he could. She was the same height as his wife—five feet six—and red-headed, with strikingly blue eyes. Slightly bigger in the bust. I managed to get out of him than his wife. Good-looking, if one liked that kind of looks.

"I don't suppose you know the actual dates of the week-ends?"

He gave me a queer look.

"It's curious, but I think I do." He felt in his breast pocket and produced one of those little personal diaries. "I jotted some of them down. I don't mean that this is a purely personal diary. It's just the briefest notes about all sorts of things. Business affairs, reminders, and so on. I think you should be able to read my scrawl."

There was the usual little thin pencil along the spine of the small diary, and the notes had been written with that. The writing was very small but reasonably clear, and the jottings themselves just as he'd described them. I was interested in things like *M. away.* or, occasionally. *M. with H.B.* I noted them for the previous three months, and even while I was writing them down, I saw a curious and highly relevant pattern. It was the last thing I'd call Matching's attention to, but those weekends went in threes with a gap of one. Such a gap—I imply that a gap means that she spent that particular weekend at home—occurred on Saturday, January 2nd.

"Thank you, Mr. Matching." I gave the small diary back. "I hope it'll be helpful. No more questions, but may I thank you for giving me so much of your time."

I got to my feet. He fetched my hat from the stand. "Could I ask a question myself?"

"Please do."

"Well—er—perhaps it's rather premature, but have you any ideas?"

"Only vague ones. I'm afraid. As soon as there's anything definite to report. I'll get in touch with you."

The buzzer went. "Excuse me just a moment."

He picked up the receiver. The very first words made him stare.

"Who? . . . But why? . . . Good God, no! . . . Right. Come in for a moment, will you?"

He replaced the receiver. His hand was still on it for quite a few moments.

"The Jaguar's been found!" he told me. "At Sevenoaks station. Apparently it's been there for some days. But why? Tell me why?"

Jean Lindman came in. He waved his hand impatiently.

"Wait a moment, Jean. Let me think this out. Or ought I to go down there."

"You're seeing Colonel Harries at three," she told him. "I doubt if you can get in touch with him now."

"Dammit, we can try!"

"He's now on the train," she reminded him. "He'll come straight from Waterloo to here. But why not get in touch with Sevenoaks and then get your garage to collect the car?"

"All right, all right," he told her, and it wasn't very graciously. "Get them for me and I'll talk to them here. You'd better stay, Travers."

The car had been checked only that morning. Cars, apparently, were often left all night, but the Jaguar became noticeable because it bad been in the same spot for at least four nights. One of the staff connected it with Mrs. Matching, the registration had been checked, and then Grange House rung. Robert Gambet had just referred back to Walton Street. Now Sevenoaks, who knew Matching well enough, were agreeing to ring the Aldways garage to get the car to Grange House. The keys weren't in it but the near door hadn't been properly closed.

"You'd like me to see the car and make some enquiries?" I said. "I thought of going down in the morning in any case."

That discovery had been the very devil of a shock. He took a moment or two lo grasp what I'd said.

"The car," be said. "Why should she leave the car?"

"Obviously because she wouldn't be wanting it," I told him. "She went somewhere by train."

And somewhere easy to trace, I thought, with all the luggage she'd taken with her.

He went slowly across to the corner cupboard just beyond the desk and poured himself a drink. He'd taken a pull at it before he remembered to ask me if I'd have one too.

"Thanks, but I'll have to be getting away." I gave him a business card. "Give me a ring if you think it's necessary."

He pressed a button. Jean Lindman came in again. "See Mr. Travers out, will you." He held out a hand to me. "Sorry this happened to crop up."

"Don't worry," I told him. "We'll soon get it all sorted out."

A man who looked like a dealer was talking quietly with that elderly assistant and I couldn't speak to Jean Lindman till we were at the outer door.

"This is urgent, Miss Lindman, but ring my office and ask for Hallows—you've got it?—Hallows. Tell him to meet me at the bookstall at Charing Cross Station as soon as he can. Then get Mr. Matching's garage and vouch for me. Say I'm coming down at once to see the car, and he's not to take it to Grange House but keep it in his garage till I get there. All right?"

She nodded. There was even a little smile.

I made my way back to Bond Street Station, and I wasn't thinking so much about the actual case as about Jean Lindman—and Julian Matching. There are some things you just can't disguise and what she thought of Julian was one of them. I noticed it when we were in her room and she'd heard him come in. "Julian!" she'd said. Nothing unusual in that, considering the circumstances, but it hadn't been all alarm or surprise. There'd been a sudden look on her face: a scarcely noticeable smile.

And what about him? To him she was just a very likeable person—I dared say he'd even call her a friend—and, above all, a highly efficient secretary. Love, I thought tritely, was an amazing thing. Matching could suddenly fall with a tremendous thud for little more than a pretty trollop, and for years there'd been right under his nose a someone like Jean Lindman. Still, that's how things often went, and I gave myself a smile. Ludovic Travers. Matchmaker. Broken hearts re-set. Terms, free, gratis, and for nothing.

4

GRANGE HOUSE

WE WERE lucky. A not-too-slow train left at three-fifteen and we were on it. The twenty-five mile journey didn't leave much time out of an hour, but we didn't waste it. It took most of it to make Hallows familiar with what had happened at Walton Street.

Almost as soon as he'd left me that morning to go to Somerset House, he realised that with a little more to go on, he could save quite a lot of time. So he turned back to the United Assurance building and rang John Hill from the ground floor enquiries room. It took quite a few minutes for Hill to unearth the information required—the dates of the Matching-Hyson wedding and Moira Matching's birthday. I thought the latter must have been obtained through Jean Lindman, not that it mattered.

Everything was then easy enough at Somerset House. On payment of the usual fees he was given the two copies of certificates. The birth certificate gave the names of Moira's parents as Frederick and Nelly Hyson of 71 Dorset Crescent, Hammersmith: ages, twenty-eight and twenty-seven respectively. The occupation of the father was given as *Factory Hand*. So much for her description of her father as the owner of a chemist's shop.

The wedding certificate gave the names of her parents as Frederick and Eleanor Hyson, deceased. The change from Nelly to Eleanor was from non-U to U. Doubtless Moira had thought Nelly too old-fashioned and not well fitted to the rest of the romantic accounts of her life and career. But she hadn't taken the risk of describing herself under an assumed name. She had definitely been married as Mary Hyson, though known as Moira, and it was as Moira that she always insisted that she should be known.

Hallows didn't leave it at that He was early back at the office and had at least half an hour on his hands, and as, like myself, he has at least one friend or old acquaintance in virtually every police division, he rang Hammersmith. Moira must have had some reason for choosing for her father the business of chemist, so what he wanted to know was whether any manufacturing chemist had had works in that district around 1940. The answer came pat. There wasn't even the necessity of getting Hallows' friends on the line, since the sergeant on desk duty had lived in the neighbourhood all his life. Grove and Craxton, who were among the biggest manufacturing chemists in the country, bad had a factory there long before 1940. It was still there.

"Then you can also tell me where Dorset Crescent is?"

"I certainly can," the sergeant told him. "It's in that very district. Used to be one of those posh districts in my father's time, but got a bit run down."

So much for that. Norris, the managing director of the Broad Street Detective Agency—I appear somewhat nebulously as chairman—is a retired Yard inspector and bis old friends and acquaintances would fill a page of the telephone directory, so Hallows passed the buck to him. Given the names of the parents killed in 1941, and that their daughter Mary and an older brother had been adopted by an aunt whose only known address was somewhere in Fulham, could the police find the name and address of that aunt, ignoring whether she were now alive or dead. Norris said he'd get busy at once, using the well-tried reason that the aunt had come into some money and we were doing the tracing.

That's the kind of worker Hallows is: quiet, unobtrusive, patient, tireless when on a job and known in the business as about the best there is. He often reminds me of a cooped ferret in the rabbitting days of my Suffolk boyhood. You put it quietly into a burrow and left it to do its job, and in less than no time the rabbits would come hurtling out. When there were no more, out the ferret would come, too. It'd peer up for a moment, then with nose to ground move off in search of another burrow. One often hears nowadays the crack about not keeping a dog and barking oneself. That applies to Hallows. You can give him a job and forget all about it. In nineteen cases out of twenty he'll do it far better than you could have done yourself.

There'd been a fairly sharp thaw all day and the roads were reasonably clear. Aldways is to the north as you come down from town, and the taxi took ten minutes to take us there. There was only one garage.

We walked in by the car entrance and ran slap into the proprietor, a middle-aged, strongly built man named Oldfield.

"You'll be the gentleman I was rung up about," he told me. "Name of Travers?"

I showed him an Agency card. I didn't try to hoodwink him into taking it for a police card. There was no point in it I was an enquiry agent interested in the theft of the car. The whereabouts of Moira Matching was no business of his, even if I did do some explaining.

"Mrs. Matching happens to be away," I said, "so she couldn't collect the car."

"Thought I hadn't seen her for a few days."

"She's often out with the car?"

"Very few days she isn't. Parks it at Sevenoaks pretty regularly."

"Right," I said. "Let's have a look at it."

We went through to the largish repair shop and there it was. As far as I could see, it hadn't even a scratch.

"This near door wasn't properly closed, so I had no trouble starting it," he told us.

"What about the luggage compartment?"

"Locked," he said. "I wouldn't do anything about that without authorisation."

"And quite right, too. There may be spare keys at Grange House. In fact. I'm pretty sure there are. Any reason why we shouldn't take the car away?"

"We'd better give a receipt," Hallows said. "That'll regularise it all round. How's the petrol?"

The tank was about a quarter full. Two or three minutes and Oldfield was backing the car out Grange House was half a mile on. I drove past the green with the church in the background, past the last houses and a tiny straggle of bungalows and a quarter of a mile on we were there. It was an architect's nightmare and bigger than I'd thought.

At the near end was a kind of semi-circular tower, just beyond which was the tradesmen's entrance. The whole house was adorned with miniature steeples and crenellations, but a Virginia creeper mercifully covered most of the red brick of the front. A probably later imitation Georgian porch had been built out over the main door. The short drive-way made a complete circle, but a kind of tangent way led on to a large garage. It was empty and I drove the Jaguar straight in. Through the garage window I could see what had at one time been stables. Gardens seemed to stretch back for quite a long way.

We walked back to the front door. Robert Gambet opened it. He was about fifty, rather thin, hair balding slightly and worn to just below the ears. It gave him a definitely Edwardian look. I told him who I was and why I was there. Except for an occasional slight nod he didn't move a muscle.

"I understand, sir. Will you gentlemen come in?"

It was the usual quiet voice of the trained servant.

"We'd rather you came to the garage," I said. "A few minutes and it'll be dark. The luggage compartment is locked and we ought to open it. We'd like you to be there."

"I'll inform my wife, sir."

He left the door open and we heard him calling. A voice answered from quite near, and almost at once Gambet was back and his wife with him. I'd say she was a bit younger than her husband: a competent looking woman, pleasant faced and with no grey that I could see in her dark hair. Her husband was about five-foot ten: she was almost as tall.

"Would there be anything to bring in, sir?" Gambet said.

"Not that we can't manage ourselves," I said. "Pardon me, but you're Mrs. Gambet?"

"That's right, sir."

"And Mr. Matching calls you what?"

"Eva, sir, and my husband is Robert."

I held out my hand. "I'm glad to meet you, Eva, and you. Robert. We may be seeing quite a lot of each other. This is also a Robert— Robert or Bob Hallows. Now we'd better get that door opened."

"You'd like some tea later, sir?"

I said we'd like it very much. She disappeared across the dim hall. Gambet closed the door behind us and we walked the few yards on.

"No spare keys that you know of?"

"I can't say, sir. If there are they might take a lot of finding."

"No time for that," I said. "I want that door opened at once."

Hallows looked round for a tool and came up with a large screwdriver and a couple of tyre levers. Once we'd forced a slight opening a lever opened it further. An outsized wrench did the rest of the trick.

What had we expected to find? We'd neither of us mentioned it, but there'd have been no surprise if that boot had held Moira Matching's body. It didn't. It was full of baggage, packed higgledy-piggledy in. There were at least six cases, some of them brand new, and each one that we could see had either been opened or hastily packed. Articles of clothing protruded and one case hadn't even been closed.

"Is there a key, Robert, to Mrs. Matching's room?"

"Yes, sir. It's still in the lock."

"Right," I said, and began putting on my gloves. "If you show us the way, Hallows and I will take all this luggage there."

It took two trips. The room itself was at the far end of the corridor that led right from the landing: beautifully furnished in the modern style and with windows that overlooked the front. I locked the door and pocketed the key and then we went back to the garage. Hallows had a torch and we went over that luggage compartment almost inch by inch. We went over case front. We even had a look at the engine and the tyres. We'd have learned just as much if we'd had tea instead.

I closed the sliding doors and we went back to the house. Tea was ready and we were shown the downstairs cloakroom and the door to the lounge. It was the room I'd already heard described: television set, radiogram, cocktail cabinet, modern furnishings, a mirror wall with a trailing evergreen and, mercifully, an incongruous but welcome fire in an arty kind of grate. Robert brought in the tea on a large, very modern papier mâché tray. Even the tea-things had futuristic designs.

"Will that be all, sir?"

"Yes," I said. "But I'd like a brief word with you. Everything that's said and done from now on is strictly confidential. Understand?"

"Absolutely, sir."

"Tomorrow morning we'll be down fairly early to see you and your wife. You're not to know that."

"I understand, sir."

"What time does Mr. Matching usually get in?"

"At about six o'clock, sir. He leaves in the morning at about twenty to nine to catch the nine o'clock, and leaves bis car at the station."

"Right," I said. "We'll wait till well after six o'clock."

We had an excellent tea and took our time over it and it was after five o'clock when Robert Gambet took out the tray. He'd made up the fire, brought the cocktail cabinet handy and showed us how to manipulate the television set and the radiogram. The telephone, he said, was in the hall. Hallows rang the office, who'd inform our wives, and then we made ourselves comfortable and talked. After five minutes it almost looked as if there wasn't anything more to talk about The whole thing was inexplicable. All that seemed reasonably obvious was that Moira Matching had left so hurriedly that she'd literally crammed those cases with this and that. That wasn't too surprising. After all, she didn't know for sure when her husband would recover from that dose of chloral hydrate.

"Even then there's something wrong," Hallows said. "She could keep her room locked and she had all the time in the world to pack those cases beforehand: then all she'd have to do was get them out to the car."

"I know," I said. "At any rate she drove straight to the station, so why didn't she have the cases taken out? Only one reason, surely. She had to go somewhere else in the same hurry and she intended to come back for the car."

"I don't like it," he said. "I don't know why, but I've got the feeling something's wrong. She's had five days to get back in."

"What about the weather? Suppose she was leaving the car during the weekend and intended to pick it up on the Monday. That was when the snow came. Mightn't she have left it there till the weather changed? You know: hoping it *might* change."

"Could be," he said. "Then there's that business of the unlocked near door. She locked the off-door and took the keys. Would she be all that careless? A car still worth well over a thousand pounds? And the trunk crammed full of luggage?"

That's how it is. You can talk and talk and nothing comes out. Maybe something's been said that you'll remember later: something that was a vital clue if you'd only gone a bit further or seen a connection. But we did go on talking, about the hurry in which she'd left the house, shown by that hastily packed luggage, and how the same urgency might have made her forget to make sure that near door was properly locked. That brought us back to why should the luggage have been hastily packed when she'd had time to pack it beforehand. And the logical answer to that was that she hadn't known until the last moment that she'd be leaving so quickly. What, then, had changed her mind?

There it was, as I said, going round in circles, and if you stopped at one point, then you thought of another and the circle got still wider. Only one definite thing did arise. Moira Matching had definitely left that car at the station, and the time, as we worked it out, would be between half-past eight and nine on that Saturday night The best thing to do was to put another man on the job to try to follow her movements from there. The station should have been far from busy at that time of night, and if she'd been wearing that mink coat and Eva Gambet could suggest what kind of hat, then there'd be quite a good description.

I wasn't supposed to know about that mink coat, so all I asked was what Moira Matching might have been wearing. Also, I didn't know how much the Gambets knew, so I had to divulge something about the time. The fur coat was suggested at once.

"What kind of fur?"

"Oh, mink, sir." There was something awestruck in the tone. "A beautiful coat! Madam told me herself it had cost over two thousand pounds!"

I let myself be suitably awed. "Aren't there different colours of mink? Mutations or something?"

"Well, this was a pale brown. Almost a fawn."

"And any special hat to go with it?"

"Yes, sir. She had it specially made. That was mink, too. A Russian style of hat. Fairly high-crowned."

She showed me with her hands: something like a fur tarboosh, but oval instead of circular. I got on the phone at once to Norris. We have a photographer who's always ready to do a rush job, and he was to superimpose the coat and hat on one of the photographs. I said we'd like it by nine in the morning. I'd also be wanting another operative.

I was turning back to the lounge when I thought I heard a car, so I took a look from the front door. It was Matching and he was closing the drive gate. I stepped out and was full in his headlights when he got in again, and he drew the car in to where I'd backed.

"Here you are then, Travers. I stopped at the garage and they told me you collected the car."

"It's in the garage," I told him. "Would you leave your car here? I'd like you to drive us back to Sevenoaks if it isn't too much trouble. Also I'd like you to have a look at the Jaguar."

I told him just what had happened, and as soon as I came to that matter of the luggage, he stopped dead in his tracks.

"But that's . . . it's incredible! This is driving me crazy. What the devil does it mean?"

"Don't know," I said. "We took that luggage up to her room, so maybe you'd like to see it unpacked. You can see the car itself at any time."

Robert Gambet was in the hall as soon as we went in, Matching waved him fretfully back.

"Don't bother me now. Just have dinner at the usual time." He turned to me. "You'll stay for dinner?"

I thanked him and said I couldn't. Hallows came out and the three of us went upstairs. I unlocked the bedroom door and we went in. Matching was looking deathly pale.

"Sure you're all right?" I said. "You're not looking too good. What about some brandy?"

"Perhaps yes," he said. "It's been a terrible shock. Do you know what I thought when you mentioned that locked boot?"

"I know. We thought the same thing. Thank God it wasn't." I drew a chair across. "Just sit down and take it easy."

Hallows came back with some brandy. A minute or two and Matching was more like himself. All the same, we brought those cases to where he was sitting and began unpacking them. Hallows re-packed each case as soon as it was emptied. In none of them did we find a thing of any consequence: all they contained was clothes and shoes. There were two hats in the one hat-box but not that Russian hat. Matching made never a comment: he just leaned forward in his chair and watched.

"Well that's that," I said, when the last case was re-packed. "Nothing there to tell us where she's gone."

"Yes, but why leave the car with everything in it?"

I told him that weather theory. A minute or two and be seemed to be accepting it. He moistened his lips and suddenly looked up.

"Why not use it as a trap? Take the car back and have someone waiting when she comes to collect it?"

"That's what we've arranged—in a way," I told him. "I'll leave word about it tonight at Sevenoaks and in the morning we'll have our own man there. No need to take the car back. She'll see it's gone and she'll have to make enquiries."

We went downstairs again and he walked steadily enough. I still had the bedroom key. As I'd told him, we might have to go over those cases for prints. We wait for a moment to the lounge.

"We can't possibly let you drive us to the station," I told him. "Couldn't Oldfield come and fetch us?"

Robert Gambet arranged it while Hallows and I had a drink. We had whisky: Matching had another brandy. We said nothing about the morning and it was about half-past seven when we left.

We had only ten minutes to wait for an up train after I'd arranged about the Jaguar. Hallows opened the ball as soon as the train was on the move.

"Lucky he didn't ask us what we thought. What would you have told him if he had?"

"Anything I thought would satisfy him."

"And what do you think *has* happened?"

"You tell *me*."

He laughed. "No, sir. I did the guessing last time, when we were with Mr. Hill."

"I don't think it's guessing any longer," I told him. "Take those cases we undid. Not a single one was locked or even had a key in a lock. Then those really beautiful frocks and things. She'd obviously packed them in tissue paper with extreme care, but what were they like? Everything crumpled up, paper and all. And the pockets of two of the short coats were inside out. Also there wasn't a single scrap of correspondence or things like bank statements or a cheque book or a passport. So what?"

"Yes," he said. "I thought when we first saw those cases that no woman would ever have been in that much of a hurry. You know what I think? That jewellery was the . . . well, the centre point. That confederate of hers was just stringing her along. She was the patsy."

We had our own little Summit Conference and reached agreement Moira's boy friend had planned the whole thing, beginning with the sacking of the Gambets, followed by playing the role of Martin J. Hamstall. On the Saturday night, sure now that the jewellery was in the safe, he was waiting outside the house ready for the signal that the Mickey had knocked Matching out. He took the keys of the safe, replaced them after he'd taken the jewellery, and meanwhile Moira had been taking the cases to the car. Then off they went. *But to where?*

That's when the obvious ended and speculation began. That Jaguar certainly didn't go to Sevenoaks. It went *somewhere*, and that's all we could say. And at that somewhere, something terrible happened. It was more than likely that Moira Matching was no longer alive. Could "X", that lover-confederate, let her go on living? He was still "X", the unknown. She'd still be known, and capable of being found. Very well then. Everything pointed to the fact that as soon as she was dead he'd gone through every one of those cases and any others that might have arrived beforehand. When he was sure there was nothing that could in any way lead to himself, he re-packed the cases, put them into the boot and locked it, and drove the car to Sevenoaks station. If he took a train from there, then we'd be wasting our time in bringing another man down. Our man wouldn't want Moira now: he'd want "X". And about "X" we knew nothing at all. "X" might be anyone. "X" might even be a woman: say, Hulda Bland.

"That's it then," Hallows said. "We keep one eye out for the lady in case she's still alive but we're really after 'X'."

"That's it. We don't neglect her life before then but we concentrate on the last six months, when she began spending more and more time away. That was when 'X' and she got acquainted."

"We start with Hulda Bland?"

It seemed the best approach, once we'd seen the Gambets again. All the same, after we'd slept on it, we both might have other ideas.

"What about the client?"

"He'll have to be strung along, too," I said. "At least till we're sure. He's still absolutely besotted about that woman. You saw how he reacted tonight."

"And what about the police? If it does turn out to be murder, where do we stand?"

"Until it *is* murder, nicely balanced on a tight-rope," I said. "No one could prove we had reason to suspect murder. We can afford to be thought fools. So we'll go on behaving as if such a thought never entered our minds. Also I gave my word that the police shouldn't be called in."

"Good enough for me," he said. "Maybe it isn't murder. Maybe 'X' has got her safely parked somewhere."

He said it like a man who doesn't believe it. I didn't believe it either.

5

THE MAN WHO SHOULD HAVE DIED

THE morning brought some news about that aunt who'd adopted the Hyson children on their parents' death. She'd been Nelly Hyson's sister, a widow named Gifton who'd kept a little sweet and tobacco shop at 22 Lower Norgate Street, Fulham. She'd died five years ago which would be when Moira was eighteen.

Enquiries at Fulham could wait. Just after nine o'clock I rang Grange House, ostensibly to enquire after Matching's health. Robert Gambet said he'd fully recovered from his slight indisposition and had left earlier than usual that morning to catch the eight-twenty. We went by car and took French with us: another operative who'd been with us for years. He had a couple of photographs—Moira in mink and Moira without—and he'd been told everything that was strictly necessary. We dropped him at the station. If nothing happened there, he was to try the local hotels, just on the off chance.

It had thawed all night and was still thawing. The roads had been so good that it wasn't much after ten o'clock when we reached Aldways. I pulled up at the garage. Oldfield himself came out to attend to us. I had the tank topped up for the good of the house. He told us he was getting that trunk door put right at once.

"The car was stolen on Saturday night," I told him. "You didn't happen to see it some time about half-past eight?"

"Never a hope," he said. "We always close at six."

"Well, we think the job must have been done by someone who'd given the place a good looking over, otherwise he wouldn't have known it was actually in the garage. Someone she may have given a lift to. Did you ever see anyone with her these last few weeks?"

"Never saw anyone with her. Always had that car out alone. Never even saw Mr. Matching with her. Between you and me, he was just a bit scared of how she drove."

We moved on to Grange House. A furtive sun was out and we could get a good idea of the lay-out. The usual lawn with a herbaceous border at its back was at the front, which faced due south. Behind the house were the buildings, solidly built of brick, that must once have been the stables, and entry to them was by a way that turned abruptly to the right and past the side door as you came into the short drive. Beyond them was a kitchen garden, backed by some very old fruit trees and beyond them what looked like a shrubbery, planted years ago as a windbreak. Nothing looked well kept. Even the border had plenty of weeds and the kitchen garden was a mass of them, almost smothering the stalks of brussels sprouts and a few greens.

Gambet actually seemed pleased to see us. He said he'd kept up the lounge fire and he'd bring the coffee there. I said I'd like it in the kitchen, if he didn't mind. I'd always liked kitchens. He smiled.

"It's curious how people do," he told us. "I think it's because in the old days it was the cosiest room in the house."

Eva Gambet got busy with coffee, and Hallows and I made ourselves comfortable. It was hard to imagine that kitchen as it had been in Victoria's days. Now it had everything. Even the windows that looked out past the stables had a fine view towards rising farm-land and woods.

"You're glad to be back?" I asked.

"Quite glad, sir," he told me. "We like it here. It's quiet And it's lovely in the summer."

Eva brought the coffee and the four of us sat round an enamelled-top kitchen table. It was good coffee. There was a fruit cake, too.

"Mr. Matching has told you both that you're to give us all the help you can?"

"Yes, sir. And well both be pleased to do so."

I had to warn them that everything that was said and done was to be strictly between us. I didn't anticipate any great difficulty about that.

"Mr. Matching himself," I began. "What has he been like as a master?"

"We couldn't wish for a better."

"Can you tell me why?"

"Well, sir, he's always considerate. A bit reserved perhaps, but very considerate. Take just one thing, sir. He didn't care for either wireless or television, not after the first few months, and he used to sit in the study and read till it was time for bed, so, when madam was away for a weekend, he'd tell us to make free of the lounge. Not many masters would have done that, sir."

"They certainly wouldn't," I told him. "But in case you're wondering why I should be asking you about Mr. Matching, it's because I have to get what I'd call the atmosphere of the house. Unless I knew what he was like and how you felt about everything, then I couldn't get that atmosphere. Now I think I *have* got it, I can come to the other member of the household—Mrs. Matching. She's gone away. We can't say if it's for good. In any case, Mr. Matching wants her found. Anything you can tell me may help us to find her. Which brings me to a preliminary question. What'll be your attitude if we do find her and Mr. Matching decides to have her back?"

"She won't come back, sir," Eva Gambet said. "She hated him. You could see that in every look and word. She wouldn't have stayed as long as she did if she hadn't been trying to get out of him all she could beforehand."

"I see. Then would you mind starting at the very beginning and telling me just what happened as things went on?"

It was a longish business. The first few weeks were idyllic and Moira the cooing turtle-dove. The Gambets did find her difficult: she was so obviously out of place. She was too free-and-easy and used to spend too much time in the kitchen, making herself at home and generally cluttering things up. She was untidy from the very first and, after the first few weeks, never made even a pretence of doing anything in the house. Matching had hoped she'd take an interest in the garden, like his mother, but except when she took an occasional walk round, the garden mightn't have been there at all.

That was the first phase. The second began in the middle of the first summer when she managed to acquire the Jaguar, and then she began to spend almost every day away from the house: usually not till after lunch but occasionally all day. Sometimes she'd obviously been doing a lot of shopping in town. The first quarrels occurred. Practically every evening she'd have the radiogram going full blast, and always modern dance music. She drank consistently but not heavily, and neither of the Gambets had seen her under the influence. That period lasted till the following summer. That previous autumn was when she'd acquired the mink coat. She'd also by then quite a lot of new clothes and jewellery. She also adopted a far more reserved attitude towards the kitchen. Gambet could only describe it as "putting on the madam".

The third period was from that early summer till her going away. The weekends we'd already heard about, and the increasing virulence of her attacks on her husband, interspersed with short periods like the first idyllic days. And we'd heard about the separate bedrooms. The Gambets now told us of her hostility to them personally. More than once when she was asked if, for instance, she'd be in for lunch, she flew into a rage and made accusations of spying. The Gambets, by the way, insisted that through all this Matching had been most forbearing. He'd go far out of his way to avoid a quarrel.

"Tell me about the actual dismissal?"

"It was on the Thursday morning, just over a week ago," Gambet said. "The master had hardly left the house when she came in here looking as pleased as could be, and told us we wouldn't be any longer required. Legally she was within her rights, sir. It's the madam who controls the kitchen, but I rather forgot myself. I said that we'd been engaged by the master and he was the one to dismiss us. She said I could ring him in town and he'd tell me he *was* dismissing us. I didn't actually do it, sir, but I found out later she was right. It was the old story. She'd got round him again. Anything for peace and quiet."

"That's what I've gathered," I told him. "But now to more confidential matters. Did she ever bring a male friend here in Mr. Matching's absence?"

"Never, sir."

"Did you ever hear her telephoning to what you might think now was a male friend?"

"Never, sir."

"You have time off?"

"Yes, sir. Thursday is our regular day, subject to anything special happening."

"Then when you returned, or the next day, did you ever see any signs whatever of a man's having been here? Special cigarette ends? An extra glass? Anything like that?"

He shook his head.

"No, sir. I can't say that we did. But about the telephoning. I didn't mention it because I thought you'd noticed the telephone in her bedroom. She had that extension put in some months ago."

"Miss Bland came here only the twice?"

"That's right, sir. I think the master disapproved of her, and at that time madam was anxious to keep in his good books."

"What were Mrs. Matching's interests, other than playing endless jazz records?"

"That I wouldn't know, sir. She had no other special interest here. She smoked a great deal, of course."

His wife interrupted him. "But she almost cut that out entirely during the last month or two."

Hallows caught my eye. He was thinking what I was. Cigarettes aren't good for the throat, so maybe Moira was thinking of taking up a singing career again.

"Just one other thing," I said. "The gardens lode a bit neglected. Why?"

That was easy to explain. There'd been an almost fulltime gardener up to a year ago: another oldish retainer who'd been there some forty years. In the early spring he'd been taken ill and undergone a major operation. He'd made a very slow recovery and the Gambets were of the opinion that he'd never be coming back. Matching, for sentimental reasons, wouldn't take on another man till he was sure of that, but had induced another gardener—an old-age pensioner—to slip along from time to time and do anything really necessary. Even he hadn't been along since the late autumn.

"I used to see to the grass myself," Gambet said. "A nice bit of open-air exercise, sir. And not hard work with a motor-mower."

Coffee had long since been finished. I got up. "Just one other thing. Perhaps one of you would show us over the house. Just a matter of getting the feel of everything."

A door to my left led straight into the study, and Gambet took us there first. It was the only room that hadn't been modernised: Victorian fireplace. Victorian furniture, and not uncomfortable as far as concerned the chairs. There were hundreds of books, most of them dating far back: a very old edition of the *Encyclopedia Britannica*, handsomely bound works of Scott, Dickens, Thackeray and Trollope and some early editions of Hardy and Meredith. Some of the shelves had much more modern books and there were scores of paperbacks—Westerns, crime stories, adventures.

"Did Mr. Matching read these?" I said.

"To tell you the truth, sir, he didn't read much else. He said it was a relief after working in town. You see, sir, he liked going to bed at about ten o'clock, as I understood be did when his mother was alive, and he'd read till madam went up. And here, too, as I told you, sir."

He smiled, then caught my eye.

"He'd regularly pass them on to me, too, sir. He knew I liked crime books specially, and when I'd finished with them they'd be handed in at the post-office for charitable institutions. I'm afraid I was a much slower reader, sir."

"And Mrs. Matching: what did she read?"

"Magazines chiefly, sir. There was one called *Modern Jazz*, and various film magazines. I had a private understanding with the master to get rid of them at the end of a week. He didn't like them lying about."

We went straight through the lounge and across the hall to the dining-room. That, too, had been modernised, though on the wall above the mantelpiece was an oil of Matching's mother, painted by her husband. Whistler could have gone on sleeping soundly in his grave. In any case it had been painted when she was in her thirties or early forties: it hadn't quite got the matriarchal touch.

We went upstairs. The only room I wanted to see was Matching's bedroom. Its furniture was less modern: high-class Scandinavian. The outsize bed hadn't been replaced by a smaller one, and there was a brown, deep-pile carpet to match the colour of the beech. In the wall above the one pillow was a fluorescent reading light. Between that room and Moira's room was a really superb bathroom, fully tiled and with a sunk bath. A communicating door had been specially cut through to her room.

"Madam used to spend quite a long time in her bath," Gambet said. "These last few weeks she didn't even trouble to come down, even in negligée, to see the master off. If she weren't going out till after lunch she'd have her breakfast brought up at half-past nine or ten, and she wouldn't come down much before eleven. Which reminds me, sir. Will you two gentlemen be staying to lunch? I assure you it'll be no trouble."

I thanked him and said we hoped to be away before midday. That communicating door from the bathroom to Moira's room was locked on the far side. I gave Hallows the main door key. He was going to search every inch of the room and try to get prints from the suitcases. I went down with Gambet and on to the garage.

It would have been wasted time to look for prints inside that Jaguar. Oldfield had handled it. Maybe one of his men had handled it, and I'd no intention of getting their prints to make comparisons. Even if I did get a print which wasn't theirs, what then? There were ways and means of having it checked at the Yard, but I was pretty sure that job had been pulled off by an amateur. Even if it hadn't, there'd have to be far more definite evidence before I had to tell Matching that the police must take over.

No. What I was looking for, this time in broad daylight and not with the help of a torch, was anything whatever that would throw light on what had happened that weekend, and after another half-hour all I had was negatives. The spare wheel hadn't been used, nor any of the tools. The car was maroon with maroon upholstery, and that made it difficult to look for traces of blood, but when I'd finished I was pretty sure no blood had ever been there. Nor was there any point in sending mud from the wheels to a laboratory. To me that mud was just mud, and I'd be throwing away quite a lot of Matching's money merely to be told so in scientific terms. And, of course, there was no means of knowing what the petrol consumption had been. We'd never be able to find out what the mileage had been at the time the car had left Grange House, or how much petrol had actually been in the tank.

I gave the job up, washed my hands in the downstairs cloakroom and went up to Hallows. He'd just finished, too: gone over every inch of drawer space and come up with only one thing. He look it out of his wallet. Something that had been caught in the crack at the very back of a dressing-table drawer.

It was an admission ticket to the Alhambra Dance Hall, Lewisham, priced at half-a-crown, and with the words ADMISSION ONLY. It was the usual size, about two inches by one, of the usual coarse, thin cardboard and carried the number 2278 in the top right-hand corner. It wasn't at all faded: in fact it looked as clean as if it had been issued the previous night.

"Look at the back," he told me.

On the back was some very small print. *This ticket is issued subject to the Regulations and By-laws. . . .* My eye took in just that much and then I was looking at what had been written in ink clean across the print:

AMONG MY SOUVENIRS

"Among my souvenirs," I said. "That rings some sort of a bell."

"The title of a popular song a few years ago," he told me. "I showed it to Gambet and he's sure it's madam's writing."

"Part of a collection?"

"Looks like it. Probably the only one of its kind or she wouldn't have written on it. Might have been part of a collection of theatre programmes, cuttings and so on."

"Must have had some special significance," I said. "We might do worse than call up at that dance hall on the way back. It's on our way."

"Just one thing," he said. "I had a vague idea someone had been in here after we left last night. I may be wrong but something told me those cases weren't just as we'd left them. They hadn't been opened at all. Just moved. Or maybe I was wrong. After all, door keys always come in pairs."

"You mentioned it to Gambet?"

"Didn't seem worth it Besides, I wasn't sure. We can still ask him."

Gambet was doing some dusting in the hall. He believed there were spare keys, though there'd never been occasion to use them. He didn't even know where they were kept, unless it was in the study.

"Any particular key you wanted, sir?"

"No, no," I said. "Just one of those things that occurred to us."

I looked at the grandfather clock. It was a quarter to one.

"You'd like a drink before you go, sir? Beer, perhaps?"

"Thank you, no," I told him. "We ought to be on our way in a few minutes. Any of those magazines that Mrs. Matching used to read still in the lounge?"

He didn't think so. He thought he'd taken the last two or three and put them in the dustbin and that had been emptied the previous day. In any case we did go into the lounge again, maybe for a quick warm-up before starting back. It was still thawing rapidly but the air was raw and cold.

"Think I'll have a quick look for those keys," Hallows said.

We went through to the study and he slipped on his gloves. He tried the drawers of the bureau without luck. That study had french windows that led to the side and back gardens. I tried them and they were open.

"Might as well have a look at those outside buildings," I said. "Shouldn't take a minute. Nothing like rounding off a job."

Those buildings faced outwards. The parts that had been stable and coach-house were empty except for the motor-mower and a collection of junk that had accumulated over the years. The end section that must have been a feed and bedding store was now divided. The larger part nearer to the house had had a special doorway cut and was now used for fuel. The smaller half, facing the kitchen garden, was a garden shed. Hallows is what they call an enthusiastic gardener. His summer speciality is roses, with chrysanthemums to follow in autumn, and fine stuff they are. I know, because occasionally he gives some to my wife.

He gave a smile and a sort of "Ah!" when he looked in that shed. It had a long potting bench under which were pots of all sizes and heaps of sand and peat and there seemed to be every possible kind of tool. There was a stack of seed-boxes and even some scales. On a shelf were packets of fertilisers, fungicides and insecticides and, in one corner, a portable sprayer.

"Wouldn't mind a place like this myself," he told me, still smiling away. The smile suddenly went.

"Hallo? What's this?"

This was a spade. His hands were still gloved and he took it off its nail. He took it to the door where the light was even better.

"Funny?" he said. "What do you make of it?"

"Make of it? Nothing, except it's a spade. Looks like stainless steel."

"Remember what Gambet told us about the gardener?"

"Only that he's ill."

"That's because you're not a gardener. Nobody's worked in this garden since Gambet gave the lawns their last cut. Yet this spade's been used within the last few days."

It looked clean enough to me, and I said so.

"Not the right kind of cleaning," he told me. "See the mud still here? Now look at this other spade, and this fork. Just a slight rust where the oil-rag missed but no mud. Whoever used this spade thought he'd cleaned it well enough, but he hadn't. And he didn't know about the oily rag."

"So what?"

"Don't know," he said. "Wouldn't do any harm, though, to have a look round."

There was not a single vegetable in that garden except the few greens and the scarcely visible tops of some now rotting carrots, and never an inch of soil seemed to have been disturbed. We moved along the grass path to that quarter acre of orchard.

"Trees haven't been grease-banded or winter sprayed," Hallows said.

The path had ended, and beyond the small orchard was rough grass that had once been a wide path. Beyond that was a dense mass of overgrown shrubbery, evergreens mostly, and to the sides you could see the tall, overgrown hedge that marked the boundary. Beyond that lay a thin strip of falling meadow-land and still farther a wood and the buildings of a farm.

Hallows said he'd have a look round. I lighted my pipe and had a look at the view. A moment or two and he was calling "Come here a minute, will you. Round to your left."

I went round and made my way along the narrow space between hedge and shrubbery. Then I saw him. He was in a gap that had been left where some large shrub or other had died. He pointed downwards.

"What d'you make of that?"

I didn't see anything, except maybe that where he was pointing seemed even more free from weeds than the rest.

"Someone's dug a deepish hole here. Look, sir. This is it here to here. See that surplus earth scattered under here when it was filled in again? See how it's slightly sunk?"

"Good God, yes!" I said, and then I was fumbling at my glasses. "You can't think it's a grave?"

"What else could it be? Something's been buried here. Otherwise, why dig the hole?"

My body seemed suddenly chilled. It was quite a time before I could speak. I was supposed to give the orders, but I hadn't any to give.

"What's the best thing to do?"

"Open it," he said. "I'll fetch a spade and get to work. I've probed it and it's only about two feet deep. We needn't open the whole of it."

He went off for the spade. That hole, now I could clearly make out its outline, was about four feet six by eighteen inches. I saw the stick Hallows had trimmed and sharpened and used as a probe. I thrust it down and at about two feet it came up against something hard. I tried it in another place and the same thing happened. Then Hallows came back.

He worked methodically from about a foot and a half along to the end of the hole. I'm no gardener nowadays but I saw the subsoil on top with only a little clay and the far better soil as he dug down. Only five minutes and his spade hit that something hard.

"The bottom," he said. "There's nothing there! Just the hard bottom."

He began again, this time at the opposite end. Another five minutes and that was cleared, too. That hole was absolutely empty. Someone had dug what might have been a grave. But there'd been no burial. Just a filling in.

He was puffing a bit and I handed him a cigarette, as much to sooth my own nerves as his.

"You know what I was thinking? That we were going to uncover Moira Matching."

"Me, too," he said. "Preposterous, perhaps, but that's how it was. Funny to be employed by a man to find his wife and then think he might have killed her himself."

"Matching wouldn't have killed her," I said. "It's the last thing he'd have done."

"I know. But that doesn't stop you from thinking." He nodded down. "When you suddenly come up against something like that."

"And what now? Fill it in again."

It didn't take long to fill it in. By the time he'd finished the job and scattered some of the dead leaves over it and around, you'd never have known it was there. As we stepped out he ran his eye along the boundary hedge. It was gapped here and there. Anyone could have got through.

"Couldn't have been anyone from outside," he said. "He'd have brought his own spade. You going to mention this to Mr. Matching, sir, or not?"

I said I'd think it over. How Matching could throw any light on the matter I couldn't at the moment see. So Hallows cleaned the spade—it hadn't been the one we'd first seen—and gave it a wipe with an oily rag. He gave his own shoes a bit of a clean and then we went back to the house. A minute or two and we were on our way. We stopped at Oldfield's garage and told him he could now collect the Jaguar, then we pushed on to Sevenoaks. It was then after one o'clock. That dance hall wouldn't probably be open till at least two, so we found an hotel and had lunch.

It was about half-past two when we found the dance hall. The front entrance was closed so we went round to the back.

That door was open. There'd be an afternoon session from three to five-thirty and a main evening one from seven-thirty to ten-thirty. That's what the manager told us. I'd given him my card and said we were trying to trace a missing person. He had a look at the photographs and could only shake his head. We showed him the admission ticket.

"Can you tell us anything from that? Date, for example?"

"Only that it's prior to September last," he said. "After that we had coloured tickets, changing the colour every now and again."

"With forgery in mind?"

"That's it," he said. "We had a few cases. Plenty of bright boys round here, you know."

"You have them printed in big batches?"

He did. Fifty thousand at a time. The numbers always went from one to fifty thousand. That ticket Moira had kept might have been for any session during the four years the dance hall had been open, and up to September last. In other words, you now couldn't trace even the month, let alone the day.

"Any really special show put on during those four years, other than the opening night?"

"We're always having special shows," he told us. "We change the bands, the singers, the competitions: anything to keep the customers interested."

"Every night a gala night?"

He laughed. "Well, not quite that. Say every week."

We thanked him and pushed on, but not till we'd parted with one of the photographs. He was to show it to his staff, and there'd be a five-pound reward for the right information. We were making for Old Bond Street, and as we turned into Park Avenue, Hallows asked what I'd decided to tell Julian Matching. I said it might be best to bring everything into the open. He agreed.

C.T. Haddowe was as quiet as ever when we walked in. There wasn't even an assistant behind the long counter, though one appeared at once from somewhere as soon as the door bell shrilled. He wasn't the one I'd seen before. This was an even older man. He asked us to wait a moment and disappeared through the far door. In a moment or two he was back, and Jean Lindman with him. She didn't look all that pleased to see us.

"Julian's looking horribly ill," she told me. "All this worry is really getting him down. You won't stay long, will you? I'd like him to go home and to bed."

She showed us in. I had a shock when I saw him. His face was pale and the eyes dark and sunken. The room was warm but his hand was very cold.

"You're in for a dose of 'flu," I told him. "You ought to be home and under the blankets."

"Jean's been making a fuss," he told me testily. "I'm perfectly all right. Worried, of course, but nothing more. Quite able to listen to anything you have to tell me."

"Well, we won't keep you more than a minute or two," I said. "About that passport," I went on, just to make time. "You still have it?"

"No," he said. "It's gone. She must have taken it."

"Right," I said. "If she's used it, it might be traced. There is just one other thing which we think you ought to know. Hallows had better tell you about that."

He looked startled for a moment. Maybe I'd been a bit abrupt. Then when Hallows came to that business of the hole, his mouth suddenly gaped. The voice grew hysterical.

"A grave. It *was* a grave! Don't you see? They meant to kill me!"

"No, no. That's only an assumption."

"It's true I tell you! Why did she give me that poison?" He was staring across the room, and then, suddenly, his lip quivered and his eyes began welling with tears. His head fell forward on his arms and quietly, pitifully, he was sobbing his heart out.

I was on my feet and I felt a pity, too. Many a time in my life I've come against something that's made me long for the healing outlet of tears, but those tears would somehow never come. Churchill has the gift, but I'd never have dreamt that Julian Matching could so quickly have summoned an emotion. Then Jean Lindman came in. She took one horrified look at Matching, then rounded on me like a tigress.

"What've you been doing? What have you told him?"

I put a quick finger to my lips and turned towards the door. She followed us out. In the lobby I whispered what I thought she ought to know.

"We found a hole in the shrubbery this morning at Grange House. It looked like a grave, but there was nothing in it. He thinks it was meant for himself."

"Oh, my God!"

A last horrified look and she was opening Matching's door. We went quickly out to the car. For a moment I didn't feel like moving it on.

"He was right," Hallows said. "Why the hell didn't I think of it before!"

"A Mickey doesn't kill," I reminded him.

"No, but it knocks a man out. All the easier to strangle him."

"Yes," I said slowly. "But if so, why didn't they strangle him?"

We didn't know. Maybe Moira Matching had stopped "X" from that finality. Maybe there'd been some sudden pressure of time. All we did know was that the hole, which might have betrayed them, was filled in.

"If I'd been 'X' I'd have killed her there and then instead," I said. "I'd have buried her, tipped off the police later and had the whole thing pinned down to Matching."

"Maybe she had the jewellery. He couldn't kill her if he wasn't sure of that."

"Yes," I said, and moved the car slowly on.

6

DIGGING DEEP

FRENCH came in pretty late that evening and I didn't get his report till the morning. It was negative all through. No one who'd been on duty at the railway station on that Saturday night had seen Moira Matching. Five employees had recognised the photograph without knowing the lady's name. All five recalled some previous occasion when they'd seen her but never a soul had clapped eyes on her on that Saturday or any day following. In the town itself French found the hotel where Moira sometimes had tea after a cinema matinée, but no hotel remembered her at that vital weekend. He also called on a couple of country clubs in the district but neither recalled such a woman as ever being there even for a meal.

I waited till well after nine before ringing Grange House. Gambet told me that Miss Lindman had as good as brought Matching home and sent for the doctor. Matching had at once been sent to bed. Not influenza. Gambet said: just overwork. The doctor had advised complete rest for at least a week. Oldfield had taken Miss Lindman back to the station.

It was information that affected the case. We shouldn't, for instance, now have Matching round our necks, asking for progress reports. We could just get on with the job. Or could we? After that frightening discovery of the previous afternoon, could Matching be relied on to follow his doctor's orders? And, if it came to that, just who precisely was employing us? Hill had left it vague—a sort of family affair—but to whom was I to go now if something arose that broke the terms of the unwritten agreement? That, for instance, the time had definitely come to call in the police. I rang Hill to clear the matter up, though I didn't put it like that: just said one or two things ought to be discussed. He asked me to see him at once. He didn't mention Hallows, so I went alone.

"A curious thing," he said as soon as I stepped into his room, "but I was just about to ring you when you rang me. Jean Lindman told me first thing this morning what had happened yesterday afternoon. Like to tell me about it yourself?"

I told him the whole thing, including that distressing climax in Matching's office.

"Must have been dreadful," he said. "Julian's a hard-headed business man and for him to collapse like that is pretty surprising. Just shows how torn to pieces he's been. But about that hole. You're sure it was intended as a grave?"

"What else could it be?"

"Well," he said. "I remember digging a pretty big hole or two at my place to bury broken glass and stuff like that. You know, getting rid of it for good."

"Yes, but you did bury the glass. This hole had nothing in it. And why bother about filling it in again even if it was intended to bury some sort of rubbish. Nobody was likely to go there. Also there's the question of who dug it. That hole wasn't dug by anyone connected with the house in any way. Also it wasn't just a hole. It had a definite shape. And one other thing. Hallows knows what he's talking about and he's prepared to swear that that hole was dug at about last week-end. It wasn't dug since because of the frost and snow and it wasn't dug much before or it'd have been far more wet at the bottom."

His smile was a bit rueful.

"You've certainly been piling up evidence. But *was* it so definitely a grave? Mind if I mark the size on the carpet hers so we can have a look at it?"

He marked the four corners with books. "There we are, then. What sort of a body would go in a hole like that?"

"Don't know," I said. "It'd depend on the amount of compression. Draw up the knees and use some force and you could get most bodies in."

"Julian's just my height," he said. "Five ten. I admit he's on the thin side, but it'll take a lot of convincing to get me to believe you could get him into a hole that size. And who was supposed to do the burying? Moira?"

I thought he was being a bit obtuse.

"The boy-friend. Remember that theory Hallows gave you? Well, we've seen no reason to change it."

"What about Moira in the hole? I won't quarrel with that She'd have been a deadly witness if anything went wrong." He shrugged his shoulders. "Mind you. I'm not interfering. It's your job, not mine. What I do say is that Julian's been slowly working himself up to a state of hysteria, and when you told him about that so-called grave he just went to pieces. I think he's been reading far too many of those detective stories of his."

"Could be," I said. "Too early yet to form any real conclusions. What I'm going to assume is that his mind has to be kept off the case and any necessary reports are to be made to you."

"That's right. If he should worry you in any way, just refer him to me."

On the whole a satisfactory meeting, but as I walked back to the Agency I couldn't help the sneaking feeling that he'd talked some good hard sense. I wasn't so cocksure that Julian's body could have been wedged into that hole. Moira's body, definitely yes. If that were so, then it was the jewellery that had saved her. Maybe she'd had the sense to know it and had managed to secrete it somewhere as a guarantee that at least she'd get her share.

Not that it mattered all that much for whom that grave had been intended. No one could have dug it, and later filled it in, but "X". And it was still as obvious as it had ever been that "X" was the one we had to find, and that we could find him only through Moira.

We were later than I'd intended when we set off for Lower Norgate Street. Fulham. We'd looked it up in the directory, and it didn't take much finding. It was, in fact, a continuation of Addison Road: one of those continuations of a shopping street that get shabbier and shabbier as they get farther away. Number 22 was still a little sweet and tobacco shop. An old-fashioned bell tinkled as we went in.

A youngish woman appeared from somewhere in the rear of the shop. I explained who we were and how we were trying to trace the late Mrs. Gifton's heirs. It took her a moment or two even to remember who the late Mrs. Gifton was. And she didn't know about any heirs. She'd bought the shop through an agency not long before Mrs. Gifton went to hospital, and it was her husband who'd looked the place over.

"Anyone near here who must have known Mrs. Gifton well?"

"Well, there's Mrs. Young," she said. "She's at the Bargain Shop a little way along. About four doors."

There's scarcely a street in the drab purlieus of the suburbs that doesn't have its junk shop. Ma Young, as we'd been told she was known, had merely found an attractive same. There were definitely bargains in the oddments of furniture on the pavement outside the shop. The windows were chock-a-block with glass and china ornaments, reproduction candlesticks, brass fenders, a couple of battered warming-pans, a dolls' house, coal scuttles, a phonograph complete with trumpet, framed photographs, and the whole backed by worn rugs and small carpets hung behind on strung wires. It was a fine but overcast and almost muggy morning, and the door was wide open.

Larger pieces of furniture were round the walls: seats, tops and even open drawers displayed the usual debris of a long lifetime. Hallows coughed loudly and we could hear sounds from somewhere beyond the one inner door. Then a woman appeared. She was short and stout, with grey hair worn incongruously in a sort of bob. She looked the cheerful kind, and as soon as she opened her mouth I guessed she'd lived in that neighbourhood most of her life.

"Yes, dear? Anything you fancy?"

"All depends," Hallows said. "As a matter of fact we're after information. Might be worth a bit to you."

She ran an eye slowly over him, then had a look at me. "You're not from the police?"

"No," I said. "I'm a solicitor and we're trying to trace any heirs of the late Mrs. Gifton."

Her eyes bulged. "You mean they've come into money?"

"That's it," I said. "We were told at the sweet shop that you'd known the family."

"Known 'em?" She laughed. "Polly Gifton and me was friends. Always was. She was a widow like me and we always got along well together. A bit younger than me, and yet she was took first."

"What about the two children?"

"Ah, them," she said. "I remember the day them two little mites come, just as if it was yesterday. Frank was about six and Mary was about two or two and a half. Been bombed out, you know. Before you knew it they was calling me Ma." She laughed. "That's where the name come from. You see, I was always in and out as you might say. Never had no kids of my own. Now everyone knows me as Ma. The name's Fanny, really."

She loved talking. All one had to do was put in an occasional leading question—a kind of tug at the steering rope—and off she'd go along the required course. Chronology didn't matter. So long as we had the facts we could piece them together later.

Frank was a nice boy: the quiet sort. He was never any trouble and got a job in a garage in the High Street He was a good mechanic, but when his aunt died he went to Canada and nothing had been heard of him from that day to this. Ma seemed just a bit upset about that. She always expected him to write. After all, he'd slept in one of her bedrooms. There were just the two small rooms above the sweet shop, and when Mary insisted on a room of her own. Frank had to turn out. Perhaps it was because Frank wanted to forget all about Norgate Street. He never got on well with Mary.

Mary? A regular little madam if ever there was one. That was because she'd been spoilt from the very first, and Ma owned that she herself might have done some of the spoiling. She'd been a real beauty: looked like a little angel—till she went into one of her tempers.

She hadn't done as well at school as Frank and had left the moment the law allowed. She'd been getting a bit of a handful long before that: associating with a set of which neither her aunt nor Ma herself approved. All that dancing and jazz, and coming home late. When she got that job at the factory—something to do with wireless and television sets—and had her own money, she was nothing else but a lodger: hardly time to gulp down a meal when she got in, before she was dolling herself up and then she'd be off.

Then had come the singing trio. It had started as part of the entertainment scheme at the works: Mary and two other girls of her own age calling themselves the Three Emms. That's when she began calling herself Moira. Another girl was Molly and the third—well, she couldn't remember, except that it began with M. The real sensation was when the trio won a contest at the local Palais de Danse, and it was just after that that Polly Gifton was taken ill.

The shop and premises were rented, not owned, and the sale of the business—stock included—wouldn't have brought more than a hundred pounds, and she didn't know bow much Frank had claimed when everything had been cleared up. In any case, he'd been earning good money few years, so maybe Mary had had what was left. All Ma knew was that one moment Mary was there and the next she wasn't What she did know was that she'd left her job at the factory and the Three Emms had broken up. And she'd neither seen Mary nor heard a word about her from that day to this.

"Her friends," I said. "Did you ever see any of them?"

She snorted. "Never brought any of 'em home. Ashamed she was, of her own home, and after all what'd been done for her. Between you and me, mister, that was what started poor Polly's illness. If she'd been mine I'd have told her a thing or two. Makes you sick to think of it Do you know that if her aunt hadn't been took as she was, she was even thinking of going into lodgings on her own?"

"Did you ever hear the names of any of her close friends?"

"No," she said, and frowned. "Can't say as I did. Except them Three Emms."

"No boy-friends?"

"You bet your life there were. None she ever brought home, though, like any self-respecting girl would."

"We think she did have one girl-friend with whom she kept in touch," I said. "A red-headed girl called Hulda Bland. You ever hear of her?"

The name meant nothing. It did bring a question of her own.

"Do you two gentlemen know what happened to her after she left here?"

"We've nothing definite," I said. "All we have is just an idea that she kept in touch with this Hulda Bland."

"No business of mine," she said, "but wouldn't *she* be the one to know?"

"This is a tricky business, Mrs. Young. We haven't yet found this Hulda Bland. As a matter of fact we thought we'd start at the very beginning with someone like yourself who'd know practically every-thing about Mary Hyson. You might even have been able to give us a line on Hulda Bland. But just one other question. Obviously Mary Hyson was thinking about a singing career, and if she and the trio wanted to get jobs they'd have to have an agent. Did you ever hear a mention of that?"

She hadn't. Hallows had nothing further to ask, except the where-abouts of the factory where she'd worked. I handed Ma a pound note, just for her time. At first she wouldn't take it. Hallows gave her one of our cards and she promised to let us know at once if anything else was learned. A refreshing character was Ma Young: the cheerful, indomitable kind: heart as big as a house and still with some of the moral values that quite a lot of us have forgotten.

Outside the Bargain Shop we split up. Hallows was off to the factory to learn what he could before the place closed down for the weekend. It was only five minutes away, so I took the car. Neither of us knew how long we'd be and the only rendezvous was the Agency.

I drove back till I found a café-restaurant, had some coffee and sandwiches and made my way towards Hammersmith. Ma Young had been shrewd enough in suggesting that Hulda Bland was the one we should have interviewed first If we'd told her about Mary Hyson's marriage and how she'd met her husband, Ma might have been even shrewder and suggested that the Frascoli Restaurant and the band she'd been with were the places at which to start. But it hadn't been quite so obvious as that. If there was one assumption we had to make it was that Moira hadn't made "X's" acquaintance till the last three or four months. Neither restaurant nor band could help us in that.

Now, after that talk with Ma Young, we were pretty sure we were tackling things the right way. We'd learned, for instance, that Mary Hyson had been ashamed of her home and origins, and we now knew that almost everything she'd told her husband had been calculated lies. That being so, it was more than ever vital to cut herself clean off from everything that had happened prior to the marriage. But not from Hulda Bland. Hulda was different. Hulda was a fellow-conspirator.

The two had shared a flat right up to the time of the marriage, and what Hulda didn't know about Moira was nobody's business. Hulda couldn't be dropped. And since she'd been to Grange House for two weekends, she must have been carefully coached beforehand as to what to corroborate and what to avoid. Hulda must have found those weekends pretty boring, and it was clear that she hadn't wanted a third. But the friendship had lasted. The two had gone on meeting in town and then the occasional weekends of Moira had become a regular thing, except far that vital one in every four. Julian Matching had never spotted the significance of that. Julian believed what he wanted to believe. He was still besotted about his wife, for instance, and therefore he let himself believe that she could be induced to come back to him and help to make a fresh start. The way we saw it was that she was having intimate relations with "X", and that from that point of view one of every four weekends would have been at least frustrating. But Hulda Bland must have known quite a good deal about all that, even if Moira had lied to her as she lied to everyone else. My hope that afternoon was that Hulda had been sufficiently shrewd to put three and one together and make the answer four.

Setting all that aside, we'd had no time as yet to get into touch with Hulda, and, if she really were a mannequin, then she'd be working most days. But probably not on a Saturday afternoon. No point in Moira's having weekends with Hulda if Hulda was always at work, and that was a reason why we'd planned things as we had. It was, in fact, about two o'clock on that Saturday afternoon when I drew the car in at that block of flats known as York House.

Jean Lindman, who seemed to have been suspicious about Moira from the very first, had almost certainly taken the trouble to inspect York House. It was as run-down as she'd said it was. It had a general shabbiness. Its exterior needed redecorating and there was grass between the flag-stones of the little forecourt. Stairs led up from a smallish entrance hall which wasn't too clean, and on the one visible lift was a notice—OUT OF ORDER. Another notice, with a finger pointing to somewhere beyond the stairs, said CARETAKER. The list of tenants gave Hulda's flat as Number 7, which meant the first-floor. I walked up to the first-floor landing. Hulda's flat was the first on the right.

Someone was in. You could hear the music from the top of the stairs, a good fifteen feet away: not jazz, as I embracingly call it, but dance music with a steady beat and the sugary gurgle of saxophones. I waited till the disc had run down before I pushed the bell. It was quite a few seconds before the door opened. Not wide: a foot, perhaps, not more.

"Yes?"

The startlingly blue eyes took me in from hat to shoes. I saw a good-looking red-head in a fawn-coloured jumper and black, drain-pipe jeans that set off a wonderful figure.

"Miss Bland?"

"Yes."

She wasn't wasting words and her eyes were still appraising me. Hulda knew the ropes. One false move and that door would slam in my face.

"A private matter. Miss Bland. I'm here on behalf of Mr. Julian Matching."

For a second or two she was startled. Then the lip curled. "What about him? What's his trouble?"

I handed her my Agency card. She looked at it, but always with half an eye on me.

"All right," she said. "So you're a private detective. What's that to do with me?"

"You were a friend of Moira Matching, Miss Bland. She left her husband a week ago today. Nothing's been heard of her since. We hoped you might help us."

She gave me a last, level look: drew back for me to step in, and closed the door behind me.

"You're pretty posh for a detective."

"We come all sorts and sizes," I told her. "I just happen to be head of a firm—and a friend of Julian Matching."

"Sit down," she said. "What's all this about Moira?"

That sitting-room was only twelve by nine: the worn, stan-dard-sized carpet fitted it exactly. Into it was crowded a small settee and a couple of easy chairs. The gramophone was on a little table in the space between a small, reproduction desk and another door. On the desk was a telephone and, flanking it, a wireless set. An electric fire was going full blast and the air was hazy with tobacco smoke. In an ash-tray on the floor in front of the other chair a cigarette was still smoking.

"Mind if I take my coat off? It's rather warm in here."

"Suit yourself," she said. "Put it on the settee."

She took that other chair, picked up the cigarette and stubbed it out.

"Now what's this about Moira?"

I told her just as much as I thought she ought to know. What really shook her was the Jaguar.

"Did she ever drive it right to here?"

"Once or twice when the days were long. Other times she'd leave it at Bromley or Sevenoaks and come up by train." She frowned. "I can't make it out. Leaving the car there all that time. And all her clothes and things."

"That's why we think something serious must have happened to her," I said. "Would you have abandoned that car and half a dozen suit-cases full of clothes?"

"Depends," she said. "You say you're a friend of his?"

"In the way of business—yes."

"I see."

She lighted another cigarette and leaned back in the chair with her slim legs crossed.

"It hadn't occurred to you that she might have left that stuffy bastard for good? Other men can buy Jaguars and clothes."

"That's just what did occur to us. That's why we hoped you could help."

"Me?"

"You were her friend. She was always spending weekends here?"

She frowned. "Who told you that?"

"She told her husband that. That was her excuse for being away so much."

"And how many weekends was she supposed to spend here?"

"I have the actual dates."

I took out my notebook.

"Her husband was getting a bit suspicious so he actually made a note of the actual dates. The last occasion was three weeks ago today and there were two consecutive weekends before that."

"And when would she get home?"

"Just about in time for the evening meal on the Sunday." She laughed. It wasn't a pleasant laugh. "You knew Moira?"

"No," I said. "Never saw her in my life."

She passed me the packet and lighted another cigarette for herself.

"Well, I knew her. We were kids together. In the same classes at school." She laughed. "Soil of chalk and cheese if you know what I mean. I was always getting into trouble but she was the teacher's pet. And, brother, could she lie! Talk about being barefaced!"

The laugh went. "Just a minute. Why should *I* be telling tales? Suppose she comes back. Where do I stand then?"

I gave her my word that everything was in the strictest confidence. Nothing was being written down so she could always deny having mentioned a thing. I did add a couple of scarers, just for luck. In a day or two, if there was still no news, the police would have to be called in, and I was sure she'd rather talk to me than to them. If anything more serious had happened, then she might have to give evidence on oath.

She looked me straight in the eye. "You wouldn't be trying to frighten me? I don't scare easy. I've been around."

"You've got me wrong," I told her. "It isn't that. What it boils down to is whether you'd rather talk to me or to the police. They don't make any promises, you know."

She tried to look tough but it didn't last "All right I'll take your word for it. What was I telling you just now?"

"That she was a first-class liar."

"That's it. And she was, and I'll give you just one instance. She had to tell her husband a whole pack of lies. I knew. She had to tell me, so I could back everything up."

"But about yourself. Surely she'd never have lied to you?"

"To me?" She laughed. "Brother, how simple can you get! You didn't know her. With her it was Moira first and Moira second and Moira for anything left over. Not that she wasn't generous, mind you. She used to give me no end of clothes and never let me pay for a thing, not when we were out together."

"Bribery?"

She shrugged her shoulders. "You might call it that. Didn't do me any harm. You had to watch her, though. Never knew whether she was telling you a lie or the truth. About those weekends, for instance. She never spent more than two weekends here the whole of the last twelve months. What she used to do was get here about twelve o'clock on a Saturday and then we'd go somewhere posh for lunch and then we'd go to a picture or have a whirl at the local palais. We might have tea out and then we'd come back here and sit and yarn. If she was leaving early—six or half-past—that's all we'd do, but if she was staying a bit later, say till eight, we might have a sort of scratch meal at about seven. And that was the regular routine."

"You're referring to, say, the last few months? When her visits got more frequent?"

"That's right When she started coming nearly every week. She used to reckon she'd go crackers if she had to spend a whole week-end with that dope of a husband of hers. I didn't worry. Always a bit of fun to have Moira around."

"When she left you on a Saturday evening, where did she say she was going?"

She looked surprised.

"I told you. Going home. To Charing Cross Station and then to wherever she'd left her car. It depended on the weather. If it was bad, she'd have left it at Sevenoaks, and when it was good she'd have gone right through to Bromley."

"Did you ever actually see her get on a train?"

"Only once. Let me see: it'd be about six weeks ago. That's right. Just the beginning of December." She paused to give me one of her tougher looks. "You're still on the level? You're sure all this is confidential?"

"I'll put it in writing if you'd like it that way."

"All right, all right. I believe you. God knows why. But about that Saturday evening. She'd been taken a bit faint, so I insisted on going with her. Strictly between you and me I might have dropped a danger if I'd said what I thought, only I remembered she hadn't been sleeping with her husband for months so it couldn't have been that—if you know what I mean. Good job I didn't say anything. Next time she came, she was right as rain."

"And at Charing Cross she took the Sevenoaks train?"

"She did, and I'll tell you why. I don't like trains. Always afraid I'll take the wrong one and land up God knows where, so when we were going through the barrier I asked the man if it was the Sevenoaks train. Moira was almost snappy. She said if I'd read the board I'd have seen it was the Sevenoaks train."

"She had a return ticket?"

"That's right, and I had a platform ticket I remember she wouldn't even let me pay for that."

"Well, that seems to be all," I said. "And now let me remind you of something we were talking about earlier. She *didn't* go home on a Saturday night. She'd never get home till a Sunday evening. So where did she spend best part of twenty-four hours?"

"Search me," she said. "But if you're hinting she was spending it with some man or other, let me tell you she never even gave me the slightest hint of such a thing."

"You never even had a suspicion?"

"Me? Why should I? I didn't even know she wasn't going straight home1. I will admit she hinted several times recently she was thinking of leaving dear old Julian. You know, just toying with the idea. The last I heard about that was she'd as good as told him so. If you could believe her."

"Then did she ever give you a hint as to what she'd do when she left him?"

"Oh, yes. She didn't keep anything to herself about that She had money, so she was going to get back in the groove with some singing lessons and get herself a job with some band. She hadn't got a bad voice, you know."

"She didn't by chance mention the name of a possible agent?"

"Good God, no! She hadn't got as far as that yet."

"Of course. You said she had money. A lot of money?"

She smiled. "Depends what you mean. He made her a good allowance and there was what she could fiddle out of the house-keeping. She had her own banking account. I do know that. Also she had her jewellery. Lovely, it was, most of it. See this ring? She gave me that. I had it valued and it's worth—you have a guess."

"Fifty pounds?"

"Seventy-five. And that's nothing to what else she had." She laughed. "Moira wouldn't have been short of money. You can bet your life on that."

She'd been glancing at her wrist-watch. The well, it seemed to me, had been pumped dry, so I got to my feet.

"You've been very helpful, Miss Bland. You can rely on me to keep what you've told me to myself."

She gave me quite an appraising look. "You're quite a nice guy—really. You married?"

"Yes," I said, and probably my smile was more of a leer. "But not too much so."

"Drop in again some time," she said. "You can tell me the latest about Moira. I'm always in by seven."

"Fine," I said. "Can't say exactly when, but I'll be dropping in. By the way, aren't you a mannequin?"

"Me?" She laughed. "That was Moira's idea: sort of bolstering up those lies about herself. Thought it sounded better than model."

I let myself run a new appraising eye. "And a good model, too, I'd say."

"Don't do too bad," she told me. "What's it matter so long as the money comes in."

"And the work's not too uncongenial?"

That really amused her. "Say, you're getting quite a character. Don't think you'd better drop in next week after all, not if you're growing up at this rate." She gave me a gentle push in the direction of the door. "Sorry I've got to turn you out, but I have to go out myself. Better luck next time."

I kept her at a safe distance and let only my eyes speak for me as we shook hands. As soon as I was down the stairs again I paused for just a moment's thinking, and then I moved the car on as far as the first left turn. I hoped it might lead me round towards the flats again and it did. I came out heading for town, about fifty yards short.

I sat there with an eye on York House, thinking about that three-quarters of an hour with Hulda Bland, and it was not till twenty minutes later that anything special happened. There wasn't much traffic in that backwater, and the Ford Zephyr that passed me looked something special, and when the winking lights warned of a right-hand turn, I moved my car on. A flashy-looking man, in the late thirties probably, made for the entrance and I wasn't all that far behind. I listened as he went briskly up the stairs and he took only a few steps from the top.

"Well! Look who's here!"

The voice was Hulda's. The door closed almost at once and I went back to my car. I hadn't known that man from Adam but I moved the car on and round the houses till I was back at fifty yards short of York House. I sat on for another half-hour and then it looked pretty certain that Hulda was finding indoors more congenial than out.

7

DIGGING DEEPER

AT SEVEN that night Hallows and I were still in the office, trying to plan a move or two ahead. He hadn't had too good an afternoon but had managed to unearth a survivor of the Three Emms: a girl now married who, for the purposes of the act, had been Maureen, but whose real name was Doris. She, too, had always wondered what had happened to Moira, and he'd had to be careful not to give too much away. When he'd had to say she was married to a business man, Doris was genuinely surprised, and she didn't quite know why—unless it was that Moira had been crazy about singing and getting to be a big name. She'd been the founder and the driving force behind that trio from the start.

"Took me half an hour to get that much out of her," he said. "But she was right, you know. Considering what Moira started with, she didn't do so bad to be singing with a band at Frascoli's. Then Matching came along just when she knew she'd got as far as she was going."

"You think it was her singing that got her so far? Nothing to do with face and figure?"

That was Travers, the cynic.

"Dare say the extras helped," he said. "But she still had a lot of strength of mind: I mean the way she tried to drop the whole of that side of her when she married. Must have been pretty hard not to turn up in her old haunts and swank around with that Jaguar and mink."

"Don't forget those gramophone records that used to drive Matching into the study every night," I said. "I think that after the first few months she wanted to have the best of both worlds."

What emerged from all that was confirmation of what had been just a bit nebulous—that Moira might be carrying out those plans she'd talked over with Hulda. But it might be a new Moira, with dyed hair and another name. And there was the other snag, that Moira might have been deliberately lying. All the same, it was something that had to be tried out. Where Moira would go for singing lessons was a pretty wide field and I thought that part of what she'd told Hulda was camouflage for something else. Innate vanity wouldn't let her admit that her voice, after only a couple of years, wasn't what it had been.

"We might try the agencies and see if they've heard of her again," Hallows said. "I don't think what you learned from Hulda about going back from Charing Cross on a Saturday night to where she left her car gets us anywhere. You get on at Charing Cross with a return ticket and all you have to do is get off at Waterloo or London Bridge. That doesn't give the sign of a clue as to where 'X' actually hangs out. But to go back to Hulda. You think she was telling you the truth?"

"I think she was," I said. "She was pretty frank. Made no bones about telling me what sort of a liar Moira was."

"I wonder," he said. "There's something I can't help thinking. That rather showy looking gent who called on Hulda after she'd told you she was going out. Mightn't she be a tart?"

"Don't think she's a pro. She might be ready to make some extra money on the side."

"You'll own she told you one lie," he said. "What if she told you a whole lot more?"

"Such as?"

"Well, just that on Moira's weekend visits they *each* had a boy-friend and made a bit on the side. A couple of call-girls, if you like, operating from home. You said Hulda had a telephone. So suppose Moira fell for one of the customers and fixed up a private arrangement with him instead. That might make him 'X'."

"Could be," I said. "The trouble'd be to prove it."

He said there might be a way. What he suggested was a visit to York House in the morning. Nobody knew him there, so he'd have a chat with the caretaker. A decent tip might produce quite a lot. It seemed a sound idea to me and better than twiddling our Sabbath thumbs. That's how it has to be in our line of business. You probe and you probe and you come up with ideas. You try them out and nine times out of ten there isn't one that was worth the while. So you begin all over again. Maybe you get a hunch—like that call-girl one—and you try that out, too, though nineteen times out of twenty you've wasted your time. You go back to old ideas with perhaps a new outlook, or something may turn up out of the blue: something you read in a newspaper, a chance word or merely remembering something you'd thought unimportant before. It's slow work and patience the prime asset. And there's always that other asset—that you can go on trying. Your best may be a bit laborious but it's the client who pays.

On the Sunday morning then. Hallows went to York House. I and French spent all the morning and some of the afternoon at London Airport, checking the week's passengers. All we got for our time was the certainty that the Matching passport hadn't been used.

I was having tea at the flat when Hallows rang. His morning had been a wash-out, too. The flashy gentleman I'd seen was a local book-maker, and Hulda's boy-friend. The grapevine had it that wedding bells would soon ring. According to the caretaker, rules and surveil-lance against the use of rooms for purposes of prostitution were pretty strict. Anything of that sort would be spotted at once. All the same, the caretaker would be keeping an eye open, not that you could place much reliance on that. A man had to promise something for a two-pound tip.

"Right," I said. "We'll make a fresh start. If neither of us comes up with anything better by morning, we'll drop in at Frascoli's."

We timed the call for ten-thirty, even if we had to use the service door, but it took us a good few minutes to see the manager, an Angli-cised Italian named Ragoni. We had to show him a photograph of Moira Delane before he remembered her at all, and then it took him quite a while to check the dates. The band, he announced, was the Harry Taylor Sextet and the two vocalists were Moira Delane and

Billy McCrae. The band hadn't had a return date and he'd no idea if they were even still in the business.

We walked along to Charing Cross Road, bought a theatrical paper and over a coffee had a look at announcements. We found the Sextet in very small print. The Harry Taylor Sextet, vocalists Helen Dawn and Billy McCrae, were appearing that week at the Palais de Danse, Holloway. We grabbed a taxi.

It was half-past eleven when we got there and again we had to use a side door. The band was there, rehearsing in a back room, and we might have had to hang about till the break if I hadn't had a card sent in with *Enquiries about Moira Delane*. Taylor himself, shortish, clean-shaven and plump, and as little like a band-leader as could be, came out to the vestibule. He picked me out as the writer of the note.

"Moira's not got herself in any trouble?"

"Strictly between ourselves," I said, "she and her husband haven't been hitting it off lately and a week ago she left him. He wants her found. We wondered if you'd seen her. Her last engagement before she married was with you."

"Haven't seen her for—oh, a couple of years. But what made you think she'd come to me?"

"Because we know she had a hankering to get back in show business again. You ought have helped."

"Well, I haven't seen her." He looked at his watch. "Now if you'll excuse me—"

"Just one question. Who was her agent?"

He thought for a moment.

"Can't say off-hand. Wait a minute, though. Billy might know. He's somewhere around."

It was best part of five minutes before he reappeared.

"Joe Wintle was her agent, so Billy says, and he ought to know."

"You don't happen to know his address?"

"Look it up in the telephone directory. Joe Wintle—W-i-n-t-l-e."

"Thanks," I said. "You haven't time for a drink with us?"

"Some other time."

He was already on his way. We split up forces. Hallows would get a quick bite, then hang around and try to attach himself to Billy McCrae. I was seeing an old friend of mine—Tom Holberg.

Tom runs one of the best theatrical agencies in town and he also has the idea that he owes me a debt. It's the other way. Tom doesn't know it, but he's solved at least a couple of cases for us, which is why I give him every Christmas a box of twenty-five cigars. Tom loves cigars. I was in the office one day when old Solly Bax, Tom's uncle, came in.

"Tom, why you always making now like Churchill with them big cigars?" he asked plaintively.

You see why I give only twenty-five. I think Tom has a shrewd idea where they come from but he's never mentioned it. I do know that he'll keep most people waiting if I send in an urgent chit. He didn't happen to be busy that Monday morning and he saw me at once. A minute or two's talk and I got down to business. I asked how Joe Wintle ranked as an agent.

"Joe's all right," he said in his usual mild way. "Never quite gets the breaks. Handles the small fry—mostly."

"Ever hear of a Moira Delane, Tom?"

He rubbed his chin. "What was she?"

There aren't many people I'd trust as far as Tom Holberg, so I spread the whole story. He shrugged his shoulders.

"I still don't know her. So what is it you want I should do?"

As I told him, it was a question of time. If Wintle hadn't heard a word about Moira since she came off his books, then there'd be no need for me to see him. Tom pressed the buzzer. A minute later, Wintle was on the line.

Did you ever hear that famous record made by the late Tom Clare about a certain tenant of the name of Cohen who rings his landlord about a damaged shutter? The next three minutes were almost as funny. Tom Holberg had used business as an opener and be couldn't have chosen a bigger time-wasting topic. Wintle's voice went on and on, with Tom grimacing helplessly at me and doing his best to get a word in. As soon as Moira's name was mentioned, Wintle seemed to be accusing Tom of trying to steal a client. Tom's a hard person to rile. It was a shame that Wintle should even think such things. In any case, the lady was no longer in the business. Who told him so? Nobody told him so. A minute of that and Tom cupped the receiver.

"You speak to him, Mr. Travers. Please!"

I lifted the receiver. "Mr. Wintle, my name's Travers and I'm here with Tom in his office and I'm the one who's enquiring about Moira Delane. . . . Just listen a minute, Mr. Wintle. It isn't that at all. She's disappeared. Been gone for over a week and I'm trying to trace her. . . . See you? Only too glad to. I'll be with you straight away."

I replaced the receiver.

"I can't understand it. Tom. Soon as I told him she was missing he said, 'Oh my God!!!' just like that. How far away is his office?"

It was the nearer end of Tottenham Court Road, so I cut through Soho and made it in ten minutes. Compared with the Holberg office this was a poor relation: three or four small rooms maybe, on the first floor above a shop. In the tiny enquiry office a girl took my name and rang through. An impatient voice was plainly telling her to send me through at once.

Joe Wintle looked about sixty. He was bald as a coot and far too fat for comfort. His greyish eyes looked a bit watery but they gave me a pretty shrewd look. I introduced myself and showed the Agency card. Then we shook hands and he asked me to take a seat. After that performance on the telephone he was striking me as a man who was making a tremendous effort to hold himself in check, and even then his calmness would have been my agitation. He did let me make a brief, uninterrupted statement, and it was only the two extras I added that really made him all of a tremble. I'd said, you see, that at any moment Moira might be the concern of the police. As an inducement to talk I'd also said that I hoped he and I could exchange information in such a way that the police wouldn't have to trouble him.

"But why are you interested, Mr. Wintle? She's been off your books for two years!"

He told me, and, curiously enough, as he told me he calmed down. I was the one who ought to have been agitated. Moira had been in that very room exactly three weeks ago to the very day. He looked in his diary and showed me the entry. It was the first working day after Christmas, and the afternoon, and things were slack. He'd known, of course, about her marriage—he'd even sent a small present—but he was careful to let her do the talking. He did tell her she was looking younger than ever, to which she'd replied:

"Joe, I want to go back to where I left off."

He'd shrugged his shoulders. "It's not going to be easy, Moira. Things are different. The competition is pretty fierce. Every day I'm turning down girls like you."

"Not like me, Joe," she'd said. "They haven't got my looks for one thing, or my money. See this coat, Joe? It's worth a couple of thousand pounds. See this ring? It's worth another five hundred and there's more at home. You'd like to see my bank balance, too?"

He'd thought for a moment. Things were getting interesting. "You mean you want to buy yourself a job? And what about your husband? What's he going to say?"

"Count him out, Joe. I'm leaving him. Not till I'm ready, though. In a week or two, maybe. But that's my business. And I'm not going to buy myself a job; you're going to do it for me."

"But how? It's the first time I've had such a proposition put up to me."

"Publicity," she'd said. "If necessary you can have a couple of thousand pounds. But there won't be only you and me in it, Joe. I happen to have a friend who can pull a lot of strings and he'll have a say in how it's spent. I wouldn't even mind changing my name. I could be billed as one of those sensations from France, or Mexico, or something like that. I wouldn't let you down, Joe. Give me a week or two to work at some records and I'll have the whole thing pat."

"All right, Moira. Bring your friend along and we'll have a talk. When'll it be?"

"I'll let you know," she had said. "It mayn't be for three weeks or so. What do you think about it, Joe? You think I can do it? Get right up to the top of the tree? And don't try stringing me along. My friend wouldn't stand for that."

"And what *did* you tell her?" I said.

"Told her it was up to her. If things were like what she'd said, I'd guarantee within a couple of years or so to have her right up in, say, the top ten. Moira was always a cut above the average, only she was in too much of a hurry. That got her in bad with people. If you ask me, that's why she got married. Wanted to get too far too fast, and then it got her down."

"And that was all?"

"Just about She promised faithfully she wouldn't keep me waiting more than three weeks. Almost as good as a firm date."

That was when he remembered other things.

"Today!" he said. "She should have been here today. I remember thinking about it when I came in this morning. Now you say she's missing."

A moment and he was leaning forward across the desk, and he'd conjured up from somewhere a ghost of a smile.

"It might mean anything. Maybe she's off on a private honeymoon with that friend of hers. It needn't mean she's what you called missing. Not the way you said it."

I had to disillusion him. All my life, I said. I'd been in much the same line of business, and things were far more serious than just a woman leaving her husband. I wasn't in a position to tell him more, except that I hadn't been exaggerating when I'd said it might at any moment be a matter for police enquiries. There was even the possibility that she might be dead. I said I wasn't a betting man but I'd risk a considerable sum that he'd heard the absolute last of that proposed deal.

"Oh, my God!" His hands were trembling as he leaned back in the chair.

"Tough luck on you," I said. "I'm sorry to have had to put it like that, but believe me, it's the truth."

He shook his head bewilderingly. "Why does it always happen to me? You know Tom Holberg. But for always the bad breaks I might have been where he is now. Nothing but bad breaks. It gets you down."

He leaned forward again. "She comes in here and as good as puts a couple of thousand pounds right under my nose and hardly any strings except that friend of hers, and believe me, Mr. Travers, I know my business and I could have handled him. And then what. She's disappeared and you say the whole bloody thing's off." He took a quick breath and was off again. "And if I did get her somewhere near the top, think of the money! All we had to do is what she said, and think out a gimmick. Alma Cogan's got a gimmick. Vera Lynn's got a gimmick. All right, so we think up a gimmick."

I've often been called a sympathetic listener. I often have to be, but generally it's a gross over-statement. I'm just prepared to listen to anyone's troubles provided they look like easing my own.

"Yes, a bad break for you," I said.

"Nothing else but," he said. He leaned forward once more. "Take Rocky Carlisle."

He saw the immediate blankness on my face. "You don't know him?"

"Sorry. Never heard of him."

He looked for a moment as if I were someone from outer space. It was then that I had the hazy idea that this Rocky Carlisle must be a pop singer, or crooner, or skiffle merchant—call them what you will—and, strictly for the purposes of this story, I'm telling you that I loathe the whole tribe, and the higher up they get, the deeper the loathing. I'm old-fashioned? Maybe I suffer from intellectual arrogance? Maybe. But what about yourself?

Maybe you have your own particular hates; rattling bedroom windows, politicians, fish-and-chips, grand opera, shrill voices, the smell of cats, queues, spinach, action paintings, the Third Programme, or something else, but my phobia happens to be crooners—let's call them that—and I love the radio or television switch that enables me to turn them off. They make me suffer acute physical and mental torture, what with their beat-skipping, ersatz emotions, maudlin lyrics, eye-rolling, guitar vamping, and all the flummery that still can't conceal the absence of a voice. Maybe I'd make an exception of the old Fred Astaire, but I'd swop a couple of even him for Jimmy Durante or Marie Lloyd.

"What about this Rocky Carlisle?" I said.

"I'll tell you," he said with that tremendous patience that foretells catastrophe. "He's about twenty-four or five, but what I'm telling you about was two years ago. He had a window-cleaning business: you know, one of those one-man things with a motor-bike and side-car and an extending ladder. Anything he wanted for the job. So what happens? One day he's cleaning away at a window and singing away like he always did, and who should be inside calling on his old mother but Mickey Malone!"

I tried to look impressed.

"You see? Mickey's one of the best in the business. Came up the hard way himself and always good for a touch. So what's he do? Has this window-cleaner in. Next thing you know, he's made a record. Mickey gets it plugged. Then there's something about him in the papers. Next he's on *In Town Tonight*. Next he's in Mickey's Hour on television and before you can say 'Bob's your uncle' he's a riot. And what's he making now?"

"Don't know. You tell me."

"What d'you make yourself, if it isn't a rude question?"

"Just about enough to pay sur-tax on."

"Well, I'm betting you, Mr. Travers, he's paying more in taxes than you and me have made in the last ten years. But that isn't the point. But for a bad break, he'd have been with *me*. I know it. I can't tell you how, but it's as true as I'm sitting in this chair. Now he's with Dick Fuller and Dick could kick out the rest of the customers and still be sitting pretty."

"Yes," I said, "that's what I call a bad break. It worked just the other way with Carlisle."

I just managed to head off another instance of that hoodoo that seemed to be devoting all its energies to the frustration of Joe Wintle, and get him to think back again to that interview with Moira, but I didn't leant anything else. I offered to stand him a lunch, but his buzzer had told him quite some time before that a someone or other was in the waiting-room, and his reply had been curt, "Let him wait." So I gave him a card and we agreed to keep in touch. Then even when he was seeing me out he was back again, still nursing the unconquerable hope. Maybe things weren't so black as I'd painted them and Moira would turn up after all. I hadn't the heart to disillusion him. I didn't exactly know why, but I liked him. Maybe his troubles had made him something of a bore, but if it came to that, there were times, no doubt, when I was very much of a bore myself.

It was pretty late for lunch, but I knew I could still get a meal at my club. No use, in any case, getting back to the office till Hallows returned, and that mightn't be till three o'clock. That was when I did get back and he was already there.

I made a tape-recording of that interview with Wintle as far as it concerned Moira—that Carlisle stuff didn't matter—and Hallows heard it a second time when I played it back. For us it bad been one of those perfect breaks, a something clean out of the blue. The trouble was that all it did was confirm. What we'd desperately needed was something really new. The fact that Moira's friend was almost certainly "X" was about as much news as the death of Queen Anne. All we ended up with was *if only's*. If only Moira had told Wintle the friend's name, or given even a hint about his line of business. We weren't even cheered when we remembered that that interview with Wintle had confirmed most of what Hulda Bland had told me on the Saturday afternoon.

Hallows had had no luck either. He'd managed to get hold of Billy McCrae and had stood him a lunch. All he'd learned was that Billy had considered Moira a good enough scout. With her face and figure she'd been pestered enough by men, but she definitely knew the ropes, and she'd had her eyes on a Target Matching, according to Billy, had caught her on the rebound, after she'd set too high hopes on a certain contract that went bust. He'd seen her only once since her marriage, and that was last August or late July, and then it turned out that he must have been the man John Hill had seen her with that day in the Café Royal. They'd run into each other on Swan and Edgars corner and she'd insisted on taking him across for a drink.

As far as he remembered, she'd said she was sick to death of life among the yokels. She talked of the old days: the days which memory distorts and colours a rosy red. There'd been no actual mention of leaving her husband.

That was all Hallows had learned. McCrae was a nice chap, he said, and married and with a couple of kids, not that that helped. Another day had pretty near gone and all we could do was plan or pray for a fresh angle. It was five o'clock when he left and we still hadn't found it.

8

GLEAM OF LIGHT?

BERNICE had work of her own that evening or she'd have found me pretty poor company. Until it was time for bed I didn't move from my chair but just sat there trying to think. It isn't often I get that almost frightening feeling of absolute blankness: that mental impasse that leaves no way to tum except perhaps backwards to the road by which you've so far come. And the infuriating thing was that I was up against a problem that ought to have been easily solved. It should have been simply this. A woman deceives her husband over a period of months and spends with some other man quite a few truncated weekends. She finally leaves her husband for that man. Puzzle—find the man. Or find the woman.

It wasn't as if we had no information on which to start: on the face of it we should have had plenty. And yet we'd been busy as beavers for over four days with a real result of absolutely nothing. And what was now nagging at me most was just one question. Why had Moira Matching considered it so vital and been so able to cover her tracks with such elaborate care? Moira Matching, intellectually a nitwit and her only two assets a driving ambition and the art of fluent lying, and yet she'd been able to disappear with never a trace and without any clue whatever to the man to whom she'd gone. Nothing let slip, for instance, to Hulda Bland and nothing definite in that interview with Joe Wintle; though even if anything apparently vital had been disclosed, how could one know whether it was truth or lies?

When bedtime came I was really mentally tired. All the old devices had been tried—writing things down and malting them ask questions and looking for answers to those questions, and knowing most of the time it was just a verbal hash of all we'd been doing the previous four days. I knew I shouldn't sleep if I didn't do something about it, so I went to bed outside a pretty big hot whisky and I hoped I shouldn't wake in the night and start all over again. I was lucky. I woke up only an hour before my usual time.

I didn't lie on long. I got up quietly, spent a far longer time over a bath and shaving, and then made early morning tea. I was a bath and a shave ahead of schedule, and by the time I'd dressed it was still only seven o'clock. I didn't want to sit there and think till the newspapers arrived, so I said I had to be early at the Agency and I'd have an early breakfast. Then, before I could actually get to the house phone to order it, something happened.

I couldn't swear to the actual train of thought that made me think of Charing Cross, unless it was a mental flash of a journey I'd made a thousand times—from the flat to the Agency—a short journey that began within a few hundred yards of Charing Cross Station and passed it as I turned into the Strand. All I know is that I whipped out my notebook, then dialled Hulda Bland's number.

It must have been almost a couple of minutes before a sleepy voice answered.

"That you. Miss Bland?" I said.

"Yes. Who is it?"

"Travers. Remember me? I saw you Saturday afternoon."

"Oh, my God! Why do you have to ring at this Godforsaken time?" Almost before that last word, she was suddenly awake. "You don't say you've found Moira!"

"Not yet I want to put some money in your way."

"Money? Say, you're not getting ideas?"

"Not the sort you're thinking about," I said. "Strictly business. You might be interested to know, by the way, that that yarn she gave you about having voice-training lessons was sheer hooey."

I told her about the visit to Joe Wintle. As I pointed out, it was the first time we'd had any actual connection between Moira and the so-called friend. And, unless she'd been lying again for her own purposes, that friend was a shrewd individual and probably connected with show business.

"I'd like you to think all that over," I said, "and if you can come up with anything whatever that gives us a lead to that friend, you're on to twenty pounds. Expenses paid if you have to go anywhere or do anything special."

She wasn't too enthusiastic, or was it hopeful, but she said she'd try.

"Just one other thing," I said. "Something it's necessary to confirm. Am I right in saying Moira always left her car either at Sevenoaks or Bromley, according to the weather?"

"That's right. Fog, chiefly. If the weather forecast was fog, then she'd only go to Sevenoaks. We nearly always used to mention it—or I did—when she was leaving on a Saturday night. 'How far're you going to-night?' I'd say, and she'd say either Sevenoaks or Bromley."

"Fine," I said. "That's got it clear. By the way, you went down there twice, so you went the same way."

"No, I didn't. It was nice light evenings both times, so I went by coach and she picked me up at Sevenoaks. I don't like trains."

"I know the journey. Through Lewisham and Catford and Bromley. A bit suburban till you get through Bromley." When I rang off I was as elated as if the post had just come with an anonymous gift of a fortnight free from all worries on the Riviera. What I'd unearthed mightn't be much: it was the contrast that mattered: the contrast between overnight blackness and a peephole of light.

Hallows had had an evening much like my own. I wasn't being clever that morning or playing any tricks, so I told him about that talk with Hulda. He was like me. The obvious had been under his nose and he hadn't seen it. He still didn't see it. I got out a road map of Kent.

"Here's the road from the bus station to Sevenoaks," I said. "That one that Hulda took four times, going and coming. About twenty-five miles. Lewisham, Catford, Bromley, past Knockholt Junction, up to the hill and then the long drop down into Sevenoaks. The road, in fact, that we took ourselves. Now look at the main railway route to Sevenoaks from Charing Cross. Here it is: Chislehurst, Orpington, Knockholt, Sevenoaks. See what I'm driving at?"

He bit his lip and looked at the map again.

"Don't know, unless it is that Bromley isn't on that railway route."

"Exactly! You can't pick up a car where you couldn't possibly have left it. And tell me this. Would you think Hulda knew much about cars?"

"I doubt it. From what you've told me, I'd say she wasn't interested. She probably hadn't even ridden in one unless it was that Jaguar occasionally or recently with her boy-friend."

We began tying the whole thing up. Hulda would have been easy enough to hoodwink. Hulda knew Bromley: she'd gone through the whole length of it on four occasions, but she knew nothing about the route by train. In order, then, to conceal the name of the actual station at which her car had been left, Moira had quoted Bromley. Now we knew that it couldn't possibly have been Bromley. In fact, we should have been suspicious from the very first. Bromley's about two-thirds of the journey by road to town and virtually an outer suburb. That's a pretty long way to drive home on a dark night even if the sky happens to be comparatively clear and there's no rain.

What we needed now was an alternative to Bromley. One such alternative could have been that Moira used no station other than Sevenoaks. That was unlikely. In so far as we could judge, the workings of that tricky mind of hers, too frequent a use of that particular station might have made her conspicuous. Also her husband used that same station regularly. So the obvious station to try was Knockholt. It wasn't too far from Sevenoaks and it had one tremendous asset: that the main road from Sevenoaks to town actually passed the station. From then on road and railway went their separate ways. The main road went through neither Orpington nor Chislehurst.

We made a further check with the autumn and winter editions of Bradshaw. According to Hulda, Moira left the flat at times that varied from six to eight. The Underground station was reasonably near, and three-quarters of an hour would be ample to allow for the journey to Charing Cross. On a Saturday night, it seemed, there were plenty of slow trains to Sevenoaks, and Moira would have been unlucky if she'd had to wait much longer than half-an-hour. All those slow trains, of course, actually stopped at Knockholt.

Five minutes later, Hallows was off to Knockholt by car. I wouldn't be needing it and it'd be quicker than taking a slow train. I didn't in fact have any plans at all so I spent an hour with Norris, and it was about ten o'clock when I thought I ought to ring Grange House for news of Julian Matching. Then I changed my mind. It might save some embarrassment if I heard that news indirectly, through Jean Lindman.

They were actually busy at C.T. Haddowe; at least a couple of well-dressed men were inspecting some candelabra. The assistant gave me the usual quick look when I went in and spotted me at once.

"You'd like to see Miss Jean, sir?"

He pushed a knob. "Go straight through, sir. She's in her office."

She actually had the door open and she gave me quite a smile.

"You're looking very pleased with yourself," I told her. "Better news from Grange House?"

She flushed slightly. "Do come in. I didn't know that I was looking pleased. After all, one's expected to be pleasant to every kind of caller."

"Of course," I said, and took the spare chair. "But how is Julian? I didn't like to disturb him myself."

"Much better," she said. "He gets up during the morning and stays up till about eight. He's talking of coming back on Monday."

"That's fine. You've actually seen him?"

"On Sunday. Not only an errand of mercy, you know. I may know the business pretty well, but there's always some' thing that can't be discussed over the telephone. You'd like some coffee? I'm having some myself."

They made their own coffee and tea upstairs, she said. "Would you mind if I just finished this job? I have to get it away."

She was sealing a smallish package: an oblong, cardboard box about six inches by four by four. A rather elaborate Victorian necklace, she said, in gold with seed pearls and diamonds, and being delivered by hand to a prospective customer in Kensington. I asked if the jewellery missing from Grange House had been taken home by Julian in the same kind of box.

"Exactly the same," she said. "It's amazing, really, what you can get into one of these boxes, even though everything's packed carefully in cotton wool."

The middle-aged messenger who brought down the coffee took away the package. She asked if I wouldn't take off my overcoat and then she was wanting my news. I said I supposed she was really one of the family, so there oughtn't to be any harm. Mind you, I didn't mention a word about Hulda Bland or train and road routes: all I did was make quite a thing out of Moira's call on Joe Wintle. All the time her eyes never left my face. I might have been telling her the date of Armageddon and the final, all-destructive bomb.

"So that was it!" she said. "Going back to where he found her. It's—well, about like the dog returning to its vomit."

I must have looked horrified.

"I'm sorry. Perhaps that wasn't a nice thing to say."

"You really hate her, don't you?"

"Yes," she said. "I think I do. I hate her for what she's done to Julian. First there was his mother, then he had to go and marry a woman like that."

Her lip was trembling.

"Cry," I said. "It'll do you good. No sense in bottling things up."

That was Travers the sympathetic listener. Chest for crying on always at hand.

She wiped her eyes.

"I'm sorry. I didn't mean to make an exhibition of myself. But what about that man she's with?"

"We'll find him, and her, too. There'll have to be a divorce, after what she's done. Even Julian'll have to see that."

"Yes," she said. "Perhaps he will. You knew he was selling the house? He put it in the hands of an agent only yesterday. Another cup of coffee?"

"Thanks, no," I said. "I ought to be going."

I made a little time by picking up my overcoat. The smile I gave her was meant to be not too serious: a bit quizzical, perhaps, and no more. Unless it was just a dash of the avuncular.

"You know, Jean—you don't mind my calling you Jean?—it's quite a story. Even our old friend Tennyson used it And Shakespeare. Viola, for instance."

She frowned. "Perhaps I'm being silly, but I don't follow you."

"Sitting like patience on a monument, smiling at grief."

She froze. "Aren't you being rather personal?"

"Perhaps I've a right to be," I told her. "I like you, Jean. I think you're too fine a person to go on eating your heart out. Also I'm in all this right up to the neck. Once this thing's cleared up. I'd like Julian to see what's been right under his nose all these years. And do something about it." She smiled, and it was a smile I was to misinterpret pretty badly.

"You're very kind. But don't worry about me. I'll make out."

"I'm sure you will."

She went with me to the lobby. I promised faithfully to keep her informed. There was quite a warm pressure of my hand as we said goodbye.

It was getting on for twelve. Hallows wouldn't be back till at least the late afternoon, so I walked on to the club for an early lunch, and all the time I kept wondering whether or not I'd made a fool of myself in speaking as I had to Jean Lindman. I didn't feel happy about it. It'd seemed a good idea at the time and behind it had been the best of motives, and yet it seemed in the chill of late morning far less tactful than it had in the warm intimacy of her office. I didn't feel any happier when I told myself that what I'd said was true. She *was* in love with Julian Matching, and had been probably for years, and all the time she'd been no more to him than a highly competent secretary. She knew it and I knew it, and now she knew I knew it. The only thing that had been wrong perhaps, was that bit about smiling at grief. No woman, even a Jean Lindman, likes to be told, even in the most flowery of terms, that she's never been quite the woman for a certain man.

Hallows didn't get back till nearly six o'clock, but he'd rung the Agency earlier in the afternoon to say that things were going well. After that overnight despair, that was an understatement worth remembering.

Everything had gone smoothly, he told me, from the moment he'd reached Knockholt. He'd only to show the portrait of Moira in mink and there it all was. She'd made fairly frequent use of that station during the previous three months, though only once, apparently, for her final three trips. That, he had taken the trouble to find out, was almost certainly because of fog. Another noteworthy thing had emerged. Knockholt had apparently never been used for any of those mid-week, half-day trips she'd regularly made to town. That made Knockholt something secretive or special.

"Something else," Hallows said. "There's a pub not more than a mile on towards Sevenoaks, so I dropped in for a bread-and-cheese lunch. Remember what Hulda told you about the night when Moira felt faint and she'd gone with her to Charing Cross? About six weeks ago Moira stopped at that pub at about eight o'clock and still wasn't feeling too good. At any rate she had a double brandy in the saloon bar. And that's the only time they saw her there. And the last I learned about her. That's what kept me so long. I made enquiries along the road nearly as far as Sevenoaks. Tried garages in case they'd have been open late on a Saturday night. Then I left the main road and tried a few villages both sides. Nothing turned up so I called it a day."

The queer thing, of course, was that after leaving the station that night, Moira had been heading straight for Sevenoaks. But she couldn't have been going there. French had tried every hotel. Also she must have been reasonably well known in the town, and the risk of recognition by someone from Aldways would have been far too great.

"Right," I said. "Let's have a good look at the map."

That was all the lay-out that mattered. From Knockholt on, there were various side-roads, some of which he'd explored. The thing to do now was obviously to explore the rest, meanwhile we looked at things from another angle.

Before we hardly knew, we had half a dozen questions on our hands. Take first the matter of times. Say that Moira was about to spend a Saturday night and all Sunday up to early evening with "X". But why so restricted a period? Couldn't she have been with "X" soon after she left Aldways on a Saturday, and at least for lunch?

It was she who had done the timing as far as concerned Hulda. She might leave as early as six or it mightn't be till eight, and one could only assume that these timings were arranged for the benefit of "X". "X" wouldn't be available on a Saturday till about seven-thirty on certain dates and only at times between then and, say, half-past nine on others. What did that tell us about "X" himself?

Obviously again he had to be someone whose Saturdays were busy ones. Even a Saturday afternoon, almost universally free, wasn't free for him.

"An actor?" Hallows said, and then washed it out at once. "Couldn't be, though. He might've been kept at a matinee but there'd be an evening performance as well."

"The hour when he was free always varied," I said. "Moira would ring him first thing on a Saturday morning and find out."

We began again. It couldn't have anything to do with the coining of darkness and the urgent necessity to avoid being seen. After all, it was dark at five o'clock long before Christmas, so Moira could have been with him before five o'clock instead of wasting time with Hulda. Hallows came up with another suggestion.

"Let's say that 'X' is living within fairly easy driving distance of Sevenoaks in his own house and as an ostensibly respectable citizen. Maybe he's also bound down by variations of times on a Saturday night. What I mean is, he might have a daughter or daily help or cook or somebody who leaves on a Saturday night and he doesn't know exactly when."

"Won't do," I said, "unless he's in a position to ask that somebody on a Saturday morning, before Moira rings him, at what time they'll be leaving.

"No," I went on. "Let's assume that for once Moira was telling the truth to Wintle. What's that tell us about 'X'? I think that 'X' was enough of a business man to know if Wintle was spending that publicity money wisely. He must also have had a working knowledge of show business and the relations between agent and client. Add that to what we've already guessed and where do we stand?"

"Moira didn't mention 'X's' name to Wintle. Might that mean Wintle would know him when he saw him? A little surprise she was keeping up her sleeve?"

"Under the circumstances she wouldn't dare to mention his name."

"Why not?" he said. "She was definitely about to leave her husband? What had she to lose?"

"She didn't give Wintle the name," I said, "because 'X' had told her not to. You can't look at things from the way Moira saw them. Up to then she didn't have the foggiest idea 'X' was simply stringing her along until he laid hands on that jewellery. 'X' knew what was going to happen, so how could he let Moira divulge his name? The whole business was an intricacy of cross and double-cross, and Moira, for once, plumb in the middle."

We left the speculation and had another look at the only concrete thing we had—the map: not that we weren't to start speculating again. Let that pub where Moira had stopped that night be on the perimeter of a circle: a circle below it to the south. What radius that circle might have we couldn't guess, or if it were to the east or west of Sevenoaks, or both. It might even be that "X" was in Sevenoaks itself: some private house as one came in from Knockholt, and set conveniently back from the main road.

Then we left everything where we might have left it minutes before. In the morning Hallows and French in their own cars would begin exploring along every side road between that pub and Sevenoaks, as far, say, as a couple of villages along each. It might be a matter of two days at the least: then, if nothing had turned up, the radius could be still further extended. Lunch-time rendezvous could be arranged. And what was French to be told to look for? Anything and everything. I said. Anything whatever that might look as if it had a connection between "X" and Moira Matching.

9

LOW-BROW HALF-HOUR

JOHN Hill rang in the morning asking if there was any news. It never pays to admit defeat and, in any case, I could tell him with a reasonable sincerity that we were working on what looked a highly promising clue. I thought I ought to ask him how Julian was.

"I saw him last night," he said, "and he's very much more like his old self. I think I've induced him to go away for a short cruise. It mightn't be for a few days but I think he liked the idea."

Hallows and French came in soon after dark with nothing to report. In the morning the search would be extended to as far south as Tonbridge. Hallows didn't seem too happy. As he said, there was too little to work with—just a photograph and the description and number of a Jaguar car. And it was lop-sided. Questions had to be confined to Moira. Our knowledge of "X" was sheer guesswork and you couldn't frame questions on that.

There comes a stage in most cases when you feel you want a little relief. I was home early that evening—the first time, really, for some days—and I'd made up my mind to have one of our old-fashioned evenings—Bernice and I in our chairs in front of the fire and reading, perhaps, or listening to radio or watching television. We had an early meal, stacked the dishes ready for the service cleaner and then settled down. The howl of a north-easter round the chimney pots made things even more cosy inside. Bernice opened her book. I stoked my pipe and suddenly remembered something. We take a couple of radio and television papers, *The Televiewer* and the *Radio Times* and, though they'd been in the flat for some days. I'd had no time to look at either. I picked up the *Radio Times*.

There're always a couple of pages, with photographs, called "Round and About", and as I was casually running my eye over them in search of a likely programme. I caught sight of a name. It was at the beginning of a couple of paragraphs about some television programme or other. The set shown at the side meant that.

> *Viewers will be sorry to hear that Wednesday night's appearance on B.B.C. Television of Rocky Carlisle in "The Wally Paget Half-Hour" is something in the nature of a farewell. But not for too long. It's only that that American tour we mentioned in a recent issue has eventuated after all and Rocky should be leaving by at least the end of the month.*
>
> *Every one of his innumerable fans will be wishing him well. Not that they need have any fears. Rocky's records, we know, have been selling sensationally for some time in the States, and, with a personality like his, how can he miss out? Those who haven't been able to obtain tickets for Wednesday night's show, and we know they are many, will still be able to sit back and enjoy it on television.*

"Have you ever heard of a singer called Rocky Carlisle?" I asked Bernice.

She frowned for a moment. "Wasn't there an article on him in *The Televiewer* recently?"

"Don't know," I said. "I probably didn't notice it. It's rather curious, really. I'd never heard him in my life and then I happened to run across his name the other day. In connection with that case we're on at the moment I had to see an agent who's notorious for his hard luck stories and he was instancing this Rocky Carlisle. Used to be a window cleaner."

"I remember," she said. "He was singing and someone heard him and started him off on a career."

"That's right: another pop singer called Mickey Malone; and this agent was telling me that he ought to have had Carlisle on his books except for hard luck. Carlisle must be making a young fortune, so you see what the agent was moaning about. By the way, I see here this Rocky Carlisle's on B.B.C. television tonight. If you don't mind I'd rather like to have a look at him. Sure you can put up with it?"

Bernice is unexpectedly catholic in her tastes. The show was due in about five minutes, so I switched on the set for the five minutes of news and turned off the light.

It was not till nearly ten minutes to eight that I had my first view of the singing window-cleaner. The show was taking place in one of the bigger halls, and as the cameras made a preliminary sweep round, you could see that the place was packed, and with more than the usual sprinkling of teenagers. The show itself began as most of that kind begin: the curtain opening to let out Paget, the compère, and then swinging back to show Paget and his band. A slick number—Wally himself on tenor saxophone—came to a crash ending and tumultuous applause. It was well staged. It didn't even bore me—as yet.

More tumultuous applause as Wally announced a croonerette. She sang what I believe they call a torch number and, if I'd closed my eyes, she might have been one of a dozen others whom I hadn't been quick enough to switch off. Everything was there: the slurs, the dragging beat, the pseudo-American accent, the tears that almost came. She followed it up with a quicker number, all about Napoli and the Sunny South, and did a few dancing steps between choruses with sultry gestures and a flurry of skirts. The audience loved her.

A couple of dancers—Gretchen and Carl—came next and they were good. The band did another number and, as the music was fading out. Wally was suddenly coming forward. He waited, smiling, till the last note and the applause had gone.

"Ladies and gentlemen, now we come to the moment we've all been looking forward to." He waved a hand towards back stage. "Ladies and gentlemen, Rocky CAR—*LISLE!*"

From the audience there was one tremendous, hysterical shriek. It momentarily drowned the band and then, in a kind of artificial opening between the sections of the band, a figure appeared. He came forward, hands raised, waited for a moment almost at the footlights till that hysterical shrieking had died away, then picked up his cue and broke into the final words of that theme song. There was an incredible hush as he swayed before the microphone, hands raised again and face upwards.

I'm sorry now that things just had to be,
For you it's always Spring, but not for me.
For me it's just a dark and blind November,
But, sweetheart, maybe sometimes you'll remember
There's still a window in my heart for you.

He stayed, still poised, till the final note of the band had gone, then he smiled. It changed the whole look of him. It gave him a boyish kind of look. The mouth widened to a grin and the applause shrieked out again, and he stood there, hands waving above his head till it died down.

He was about five foot seven or eight, slim and easy moving. His thick black hair was waved back. The mouth was loo wide to make him a good-looker, but there was something about him that made you watch him, and even, perhaps, smile with him.

"Thank you, ladies cand gentlemen. Glad you remember that song. I like it, too. I guess that's why they haven't started calling me Big-head—not yet."

A ripple of laughter from the audience. A still wider grin from Rocky.

"And now, ladies and gentlemen, I'd like you to hear a new British number, specially written for me by my old friend Pat Martin. Also it happens to be my latest recording. Ladies and gentlemen—'Why Should We Care?'"

His voice was quite a pleasing baritone and he didn't play too many tricks with it. Somehow you didn't pay all that attention to the song itself, catchy though it was: the smile, the quick movements, and the way that song came almost bubbling out, made the singer somehow more important than the song. The words were more like a banal background and I wonder why I remembered them:

I love you, because you're in love with me.
You love me, because I'm in love with you.
No one else in the world but only us two
Sweetheart, this is our own love affair.
So
Why should we care, care, care,
Why should we care.

That song was a riot. Rocky Carlisle had moved on a long way from his window-cleaning days. He was slick: smart with his feet and smart with his hands. That kind of song was his *métier* and he made the audience a part of it. I'll even make a confession. I think that if I'd been alone and had switched on the set by chance, I wouldn't have turned it off: and that, coming from me, is like Macmillan owning up to a sneaking fondness for nationalisation.

When the song ended, he stood there in the tumult of applause, hands clasped above his head, and grinning like a boxer who's just won his bout.

"Thank you, ladies and gentlemen. Pat sure did a fine job on that song."

The voice lowered. It became more confidential and the grin became a quiet smile.

"And now, if you'll allow me. I'd like to make a change in what is usually my routine. People are always writing and wanting to know when I'm going to sing something more serious, so tonight, and as I'm shortly to be leaving on a three months' tour. I'd like to sing something that seems appropriate. I hope you'll like it So, ladies and gentlemen, may I sing for you—'When You Come to the End of a Perfect Day'?"

It should have been a winner almost before he'd sung the first line, and, as far as that audience was concerned, it was. I thought he was over-playing his hand. That song wasn't in character. It lacked the vital sincerity that was needed to bring it off: not that faked catch in the throat, the eyes and hands lifted to heaven and the final, wholly out of place, high note. But I was the odd man out. The applause was literally so deafening that you couldn't hear a word of his thanks. It must have been a minute before it died away.

"Thank you, ladies and gentlemen. Thank you from the very bottom of my heart. And now, good-night . . . and God bless."

That show had over-run its time and almost at once it was faded out. I switched the set off and the lights on. "Well, what did you think of it?"

Bernice smiled. "It was quite entertaining, in a way. A pity, I thought, that he sang that last song."

"We were lucky," I said. "We might have had to listen to 'The Holy City' or 'The Lost Chord'."

"I meant his voice," she said. "If he'd had it properly trained, he might have done far more with it."

"He's doing pretty well." That was Travers, the old cynic. "He's probably making more in a month than I make in a year. Still, there we are. Would you like anything else on?"

She thought there was a concert on the Home Service. I passed her the *Radio Times*, and there was. She asked me to keep the volume low and then she could read and listen at the same time. I re-stoked my pipe and stretched my long legs out to the fire, happy enough to be doing nothing but listening. The orchestra was playing some Delius, and as the wispy sounds floated quietly about the room, my thoughts began shifting, too, and I was seeing and bearing those last ten minutes on the screen. Then I began fidgeting in my chair. Another minute and I got quietly up and made my way to our bedroom.

There's a space at the bottom of the large wardrobe where Bernice keeps old periodicals and magazines till there are enough of them for the hospital to collect. I was looking for an article on Rocky Carlisle in an old issue of *The Televiewer*—the one that Bernice had mentioned. It didn't take me long to find it. It was in an issue only three weeks old. It occupied just one page: the page opposite had three Carlisle photographs. Here it is in full.

As soon as I stepped into the living-room of Rocky Carlisle's unpretentious flat at Portland Mews, I knew—as if I hadn't known it before!—that I was in the home of a man dedicated to music. But that's the way it's always been with Rocky.

"Yes," he told me. "Even as a kid I was always mad about singing and boy! was it a great day for me when I managed to get myself into our local church choir! Even when my voice broke, I managed to hang on as a kind of boy baritone. Lucky for me they were hard up for singers or I'd never have made it."

"And when did you first think of making something more out of it?"

He grinned. I expect you know that grin. "Reckon it was after I got going with that window-cleaning round. I apologised one day to one of the customers and she told me to go on singing. She liked it."

That's how it was. Rocky always HAD to sing. No great ideas, he said, about making the big time. He just had that music in him and it had to come out, even when up a ladder.

"And soon afterwards you had that lucky break?"

"A lucky break it certainly was," he told me, and I knew it came straight from the heart. "I'd never have made it alone. Didn't know the first thing about it. That Mickey Malone was sure a big-hearted guy."

"And what were you actually treating Mickey to, that day?" I asked him. "I've heard different versions of that."

"Don't laugh," he said, "but it was 'O Sole Mio'. I had a record I used to play. A lot of my spare cash went on gramophone records."

"You were singing in Italian!"

He laughed. "Why not? You try listening a couple of hundred times to a short Italian record and you'll be singing in Italian, too. Couldn't get the hang of anything in French, though."

"What about Russian?"

He grinned. "Are you kidding? Think I don't know my own limitations?"

I wondered. What about those limitations? Rocky's come a long way, folks, but he's going a long way farther. It's no use having that thing called personality if you can't put it across, and if there's one singer in our time who can get it across, it's Rocky Carlisle. Sometimes, he says, he wonders why. You know and I know. Ifs not only because he exudes a kind of universal happiness: he has that other thing without which nothing matters—sincerity.

"One question your fans would like me to put to you," I said just before I left. "Why did you turn down that big offer from America?"

"Well, to put it frankly, I didn't think I was ready," he told me modestly. "Another year, perhaps, and I might go over far bigger. Also I'm pretty well tied up over here."

That's Rocky Carlisle, folks. When next time you hear the band break into that theme song, just take a fresh took at the man who'll sing it. It may be a far cry from a Fulham church choir and a window-cleaner's ladder, but it's still that boy who just HAD to sing. And what do we all say? "GO ON SINGING, ROCKY!"

I sat on my bed and read that article through a second time. There were some scissors on Bernice's dressing-table and I cut the article out and put it into my wallet.

Ours is quite a big flat. I even have a den of my own with a telephone extension. Bernice was still listening and reading, and the orchestra, I remember, was playing a Brandenberg concerto.

"Just remembered there's something I ought to do," I told her quietly, and went through.

It was nearly half-past eight and I wondered if Hulda Bland would be at home. She was.

"Not you again! What is it this time?"

"Some personal news for you," I said. "We haven't found Moira yet, but something you told me has given us what might turn out to be a lead, so I'm putting in the post in the morning a cheque for five pounds. If things turn out the way we hope they will, we'll be sending the balance. You know: what I promised you."

"That's nice," she said. "Every little helps."

"In the meanwhile, you haven't thought of anything else?"

"Don't seem to have any time for thinking, what with one thing and another. Still, if I do I'll let you know."

"That's fine," I said. "We're always only too glad to pay for information. Oh, by the way, I was watching Rocky Carlisle on television just now. I didn't know he was a Fulham boy?"

"Him?" She gave a little snort. "We went to the same Council School together. The kids used to laugh at him about his name. Rockwell. Rockwell Carter, that's his real name. He was born the far end of Lower Norgate Street, just where it turns off into Waterfield Road. Just short of the church."

"Extraordinary! But you sounded as if you didn't like him."

"Not one way or the other. All I know is, he ain't very popular around here. I've heard him on the wireless and he makes me sick."

"You mean you don't like his kind of singing?"

"Well, not exactly. I like Frankie Vaughan and Marty Wilde and Frank Sinatra and . . . well, it's hard to explain. I think he's a hypocrite. You'd think, all the money he's making, he'd have got his father and mother into something better than a council house. And right away on that new estate. That's what's been said around here."

"Well, it takes all sorts to make a world," I said. "Thank you again, Miss Bland. And look out for that cheque."

I went back to the living-room. Bernice had the room in darkness. That's how she likes to sit when there's something she particularly likes, and someone was playing the Rachmaninov Paganini Variations and she'd turned up the volume. I sat listening, too, till the concert ended and it was time for the news. I remember she told me who the pianist was, and I think it was Peter Katin.

I listened to the news headlines, then went back to the den and rang Hallows. His wife told me he was out. There was a meeting of the local Horticultural Society and she didn't expect him in much before ten. I asked her to get him to ring my private number the moment he came in.

Bernice went on with her reading. I began a crossword, but only for show. A quarter to ten and Bernice made her usual cup of hot milk and brought me my usual night-cap. At ten she was off to bed. I said I might be a minute or two late. Expecting a telephone call. It came almost as soon as she'd gone.

"Sorry I was out," Hallows said. "You know what those meetings are like. You just can't get away. Anything special?"

"I don't know," I said. "Just something that happened to crop up tonight. That schedule for tomorrow is cancelled, by the way. Get hold of French, if you can, and let him know. Tell him to report to Mr. Norris as usual."

"What about me?"

"Take an hour or two off," I said. "Drop in at about midday. There's a special job I may have to do in the morning. After that, we'll see."

"You wouldn't like to give me a hint?"

"No," I said. "The whole thing's far too good to be true. By midday tomorrow we ought to have a better idea."

I rang off, waited a moment or two and then rang Norris.

He's always a late bird and bound to be up. I told him the new arrangements and said I'd be along early. Then I went to bed.

But not before I'd had another pretty stiff drink. I even washed down a sleeping pill to keep me from lying awake and planning over and over again the morning moves. It's not more than twice a year that I take a pill, and maybe that's why it worked. It was Bernice who had to wake me in the morning.

10

TESTING TIME

WHAT I'd planned for that morning was an interview with Rocky Carlisle's agent Wintle had called him Dick Fuller: I found him in the telephone directory as R. Fuller Ltd., Rutland Building, Wardour Street. By the time I'd summarised all I knew about Carlisle. I wasn't feeling too happy. It wasn't that my excuse for calling on Fuller wouldn't be good: I'd had that well thought out. I was to be a free-lance reporter who'd been asked by an American news agency to get the lowdown on the Carlisle American tour.

It was when I began to visualise myself facing Fuller across his office desk that I began to be uneasy. I couldn't very well keep the talk pinned to one particular subject, but even if I did. I was about the least qualified person in Europe to chat about television and its personalities. I didn't know the patter, the jargon, the trade terms, an ignorance of any one of which would prove me some sort of fake.

And, having acquired that much measure of doubt, I wondered if Fuller would even see me at all. Could I expect an agent to discuss with a stranger the private opinions of a best-paying client? In fact, what had seemed so easy the previous night was very far from it in the morning.

I didn't like to trouble Tom Holberg again but there seemed nothing else for it. His office hours begin at nine-thirty, so I rang him just before. I said I was in a jam. I had to have some highly important information but I didn't know how to get it. What was worse, it was extremely confidential. If the suspicions I had turned out to be wrong and anything got out. I might be in for a libel or slander action that would pretty near ruin the Agency.

"You know me," he said. "Drop in and we'll have a talk."

His place is only a quarter of a mile away, and I made it in well under five minutes. I had to wait longer than that before he was free. He has an inner room where he sees certain clients and we went through. As I was placed, it was all or nothing, but I think I lowered my voice when I said I wanted some information about one of Dick Fuller's clients—Rocky Carlisle.

"What sort of information?"

I told him the absolute minimum I had to have. I said it was a job I'd thought first of doing myself, till I'd realised the inadequacies. Fuller would spot in a matter of minutes that I wasn't the reporter I was claiming to be. All the time I was doing that explaining. Tom was merely nodding. When I'd finally finished, he told me George could handle it.

George Lewis is a junior partner. Compared with Tom he's almost a fly-by-night. Tom presides like a benignant patriarch in the main office. He's the final word. George, still in the thirties, does the scouting and runs the errands; keeps his nose to the ground and entertains the younger clients. According to Tom, he was friendly with a certain Harry Reade who occupied much the same position with Fuller.

"When do you want this information?"

"Time's the vital factor, Tom. I've got to have it at the earliest possible moment."

"Right," he said. "I'll have a word with Georgie. You needn't come into it at all. I'm the one who wants the information."

"Thanks. Tom," I said. "If I could ring you from the Agency at about noon, would that be all right?"

He put up a pudgy hand and patted me consolingly.

"Maybe before then. It won't be all that hard. If there's anything there, Georgie'll dig it out."

I asked if I could ring the Agency. He waved his cigar at the phone and told me to help myself.

It was about a quarter-past ten when I picked up my car and set out for Lewisham. It was a dull, almost muggy day and there was a lot of traffic till I turned off at New Cross. There was a parking place for clients at the back of the Alhambra Dance Hall, and I drove the car in. Another car was already there and I guessed it belonged to the manager.

I went in by the side door. The whole place seemed in the stages of recovery from the previous night, and behind the strong smell of disinfectant was the sourish odour of smoke and stale scent. No one knew where the manager was and it took a few minutes to run him to earth in the restaurant He was having a coffee and asked if I'd join him.

"What is it this time? Not that ticket again?"

He remembered me. With my height and spareness and huge horn-rims, I'm always something that's once seen and never forgotten. That's why I'll never make a real detective: why I've always to delegate the exciting stuff. In my Walter Mitty moments I see myself as someone like Hallows, whipping on false moustaches and lurking in doorways and trailing an unsuspecting suspect. All things to all men, so to speak. A touch of grease paint and a wig and you wouldn't know me from Adam. Real detective stuff, not the long-legged bespectacled individual trying to squeeze just a little more information from a dance hall manager.

"That's it," I said, and took the ticket out of my wallet "The last time I saw you, you said it dated prior to last September."

"May I have another look?"

He looked at it gave a nod or two, then looked at the back.

"Among my souvenirs." He grunted. "You didn't write that?"

"No," I said. "The purchaser did—a woman. The one whose photo-graph you saw. Evidently a big night for her. Probably one of your gala nights. You don't happen to have records of artists who appeared on those gala nights? Say during the last six months?"

"Think I can remember most of them. Easy enough to check."

We finished our coffee and went through to his office. He look a kind of ledger from a drawer of his desk.

"How far back do you want to go?"

"Well, start just before last September to correspond with the ticket."

"Right. Here we are. Saturdays and Wednesdays. Wednesday's early closing day. The last for August will be a Saturday. That was George Larkin and his Skylarks with Kitty Brewer. Going back, the Wednesday was . . ."

I didn't stop him till he'd got back to the middle of July.

"That's plenty. Might have been anyone. A choice of real big names to make the lady call it a special night."

"Or afternoon. Two sessions a day, remember."

"Of course. Glad you reminded me."

"Personally," he said, "I think you're working on the wrong lines. I doubt if she'd have written what she did because the band was good. Must have met a boy-friend, or something. Or some fellow might have proposed. More romantic, if you see what I mean."

"Thanks," I said. "Maybe you're right. It's an angle I hadn't thought of. Don't expect I'll have to bother you again."

I drove back towards the High Street and rang the Agency from a telephone kiosk.

"Glad you rang," Norris said. "A call just came from Mr. Holberg. He said he'd rather you saw him than talk over the phone."

I looked at my watch. "Tell him I'll be along somewhere about twelve. And you might ask Hallows to wait."

I got tied up in a traffic jam and didn't make it till nearly a quar-ter-past. Tom was engaged but I didn't have long to wait. I knew by the smile he gave me that he'd got what I wanted. When I left him I felt on top of the world and I didn't sober up till I was back at the Agency.

*

Bertha brought in coffee and sandwiches and Hallows and I got to work. All he knew was that something pretty important had cropped up. I asked if he'd seen Rocky Carlisle the previous night on television. He smiled a bit sheepishly.

"As a matter of fact. I did. My daughter's crazy about that sort of thing so I had to grin and bear it."

"What'd you think of Carlisle himself?"

"Only just heard a few seconds of him. I had to get off to that meeting. He seemed pretty popular."

"Then you missed his last song," I said. "And the announcement that preceded it. A sort of temporary farewell song, and because he's going on a tour of the States at the end of the month."

"And so?"

I asked him to read the two clippings: one from the *Radio Times* and the other from *The Televiewer*.

"I want you to notice one thing," I said. "The rest can come later. He evidently was offered that tour by interests in the States three weeks ago—a month really, allowing a week for going to press. He turned it down. A week ago he changed his mind."

I broke in again before he could finish *The Televiewer* clipping. "You've got it so far?"

"Think so," he said. "And what comes next?"

I made a clean breast of how I'd intended to make my own enquiries at R. Fuller Ltd.

"I went to Tom Holberg instead," I said. 'Tom kept my name out of it and saw his partner. Told him there'd been enquiries from a couple of big American bands who'd heard that tour was on again. They'd been made fools of the first time and didn't want a second. Was the tour now definitely on the books, and what was the story behind the whole thing. Tom's partner met Fuller's partner and managed to get the story. Off the cuff, so to speak. Sort of two lads together, letting off steam about the boss, except it was Fuller himself who'd let off the steam. Carlisle had let him badly down. He'd known months before that a tour might be arranged and then, when Fuller had sprung the good news, Carlisle had turned the whole thing down. And after preliminary arrangements had been made.

"Carlisle's reasons were those he gave in that *Televiewer* interview, that he didn't feel himself to be ready yet for such a tour. Then, a week or more ago, he saw Fuller and told him to get busy again. Said he'd changed his mind. Said he had a right to change his mind. Wanted to know what Fuller collected his percentage for. Sort of, get busy or else. He even forced Fuller's hand by making the announcement off his own bat."

"Must be a bit of a bastard. What was his idea?"

"We'll come to that," I said. "First of all, read the rest of that longer clipping."

He spotted it at once.

"Fulham! That was Moira's old home!"

"That's right," I said. "Last night I rang Hulda Bland. She and Moira and Rocky Carlisle went to the same Council School. His name was Rockwell Carter and the kids used to rag him about it."

"Then—"

"Wait a minute," I said. "Let's get back to something else—the dance hall ticket you found at Grange House. Remember? *Among my souvenirs.* So I went back there this morning and saw that manager again. That ticket was issued prior to September last so I got him to go over the list of special attractions in August. You know what he came up with? There was a gala day on the second Wednesday in August. Two sessions as usual, and the special attraction was Fred Morgan's Band with Rocky Carlisle starring as guest artist."

"Good God!" he said. "So that's when she met him again."

"Looks a certainty. When she got married, Rocky Carlisle hadn't appeared on the scene. His real rise didn't begin till about a year later, though she may have read some of the earlier publicity. I didn't want to show my band too much to Hulda, but I'd say she and Moira discussed Carlisle and then Moira found out he was appearing on a certain date at that dance hall. Mid-week was easy enough and she could have gone there by car and still been back when her husband got home. The idea was to ingratiate herself with Carlisle and use him as a stepping stone. And she didn't say a word to Hulda."

"Yes," he said. "And Carlisle fell for her." He looked up. "Is all this leading up to Carlisle being 'X'?"

"Let's keep looking around," I said. "That *Televiewer* clipping mentions an Italian record that Carlisle got off by heart. There's a kind of echo to that in what Wintle told me Moira said in his office. A suggestion she might change her name and turn up as a supposedly famous Mexican or French singer. All she wanted, she said, would be time to work hard at some records. Don't know what you think but that sounds to me as if Moira and Carlisle had done a lot of talking together. That's not a lot by way of a clue, but it adds up. Let's get back to the jackpot question as to why Carlisle changed his mind about that American tour."

All we came up with was supposition. We just couldn't be sure. Feasibility—yes. Probability—yes, but no more. Carlisle might have been so head over heels in love that he couldn't contemplate even a few weeks absence from Moira. Then things came to a head. She decided to leave her husband for good, and the whole situation changed at once. Maybe Carlisle had moaned a bit about the loss of that tour, and that forced her hand.

"Assuming all that," I said, "then what was decided was that the tour should be on again and she'd go with him. Not necessarily on the same plane or boat. That's why he put pressure on Fuller. I'd say he'd have preferred to be there now, but, as Tom Holberg told me, you just can't do things like that. Too many home engagements to be cleared off or rearranged, and too many arrangements to be made in the States. And, if all that's so, then Carlisle has Moira nicely stashed away somewhere, waiting for the great day."

He agreed—with reservations. The facts might be as I'd said, but there were still Moira's weekends to be accounted for. She and Carlisle had had those periods of twenty-four hours somewhere in the neighbourhood of Sevenoaks or Tonbridge. They might have used a private house or a quiet hotel. So why not go on with those enquiries? Everything should be easier now we had his name. And, what was more, the odds were that wherever those weekends had been, Moira was almost certainly now stashed away in the very same place.

"Leave it a moment," I said. "Let's look at the other side of the picture. Would Carlisle be the sort of man to rig that jewellery business? He wasn't in need of money."

"All she had to do was get him to impersonate an American. She could have spun him any yarn, such as the jewellery was hers and the husband had taken it back again. Any old yarn."

"Maybe," I said. "But putting that Mickey in Matching's drink was something different. Carlisle was taking a big risk if he allowed himself to have a hand in that. Then there was the car left at Sevenoaks station with all her cases in it. No one's explained all that."

We didn't say anything for a minute. It turned out we were both thinking the same thing. Something we were loath to mention. It was Hallows who brought it into the open, even if he chose a roundabout way.

"Carlisle's a certainty for those weekends. Saturday would be when he'd be almost certain to have an engagement and he wouldn't know what time he'd be able to get away. That's why Moira left Hulda at different times."

He paused for a moment. "There could be a solution that ties the whole thing in."

"Such as?"

"Well, there's just the possibility she might be dead."

He was right. If Moira was dead and Carlisle responsible, then there was an explanation for that insistence on that American tour. It represented a kind of panic: a need to wait at a distance and not return till there was never a risk of discovery. But there was no point in our thinking in terms of murder. After all, we weren't as yet even certain beyond all doubt that Carlisle was "X". That was what had to be established. After that, it shouldn't be hard to find Moira.

"We've got to unearth the scene of those weekends," I said. "If Carlisle drives a car, then we'll have two cars to help us instead of one. Think you might find something out at that flat of his?"

He thought it a good idea. When he'd left, I rang Grange House. It was Robert Gambet who answered.

"Ludovic Travers, Robert. How's Mr. Matching?"

"Very much better, sir. As a matter of fact he had an early lunch and has gone to town."

"Isn't that very unwise?"

"Not for me to say, sir. I must say he's made a remarkable recovery. Also he said, sir, he'd be returning by an early train."

"Well, he knows best," I said. "But tell me something, strictly between ourselves. You've still got those gramophone records that Mrs. Matching used to play?"

I caught a slight chuckle.

"I'm afraid not, sir. The master told me to break them up and put them in the dust-bin."

"Don't blame him," I said. "But tell me something else. When Mrs. Matching was playing those records could you hear them in the kitchen?"

It depended, he said, on madam's moods. If there was a show on television with a dance band and singers, she'd always have it on pretty loud, but no other kind of programme seemed to interest her and then she'd put a batch of records on the radiogram instead. If she were in one of her bad moods, she'd have it at what seemed full blast, just to exasperate the master, and that was when you couldn't help hearing the music in the kitchen.

"Think back carefully," I said. "Was there any particular record she seemed specially fond of?"

"To tell the truth, sir, they were much the same to me. I believe there was at least one, though. The one there was the trouble about. Would you hold on a moment, sir? I'll ask Mrs. Gambet."

I wondered what he'd meant by trouble. It wasn't long before he was telling me.

"Yes, sir: it was as I said. It was a record of a man singing a song called 'A Window in My Heart' or something like that. It so got on the master's nerves that he asked me to destroy it, which I did, and, if she missed it, I wasn't to have any idea where it'd gone. That was about a fortnight before she went away."

"And did she miss it?"

"She did indeed, sir. There was something of a scene. And you know what happened, sir? Before the week was out, she'd bought one to replace it."

I tried a chuckle of my own.

"They say the woman always has the last word. But thank you, Robert. I was just trying to get a line on Mrs. Matching's background. That's strictly between ourselves. And give my compliments to Mr.

Matching, will you? Say I'm glad to hear he's so much better. And that I might be seeing him in a day or two."

Just another link in the chain, as it were. Moira had been so confident that her husband suspected nothing, that she'd taken a personal, sadistic delight in playing that theme song. If I'd been Julian Matching I'd have taken her by the scruff of the neck and pitched her out, and her belongings after her. That a man could have let himself be so humiliated and nagged by a woman whom he must have long since come to know as about as common as they come, was something I found incredible. You couldn't call that sort of thing love: what it had grown into was a kind of Moira-mania.

Hallows was back earlier than I'd thought, and he had a description of Carlisle's car—a year-old Mercedes-Benz. He said it'd been dead easy. There'd been only two cars in the forecourt of the flats and neither had had quite the look of the kind of car Carlisle might drive, so he'd had a word with the commissionaire. Was Mr. Carlisle in? The commissionaire said he'd come in only about an hour ago. Was he driving his car? That sports car he used to have? The commissionaire said he knew nothing about a sports car. Mr. Carlisle had been at the flats about nine months and he'd always had the car he still had—a Mercedes-Benz.

"Bad luck on me," Hallows said. "I'm representing Austin-Healey and hoped he might be interested. Might as well forget it."

He went off towards Oxford Street, turned left and round into Baker Street and a big garage handy for the flats. He hit it lucky first time.

"Mr. Carlisle brought his car in yet? The Mercedes-Benz?"

"About an hour ago," the attendant said. "That's it over there."

"Just checking to see if he'd be in. Tried to get him twice already, but he was out."

"A black Mercedes," Hallows said, "in beautiful condition. The number—YF 991. Wish it had been a better colour. Black's not all that easy to remember."

It was too late to get busy that afternoon. In the morning we'd be away before nine, and take both cars, and at Sevenoaks we'd split up the house agents between us. I'd already gone through the local telephone directory and hadn't found either an R. Carlisle or an R. Carter who'd cut a search short. There was an R. Carter, but he happened to be a doctor.

"Maybe you tried the wrong directory," Hallows said. "We've ruled out a hotel as being too dangerous, but you'd have thought a chap like Carlisle would have had a telephone in any private house."

It was debatable. Those weekends were something that even his agent or his secretary wouldn't know about.

"There is one point," he said. "If he's going to America as a fugitive from anything, wouldn't he leave instructions to sell the house? If there's anything there he doesn't want found, wouldn't he want to dissociate himself from it altogether?"

"All right," I said. "We ask for places acquired a few months ago and now in the market again. But wait a minute. I've got an idea. Would Carlisle actually go to all the expense of buying and furnishing a house? Wouldn't it have been simpler to take a furnished house on a short let? That'd explain the absence of a telephone. Heaps of people have to be away for a few months and let their places furnished. And in that case the temporary tenant uses the owner's number. All he has to do is notify anyone who's likely to ring him to call him at such and such a number. The directory wouldn't make an alteration for a short period. I know. My sister used to let her house regularly. Usually for six months."

It looked as if we'd narrowed things down. In the morning we'd first enquire for furnished properties on a short tenancy. If that failed, we'd extemporise. A mention of R. Carlisle or R. Carter might produce something. Any contract whatever would have had to be signed by one of those names.

I left Hallows digging out the names and addresses of house agents. For the first time for a good few days I was back in the flat in time for tea. While Bernice was preparing it, I thought I'd chance my luck and ring John Hill. It always pays to hand out even a little to the one who foots the bill.

"Was just thinking of ringing you myself," he said. "You have some news?"

"Not actually about the lady. By this time tomorrow, though, we think we'll know the man she left her husband for. After that it shouldn't be too hard."

"Splendid!" he said. "Splendid! I'm at liberty to tell Julian?"

"Rather you didn't," I said. "He'll get the news soon enough. You don't happen to know if he's still anxious to have her back?"

"I think he's wavering. That hole business—he still insists it was a grave—shook him pretty badly. He was at the office for an hour or two today, by the way. Jean Lindman rang me an hour or so ago. She said he was looking almost his old self."

I had a good tea, a good dinner, a nice relaxed evening and a good night's sleep. I woke to a morning of mist and drizzle but I wouldn't have been all that disturbed if there'd been snow. I just had that feeling: the one that sometimes comes when you know it's going to be a wonderful day.

11

MOTHER LODE

I WENT into the first house-agent's just after ten o'clock and ten minutes later was out again. I moved a hundred yards along the street to the second. I told the clerk I was looking for a furnished house and he showed me into the office of one of the principals—a Mr. Sands. He waved me to a chair, offered me a cigarette and asked the kind of property I had in mind. As soon as I said I wanted a furnished house he said I was lucky: he had one and one only on his books, and he wouldn't have had that but for a combination of circumstances. What period of tenancy did I have in mind? The property in question was available for barely three months.

"Three months will suit me splendidly," I told him. "Where exactly is it?"

"Packford," he said. "Do you know it? About five miles away. Little Meadows is a charming, half-timbered house with absolutely every convenience. Also, if you're coming from town by road, you can turn off just short of here to the left and save driving through any sort of suburban area. It's the first house in the village if you're coming from town and the last from here."

"You'll probably think me a bit suspicious," I said, "but how's it come to be available this time of year?"

"I'll tell you. The property belongs to a retired colonel of the name of Mortimer, and he and his wife are spending six months with their only daughter in New Zealand. They left at the very beginning of October and don't return till the middle of April, and we were the sole agents for letting the property. We found a tenant almost at once and then, just about a week ago, the tenant himself was suddenly called away to New York. As he mightn't be back for some months, he honoured his contract and settled for the whole six months but asked us to let for the remainder of the period if we could."

"I see. All the tenant's trying to do is cut his losses. What's his name, by the way?"

"Well," he said, "we don't usually divulge names unless it's absolutely necessary, but the tenant is a Mr. Carter. All the necessary business was done through a house-agent in town. If you decide to take the property for the three months, then you'll be dealing directly through me."

I passed him my Agency card. His eyebrows lifted the merest trifle.

"What I'm telling you is strictly in confidence, Mr. Sands, but my firm is being employed to help unearth a series of frauds in the Tonbridge area. It's likely to be a long business and may take the whole of three months, and I'd like to have my own headquarters somewhere near. My bead assistant would be with me and what I propose is to take a look at the property straight away."

"Fine," he said. "I'll take you there myself. You're ready to go now?"

"Look, Mr. Sands, what I'm going to say is probably unusual but I don't want anyone with me when I inspect that house. I want to form my own opinions and see just what I want to see."

I smiled.

"So what you're saying to yourself is, 'I don't know this man from Adam and what he's after is the key. Five minutes after he's entered, he'll be off with everything he can lay his hands on and that's the last I'll see of him.' So what I'm proposing to do is to have a cup of coffee with my assistant while you check my references: the Agency, my bank manager and the Chairman of United Assurance."

"Quite unnecessary," he said. "I hope I'm a good enough judge to know a rogue when I see one."

"You'd be surprised," I told him. "But I'd like it that way. I'll be back in half an hour when I hope to collect the key."

It took me ten minutes to find Hallows. It might have been he who'd had the luck that morning but for the chance of the draw. We had our coffee and both of us went back to see Sands.

"Everything in order?"

"It always was, sir." He handed me a small bunch of keys with appropriate labels. "Anything else you'd like to know before seeing the property?"

"Perhaps, yes. What about domestic help?"

"Fully available," he said. "A widow, a Mrs. Polster, who's worked there for quite a long time. If you want to see her, she lives next door to the school. I think she'll be glad to be back more regularly. The previous tenant and his wife used to come down only for short weekends."

"What was he like? It's possible I may have known him."

"To tell you the truth, I can't say. As I told you, everything was arranged through his agent. I never actually saw him. His references were quite satisfactory."

I said we'd be back by early afternoon at the latest. We were pretty cock-a-hoop when we drove off. Thanks to a bit of manoeuvring we'd have that house to ourselves for a solid hour's search. There was only one slight damper: Moira Matching was definitely not holed up at Little Meadows. But that was a bridge we could cross when we came to it. And Mrs. Polster might know quite a lot. It took about ten minutes to reach the village. We followed the one road till we were well through, and about a quarter of a mile beyond the last house we spotted Little Meadows. There was no mistaking it even as we neared, and the name was on the gate that shut off the short drive. We left the car on the verge outside.

It was all that Sands had called it—a smallish house of tremendous charm. Its upper story projected, its exterior timbering was unusually massive and its barge boards beautifully carved. A two-car garage lay just to the right at the end of the thirty-yard gravelled drive: new but with a mellowed tile roof and timbering in keeping with the house. Pale fencing, ornamental shrubs and flowering trees made a screen from the road. Except for long beds planted with wallflowers, everything between house and screen was lawn. A paving path led straight from the main gate across that lawn to the front door.

The door was of massive oak, and almost certainly reproduction. We went through to a small hall with a tiny cloak-room. Stairs led upwards from the end. The walnut, eighteenth-century grandfather clock was ticking, and a massive oak dower chest was empty. A door on the right led to a smallish dining-room with an open fireplace and fine breast-beam. The furniture was Jacobean. Dark red curtains partially drawn across the leaded windows gave a nice touch of colour.

We went back and through from the hall to a drawing-room-lounge. All the furniture was covered in dust-sheets: even the front of the tall corner cupboard was draped. There was a marble fireplace of the early Adam period that must have come from elsewhere, and a bracket clock was ticking away on its shelf. Two large Oriental rugs almost covered the broad oak planking of the floor.

The kitchen, with door and serving hatch to the dining-room, was light and fairly large. Its side window overlooked the side of the garage and the long one above the stainless steel sink looked out across the back gardens. A two-oven Aga with a water heating fitment was back to the chimney-breast of the dining-room. The large refrigerator had been switched off. On a shelf in one of the pastel-coloured cupboards, a small alarm-clock was still going.

We went upstairs. Dead ahead was a modern bathroom and lavatory combined. To the right, above the dining-room, was the main bedroom: beds stripped and furniture in dust-sheets. To the left, opening out from a low-ceilinged passageway, were two other bedrooms, one of them only about ten by nine. Each had the same rather forlorn emptiness of the main bedroom. It, and the larger of the other two bed-rooms, had its own basin. About the house there was nothing of mustiness or damp. The whole place smelt fresh and clean, and there was the faintest scent of lavender.

"Which would you prefer, top or bottom?" I said to Hallows.

He chose the top. I went downstairs and we went through that house with a small-toothed comb. Every drawer was opened and every shelf examined and carpets and rugs lifted. It took me a solid hour to go through that ground floor and there was never a thing to connect it with Moira Matching. Hallows had been luckier. He came down when I was just in the last stages. In the main bedroom he'd found three blonde hairs and he had them in the safety of an envelope. It was he who did something I'd forgotten: examined the dust-bag of the modern vacuum cleaner. In it we found another blonde hair.

We locked up the house again and tried the garage. It had been swept out and no tyre-marks were on the concrete floor: nothing, in fact, to connect with either a Jaguar or a Mercedes. We locked the garage again and had a look at the double shed by the door of the kitchen. Most of it was occupied by fuel. In the better-lighted part was a small carpenter's bench with quite a good selection of tools.

We had a look at the back gardens. There was another lawn, large enough for the croquet set we'd seen in one of the sheds, and a small summer-house stood to the right in the lee of the tall, trimmed thorn of the boundary hedge. A tall hornbeam hedge served as boundary and screen for that croquet lawn, and beyond it was an untidy kitchen garden. It had its own small gardening shed, with a motor-mower and a few tools. Hallows had a good look at them. He remembered Grange House. He had a good look, too, at that kitchen garden, but there was never a sign of recent digging.

In the thorn hedge at the far back was a small gate through which was a long, narrow meadow in a corner of which were a few sheep. Fifty yards across the meadow was a chestnut wood, with a gapped, untidy hedge, and the wood looked almost at its full twelve-year growth. There was only the faintest sign of a path from the kitchen garden gate, and in a few yards it lost itself.

I had a look at my watch. It wasn't far short of one o'clock so we went back to the main gate and had a last look from there at the house. It was a charming little place. I'd have liked it myself. Hallows reckoned the only thing it lacked was a greenhouse.

We drove towards the village. There was only one cottage near the school so we went down the short path and knocked at the door. It was Daisy Polster who opened it. She must have been best part of seventy: a tallish, spare woman with quite a pleasant smile. As soon as I'd said why we were there, she asked us to come in. Just through the door was a typical cottage living-room: fire in the grate, an old-fashioned chair or two, a white-faced grandfather dock, and

Staffordshire dogs on the mantelpiece. There was even a cat, asleep on one of the chairs. She asked if we'd like a cup of tea.

We were to have quite a chat, haphazard as all real chats are. She'd been head housemaid at the local Hall and her husband head gardener, but after the last war the Hall had been sold and then demolished. Then her husband had died and it was then that she became a daily help at Little Meadows. The colonel and his wife were very nice people to work for. The colonel himself had seen to the garden. There had been far more flowers till two or three years back, and then Mrs. Mortimer, who saw to the flowers, suffered too much with her arthritis. That was one of the reasons why they'd gone to New Zealand. The change of climate might do Mrs. Mortimer good.

"What about the tenants? How'd you get on with them?"

"To tell you the truth. I never saw Mr. Carter at all," she said, "and her only once. Much younger than I'd thought she'd be and very good-looking. Really lovely blonde hair. They had a flat in town, you know, and only managed to get down on a Saturday night and then they'd be away again on the Sunday. I understood he had an important job in London, and she had, too. That's why they couldn't spare more time. Still, it made a change."

"Seems queer to me," Hallows said. "Did you have a hot meal ready for them?"

"Oh, no," she said. "They'd always had something before they left. I did have to have a good fire going in the lounge and see the electric blankets were turned on upstairs. It was easy, really, once you got used to it. I used to leave a note saying how many hours I'd put in for the week, and Mrs. Carter would leave a note about what they wanted me to have in the house when they arrived the following Saturday."

"You liked working for the Carters?"

She laughed.

"Well, it was queer, really: never seeing them and all that. Still, I must say they never gave any trouble. Sometimes they couldn't get down at all, but they'd always know beforehand and leave a note. Very considerate they were, really. And very generous. Mr. Carter wrote about how sorry he was to leave, and enclosed a present for me."

"Didn't *she* write?"

It was curious, but that was something that hadn't occurred to her. I didn't press the point. All we wanted was to keep the talk fluid. The more she talked, the more we'd learn, and there's nothing more conducive to talk than a cold day outside and you in a cosy little room and taking your time over a cup or two of tea.

"I noticed the clocks were ticking away," I said. "Quite a surprise in a way."

She smiled. "Oh, I always wind them on a Monday morning. Doesn't make the house seem so dreary when you go in. It's companionable like. And I like to air the rooms, even if they aren't occupied."

"The colonel hasn't installed television," Hallows said. "Didn't he like it?"

"I think he was having it when he came back. There's the wireless, though. A very good set."

"A gramophone?"

"No, there wasn't. Mr. Carter had one of his own, though. And a lot of records. Of course that went away when he left. It was his properly, you see."

The time had come to get to Hallows and myself. I said, if I took the house, the positions would be just the opposite from what they'd been with the Carters. We'd be there, like a couple of bachelors, during the week, and be home in town for the weekends. She said that would suit her fine. If we wished, she could have a hot meal ready for us when we came in at night.

"That'd be splendid," I said. "I'd certainly like to take the house but unfortunately the decision doesn't rest with me. My superiors may consider it's too far away from Tonbridge, where I'll be working most of the time. What I'll do, Mrs. Polster, is to let Mr. Sands know at the earliest possible moment."

I held out my hand. "Thank you for the tea, Mrs. Polster. I hope I'll be seeing you again."

"Thank *you*, sir. I hope you don't mind me saying I hope you two gentlemen do take the house. I'm sure you'd like it there and I'd do everything I could."

There was a garage about a couple of hundred yards on and I drew the car in. It was a modest garage. The proprietor was still at his lunch but there was a push bell with a notice to ring it when the place was shut. In a minute a middle-aged man in dungarees appeared from a cottage the other side of the road. I had four gallons put in the tank and asked him to check the tyres. It gave me the chance to talk.

"I may be taking Colonel Mortimer's house for the next month or two. Nice to have a garage reasonably handy if anything should go wrong."

"Glad to do anything for you, sir. Always ready to come along, no matter what time."

"That's fine," I said. "Did the previous tenants have a car?"

"Two cars, that's what they say. I never actually saw them myself. They used to come down on a Saturday night and only stay till the Sunday. Down from London, so they wouldn't have to come as far as this."

We moved on again. It would be about two o'clock when we got to that estate office, which meant it would be open again.

"Well, there we are," I said to Hallows. "How're you feeling about things?"

"I don't like it," he told me. "I don't like that bit about Carlisle sending Mrs. Polster that goodbye note and the tip. Moira should at least have sent a line."

"Anything else?"

"Yes. Assuming that Moira was too damned ignorant to know it was her place to write a note, and assuming that she's now lying doggo somewhere till it's time to leave for America, then we start looking all over again. Unless she got another passport, which she could easily do, and she's in America herself, waiting till Carlisle gets there."

"Let's look fairly and squarely at something else," I said. "What if Moira's dead? In my judgment it's the one solution that takes care of everything. Take this morning. When we got here we didn't have very much but hopes. And what happened? Everything was handed out to us on a gold platter. We know beyond a shadow of doubt what we'd only suspected. And, so what? We ought to be hilarious but we aren't. I'm not and I don't think you are. And why? Because something keeps telling us we're only on the fringes of the case. We're only skirting round the edges. And do you know the one thing that makes it so? It's something that contradicts everything else. It's that business of the Jaguar car found at the station with most of a woman's personal possessions in it. That's the one thing that can't be fitted in. We just can't explain it. It's as inexplicable as if you and I were prepared to swear upon oath that this car suddenly for a period of, say, a minute, turned into a Rolls. Am I right?"

"You're right enough," he said. "Except that you left something out. It isn't inexplicable provided you bring yourself to face the facts. If she's dead and Carlisle killed her, the Jaguar explains itself. He just had to dump the car. It's as simple as that. That's why he wrote the note to Mrs. Polster. It's why he's bolting to America."

We were at the house-agent's. Hallows stayed in the car. Sands was in and I gave him the keys. I had to do a certain amount of talking besides spinning him that yarn about my superiors. He had to be absolutely happy about us for even as long as a week. He was like Mrs. Polster: something to be kept on ice till the real questioning came. In any case I had to talk about terms and be just a bit surprised at the mention of seven guineas.

"But that includes Mrs. Polster," he told me. "You deduct her wages from the weekly account. I don't mind telling you, sir, that the colonel would have had the place shut up entirely if it hadn't been for her. And having the place occupied by the right kind of tenant. But what I can do, as a special favour, is to make it six and a half guineas for a three-month's tenancy. If I were you, I'd get your superiors to act quickly. You never know when a place like Little Meadows might be snapped up."

"Sound enough advice," I said. "By the way, how did you advertise it in the first place?"

"In the two local papers. We always have a weekly column. As a matter of fact we had an enquiry from Mr. Carter's London agent only three days after the advertisement first appeared."

"You wouldn't like to tell me his name?"

He chuckled. "Come, come, sir. No use you thinking you can make a deal with him. The balance of the tenancy is a private matter strictly between Mr. Carter and myself. I thought I'd made that clear."

"You did," I said ruefully. "Still, there's no harm in trying."

He didn't know it but it didn't matter about that agent—not for the moment. When the real questioning came he'd be ready enough to talk, though it mightn't be to me. In any case, that was a cue for leaving. I did add as we shook hands that we'd been so busy that we'd had to skip lunch. He looked almost as horrified as if I'd owned up to cannibalism.

"Go to the Feathers. It's just along the street. I'm always taking people there. Tell you what, Mr. Travers. I'll ring them at once. By the time you've parked your car, they'll have something ready."

So Hallows and I had lunch after all, and we took our time over coffee in the lounge. We even had a liqueur brandy by way of celebration.

"Yes," I said. "We've certainly had a tough row to hoe. About as tough a one as I can remember."

He smiled. "The way you're talking, sir, you'd think it was all over."

"Isn't it?"

He just stared.

"If it isn't, where do we go from here?" I said. "Say we walk into Carlisle's flat. What's he tell us? To get the hell out of it. Can we make him talk?"

"We couldn't hold the police over his head?"

"Suppose we do. He still tells us to get out. What else can he do? If he lost his head and tried to buy us off, we'd have no witnesses. And what'd be our approach? That we thought he might help us to trace a missing woman? He'd simply swear he'd never heard of her—and he'd tell us to get out He's either got to do that or own up to—well, anything that won't land him in really bad trouble."

"Maybe you're right," he said. "So what do you do?"

"The client calls the tune, provided he leaves us in the clear. That's why we can't see Carlisle first. Can't you imagine Superintendent Jewle or someone being told all we know and learning we'd had the nerve to interview Carlisle and more or less tip him off? He'd blast us to hell and back, and we'd have asked for it."

"And what about the missing jewellery?"

Hallows isn't mercenary. Our standard fee for recovery is ten per cent, and out of that there's always a bonus for the operative or operatives employed. That's usually five per cent of ours. Fifty pounds on a ten-thousand-pound recovery mayn't be a fortune, but it's better than a poke in the eye with a sharp stick.

"The jewellery isn't affected," I said. "Even if the police take over from here, it's still on information supplied by us. If the jewellery's recovered, we get the bonus. It's happened before."

"Just thought I'd ask," he said. "And your mind's made up?"

"Practically," I told him. "I might quibble and say it's made up for me. What I'll definitely have to do is ring John Hill. If you haven't thought of anything to change it, that's what I'll do as soon as we're back at Broad Street."

He went off to collect his car. It was well after four when I rang John Hill.

"I ought to see you first thing in the morning," I said. "Things have gone as far as we dare take them. It's a pretty nasty mess and it's up to you to say what's to be done next."

"You've found Moira?"

"Don't know," I said. "I'd rather not say anything till I can make the whole report. I think Matching ought to be there."

"Just a minute," be said. "Let's not be too hasty. You mentioned a nasty mess."

"It may be a very nasty mess indeed. As nasty as they come."

"Then Julian mustn't hear it," he told me. "He's had a nerve-racking time. If necessary we'll have to present him with a *fait accompli*."

"You're the boss. And Haddowe?"

"No," he said flatly. "Just you and me. Shall we say ten?"

"You and me and Hallows at ten in the morning. Anything to the contrary, let me know."

Bertha brought in a pot of tea, and Hallows and I set about drafting a report. Not for John Hill. He wouldn't know it, but he was being seen as a matter of courtesy. Whatever his reactions and suggestions, the upshot would be precisely the same. What we knew was too much for us to handle. If we attempted to handle it the least bit further, we'd be definitely guilty of impeding the law: a something the Agency couldn't afford, even if it meant the loss of United Assurance.

Not that we could have handled it in any case. We'd neither the authority nor the available men. But, as it turned out, John Hill wasn't unreasonable. In the morning he was told what we knew and what we surmised, and I'd go almost as far to say he was badly shaken. Like most big executives, he's a stickler for strict legality, and the mere idea of a hauling over the coals by Scotland Yard was about as repugnant as doing a strip-tease in Trafalgar Square.

It was not till about half-past eleven when we left him, and as soon as we were at the Agency, I rang Jewle. He didn't happen to be in, so I asked if they'd ring me back.

12
ENTER THE LAW

I FIRST knew Jewle when he was a senior sergeant, more years ago than I like to remember. A couple of years ago he was made up to superintendent, and in that long period from just off the bottom to very near the top we'd been associated in a good many cases. I've an enormous respect for Jewle but that doesn't make us identical twins. He's Scotland Yard, pure strain. I'm by comparison a freak: a sport that's somehow evolved. The wonder is that we always get along so well.

Matthews, who was with him that afternoon, was as old an acquaintance: a young detective-sergeant when I first knew him and now an inspector. Matthews had mellowed over the years and not exactly along the lines that made our original association not only adventurous, but even at times a tacit conspiracy against authority. No more special favours from Matthews. A square deal, of course, but no blind eye or something brought out from under the counter.

I'd wanted Hill to be present but he'd turned the suggestion down. I didn't ask for his reasons. I did think he was storing up trouble. Far better tell everything he knew and get it over than have to see Jewle later and maybe at inconvenient times. Also I'd have liked Hill there to be able to confirm certain statements. The Yard, even in the persons of Jewle and Matthews, has a habit of raising its eyebrows and exchanging glances when confronted with the melodramatic.

Everything was very friendly when I arrived: handshakes, smiles, a touch or two of reminiscence and tea for three. No sooner did I get my first cup than Jewle was asking me what it was all about. Jewle is quiet, as a lot of big men are: be never permits himself the luxury of excitement.

"May I start at the end?" I said. "When I've finished telling you why I'm here you're going to say something like, 'You don't expect us to swallow that!' I'm just warning you, that's all."

Jewle smiled. "The great thing about you, Mr. Travers, is that you never change. If I'd asked you the time, there'd have been a song and dance before you said it was a quarter-past four. Not that I don't like it, mind you. It's, well it's—"

"Refreshing," cut in Matthews. "What I might call anti-cobweb."

"That's fine," I said. "Hallows was associated throughout in what I'm going to say and we drew up this account together. It's going to take a long time to read."

Jewle suggested a stenographer. I said we'd thought of that and saved his time beforehand by making a carbon. If they wanted to stop me at any time and put a question—well and good. As a matter of fact that account of our enquiries was not only comprehensive: it proceeded logically from step to step. It took me half an hour to read it and Jewle pulled me up only once.

"Right," he said when I'd finished. "Let me say one thing first On the face of it you did the correct thing in coming to us. So are we to take it you're washing your hands of the whole thing from now on?"

"Not necessarily," I told him. "Our assignment was to find Moira Matching, and we haven't done it. There was also the matter of recovering valuable jewellery. We've done neither but we can go on trying to do both, and without getting in your way. You two know as well as I do that that kind of procedure has happened before. We pass on anything new and you don't actually keep us in the dark."

He smiled dryly. I'd have liked to think there was a touch of admiration in it.

"Still the same old argument. But about what you've told us. What do you expect us to do?"

"That's up to you. I've given you certain facts."

"All right," he said, "so you've given us certain facts. A woman has left her husband for another man. That sort of thing happens every day. Admit the circumstances were slightly unusual. The husband may wish to charge her with theft, though that'd be a tricky business. He might try to prove that chloral hydrate she gave him was intended to kill him, though I don't think that business of the so-called grave would do anything to help. You say that he wouldn't do that. He wants the whole thing kept nice and quiet. Very well, then. He doesn't even want to go to the local police. So why come to us? You're supposed to be working for him. That means respecting his wishes."

"That's just fine," I said. "Never heard anything more clearly put. And what do I have to come to you with in order to get you to move?"

"You don't. You go to the local police. Surely you know that. And you'll have to give them far more evidence. It's not their job to find women who've left their husbands."

"And if I do, and it happens to be the Agency that unearths foul play, someone's going to be in a bit of a hole."

"You frighten us to death." That was Matthews. "Where's there even a hint of foul play?"

"My God!" I said. "And you're paid to think! A woman leaves her husband for another man. Very well then. That's her business. Also she manages to take some valuable jewellery with her: jewellery she'd swear was given to her by her husband. All right again. But now explain away that Jaguar. It had in it practically all her personal belongings, but it was found abandoned only five or six miles from Little Meadows. And nobody has enquired about it since."

Matthews chuckled. "Explain it? It explains itself. She wanted to make a clean break. She haled her husband, so she washed her hands of him entirely. Wouldn't keep a thing he'd given her. The jewellery's different. You couldn't expect any woman to go so far as to give up that."

"Moira Matching," I said. "Moira giving up anything? Don't make me laugh. That woman was on the make from the very first. Even you can't deny I've given you ample evidence of that, and you want me to swallow a yarn about death-bed repentance. But explain something else. Is it just a queer coincidence that this Rocky Carlisle wouldn't hear a thing about that American tour before she left her husband, and then, only a day or two after she had, he virtually thrust that tour down his agent's throat?"

"All right, all right," Jewle said mildly. "Let's cut out the excitement and look at things calmly. I think Mr. Travers has made out something of a case: not that that commits us to anything. I may be cynical but he mightn't have come here if he thought he had the chance of getting any farther by himself. On the other hand, he may have had a conscience for once and thought it the right and proper thing to play according to Cocker, and, if that's so, then we're grateful."

Matthews was grinning. "Another death-bed repentance."

"Now, now, now," Jewle told him. "You said you had a carbon copy, Mr. Travers, so I take it we can have that report. What we'll do after we've studied it, I'm not prepared to say. Frankly, I don't know. What I will say, in fairness to you, is that we'll inform you if and when we do propose to take any steps."

"Good enough," I said, and got to my feet. "And if you don't take more than a couple of days to make up your mind, we'll do nothing in the meanwhile."

It was really funny then how the atmosphere changed. I was actually told not to be in any hurry to go and we stayed on yarning for best part of half an hour. But for that report, now on Jewle's desk, I might have just dropped in for a friendly chat.

The following late afternoon I learned that Jewle was at work and the information came from John Hill. I'd rung him the previous afternoon after I'd left the Yard and given him a hint that something might be done. Now he was telling me that Jewle and another detective officer had been to Grange House. I was expecting him to be perturbed, but he wasn't. He said it was a relief. Even Julian thought so. He was even prepared to accept the fact that his wife might be dead.

"Julian's come a long way," he told me. "I'd have sworn he'd have gone on being infatuated with that woman for the rest of his life, but now I think he's cured. I may be wrong but I think he'll be far from unhappy if she really *is* dead."

It didn't matter to me one or the other if Matching were realising he'd been the world's prize fool: what was more interesting was to hear Jean Lindman's voice when I was fetched back to the telephone just as I was leaving the office.

"Are you busy this evening?"

"No," I said. "Why do you ask?"

"Well, I know it's an imposition but I'd very much like to have a talk with you. Could you come to my flat?"

"I'd love to," I said. "I might have to make it rather early. Half-past six suit you?"

It meant getting home and changing, but I made it on time. Newbury Gardens was just another modern block of flats, and 3A was on the ground floor. Jean Lindman had also done some changing: the usual jumper and skirt had been replaced by a highly attractive gown. Her hair looked different and she was wearing more jewellery. I couldn't judge the size of the flat, but the lounge in which we were to do our talking was beautifully furnished.

"You're looking more charming than ever," I told her as she was getting me a drink. "What is it? The Elixir of Youth?"

She laughed. "Just something out of bottles. Even if it were true, which it isn't."

There was a low, beautifully sprung chesterfield, and we occupied the corners with the low table between us. I lifted my drink and she smiled over hen.

"And now, why've you lured me out here?"

"To tell you about the police, for one thing. A Superintendent Jewle and another man—"

"Matthews?"

"No," she said, and frowned. "That wasn't the name. I think he was an inspector, a local one. At any rate, they had a long talk with Julian this morning."

"How'd he take it?"

"Splendidly." For some reason or other her voice lowered. "Do you know, I really believe he's actually beginning to hate that woman!"

"Really? Wounded *amour propre*?"

"I don't know. Something's opened his eyes. It doesn't matter much what."

We talked about Moira for a bit, just the same old things. Maybe Jean wanted that re-exposure as additional assurance.

"You really think she may be dead?"

"Don't know," I said. "That's for the police to find out. Wishful thinking won't get anybody anywhere."

She flushed. "You think I'm a sort of scarlet woman, don't you?"

"Heavens, no!" I said. "Any woman's the right to be in love with any man. There's no law against it. Always, of course, provided. Also, if I may say so, I do know that if Julian's ever in a position to many you, you'll make him an amazingly good wife."

"Isn't that wishful thinking?" She shook her head. "Don't let's talk about it. Tell me something instead. The police wouldn't tell Julian but I know you know. Who was the man?"

I smiled. "Sorry, but I mustn't tell you. I promised."

"Not even in confidence?"

"Not even in confidence."

There was silence for a moment, then she said she didn't like me as much as she did. Would I have another drink? I talked to her back while she was mixing it.

"Tell me, Jean: why did you want me to see you? There must be something more than we've mentioned up to now?"

"Perhaps I wanted company," she told me. "I've been worried about everything, too. You can't go on keeping things tight inside you. There comes a time when you just have to know."

She brought the two drinks to the low table.

"Think of the publicity," she said. "That can't do anyone any good. The Sunday papers, and photographs and things. It's horrible to think of."

"It needn't come to that," I said, and it must have been a bit pontifically. "'Cowards die many times before their deaths.' Plenty of time to worry when there is publicity. I don't think there will be, not of the kind you thought. In any case. I'll bet that a year from now you'll have forgotten the whole thing."

"You're kind," she said. "Far too kind."

And, believe it or not, that was almost everything that was said. Ten minutes later I'd finished my drink and was getting up to leave.

"You think it was stupid of me to drag you out all this way for almost nothing," she told me at the door.

"I think you stupid for thinking so," I said. "You just go on whistling and I'll go on coming."

But on that tedious journey back, I couldn't help wondering. Had I been brought to that flat just to be a shoulder on which to lean? Possible, of course, but something was telling me there was more to it than that. The questions she'd actually asked were little more than excuses for conversation. They'd have been almost innocuous if she'd put them to me over the telephone. And there was something else—she hadn't been in keeping. A woman can't just leave one particular self at the office and become another as soon as she enters her flat, but the Jean Lindman I'd just left hadn't been the one I'd expected to meet. I couldn't quite put my finger on the changes—they'd been too subtle for that—but the fact remained that I'd been called to that flat for a reason which I still didn't know. Or so I thought. The fact that I'd forgotten the whole thing long before I went to bed made no difference. It was something I thought of again as soon as I woke in the morning.

John Hill had insisted that we should keep an eye on things in spite of the entrance of the law. In any case we weren't actually sure when he rang me the previous afternoon that the law, as represented by Jewle, would consider itself bound to do anything at all. That's why Hallows was going to Packford to try to unearth what he could at the village pub. Packford had its television sets and weeklies, as Carlisle well knew, which was why he took precautions against being seen, but what Carlisle—the Fulham boy—didn't take into account was the fact that a village doesn't like mysteries. What it doesn't know it tries to find out, and gossip makes a kind of pool of its knowledge.

I suppose in a way that sending Hallows to Packford was a violation of what I'd promised Jewle, that we'd hold our hand till he'd made up his mind about taking action, but my conscience didn't worry me too much. But when, after breakfast that morning, the telephone went and the voice at the end of the line was Jewle's conscience took a mighty quick hand. But I needn't have worried.

"You busy this morning, or could you do us a favour?"

"Glad to," I said.

"Good," he said. "There's a little place called Martha's at the corner of Hollis Street. Could you be there at ten-thirty? We can talk things out over coffee."

I didn't ask what things, though I had the chance. He asked about Bernice, for instance, but what I said I really don't know, even if it must have satisfied him. What I was thinking was that Hollis Street at either end isn't more than a couple of hundred yards from Portland Mews. If that meant anything, it was that Jewle was on his way to an interview with Carlisle.

The next two hours were a pretty long time. Jewle arrived in a police car which immediately drove off again. The little restaurant was fairly full but we found a back table.

"You've been here before?" I said. "Nothing like laying down a little ground bait."

He gave me a queer look. Then he smiled. "You mean, have I been reconnoitring?"

"What's a little subtlety between friends?" I said. "But have you?—since you mention it."

"Well, I did have a general look round."

The coffee came. We lighted cigarettes and settled down.

"That report you gave us was one of the best I've ever read," he told me. "You know why? It not only gave conclusions: it set 'em up as Aunt Sallies and tried to knock 'em down. What I mean is, it wasn't biased."

"And so what?"

"Well, take our friend at Portland Mews. In public he seems to be a wow, but privately he isn't all that hot. In fact there are various people who find him pretty objectionable. He seems to have plenty of low cunning and he isn't too scrupulous. But, as you said, the question arises as to whether he'd go to the grim extreme of getting rid of a woman. I admit he may have been responsible for procuring whatever it was she put into her husband's drink that Saturday night, but something arises there that you didn't foresee. Why help her to leave her husband and then get rid of her?"

"Maybe it had been in his mind for quite a time. He wanted her to make the break in order to get her alone. He'd taken every precaution at Little Meadows and it's a fairly lonely place."

"Yes," he said. "There *is* that. The local inspector, a pretty good man, got us the name of the London agent through whom the place was taken, and there's no doubt it was Carlisle. What else was there? Oh, yes, the jewellery. I agree with you that he needn't have known anything about that."

He smiled.

"Extraordinary the way this whole thing's been handled. All this keeping things strictly in the family. It's a sort of Victorian survival. Matching's the prize specimen. He owns he knew his wife was likely to leave him, so why didn't he just kick her out?"

"I don't know," I said. "I guess people nowadays are more civilised. You don't try that go-and-never-darken-my-doors-again stuff these days."

I stopped. In some minute part of a second I'd seen again an old melodrama of my youth—the erring mother, clutching her baby, driven out into the blinding snow.

"I've thought of something," I said. "Something I don't think I brought out in that report. Have you caught any good abortionists lately?"

He stared. "You mean?"

I told him what Hulda Bland had once suspected and about that night when Moira had called for a double brandy at a certain pub.

"No," he said. "It's blowing hot and cold in the same breath. If she went to an abortionist, then no baby. No baby, no motive. The fact that the last thing she wanted was a baby, doesn't change that."

He looked at his watch.

"I didn't tell you, but I'm seeing Carlisle at eleven and I'd like you to come along. I've made an appointment but he hasn't a notion who I am."

He motioned to the waitress and paid the small bill. I was thinking ruefully about—of all things—a certain centurion who could tell this one to come, and he came, and tell that one to go, and he went. That was Jewle. Hallows and I grubbing around for results were a pretty pathetic contrast. There was only one consolation. If the Agency had been in competition with the Yard, we'd have been bankrupt years ago. Or in the bedroom key-hole business, which was worse.

Carlisle's flat was on the first floor, and it must have been setting him back at least six hundred a year. Not all a dead loss, of course. What should have been a lounge was now an office, with a grand piano additional to the usual furnishings. A sprightly looking woman of about forty had got up from the desk to let us in.

"Mr. Jewle? I think Mr. Carlisle will see you now. Will you wait just a moment?"

A moment or two and she was smilingly showing us through to what looked like a combination of study and lounge. Like that lounge at Grange House, it appeared to have everything, including a view over the little square. My guess was that Carlisle hadn't long been up, or maybe the pullover and narrowish trousers were his usual morning wear. The mop of hair was untidy and he was smoking a cigarette. He stubbed it out before he came across to us.

"Mr. Jewle?" He held out a band.

"A colleague of mine—Mr. Travers," Jewle said.

Carlisle was brashly brisk. "Make yourselves at home, gentlemen. What will you have to drink?"

We said it was a bit too early.

"Suit yourselves," he told us. "You'll excuse me getting down to business but I'm pretty well tied up for today. Just what did you have in mind about America? Whatever it is, it'll have to be gone over with my agent. You know that."

"As a matter of fact," Jewle said mildly, "we don't want to discuss that American tour. We're here on other business. Something we think you can help us about."

"Oh? What business?"

Jewle handed him his warrant card. "Just a little but necessary deception. Mr. Carlisle. As you've said, you're a busy and we wanted a little of your time."

It was a moment or two before Carlisle could speak. Jewle even had to reach for the card.

"Scotland Yard." He forced a smile. "Just what can Scotland Yard want from me?"

"Only what I said. A little help. To come to the point, it's to do with a Mrs. Matching—Moira Matching—who disappeared. You were a friend of hers and we hoped you might throw some light on it."

It shook him. He had to gain time. "What name did you say?"

"Matching. Moira Matching."

He smiled. "Never heard of her. Never heard of her in my life."

"You're sure?"

"Of course I'm sure. Look," he said, "if anyone asks you do you know anyone, you either do or you don't. I don't."

The bland look went. "Just a minute, though. What made you think I should know this Moira or whatever her name was?"

"Just one of those things," Jewle said. "Someone thought he'd seen her with you. Sorry I can't tell you his name. You're very well known, Mr. Carlisle. People who haven't actually seen you on, say, television, know your face. And this particular person also happened to know hers."

"Whoever he is, he was wrong. Sorry, Superintendent, but that's the way it is."

I produced a photograph. "Then it's only a matter of academic interest to show you this?"

He took it He looked far too long. "Sorry. I still don't know her."

Jewle caught my eye and we got to our feet.

"Well, there we are," he said resignedly. "The woman's disappeared. Strictly between ourselves, something serious might have happened to her, which is why we can't neglect any angle. Sorry we've had to trouble you."

"That's all right No apologies needed. Let me see you out."

My guess was that he wanted to keep us away from that secretary: at any rate, he went with us to the corridor door. I wondered what he'd be thinking when be got back to his room again.

Jewle and I walked back to where his car was waiting near a Selfridge back entrance. It had been a surprising quarter of an hour for me, and I told him so. Why, for instance, hadn't he let out only just a little bit more of what we knew.

"No point in it," he said. "We had everything we wanted. If he had nothing to conceal, then he'd have come fairly clean. As it is, he's in something right up to the neck. That gives us the green light."

I saw the point. "And what next?"

"Haven't quite made up my mind. Be all right if I keep in touch?"

He offered me a lift right back to the Agency. I said I'd time on my hands and a walk might do me good.

13

DISCOVERY

IT WAS Matthews, not Jewle, who rang me that night at the flat, not long before I was due for bed.

"You're free in the morning?"

I said I was. I didn't tell him that Hallows had unearthed virtually nothing at Packford.

"Well, the Old Man thinks you might like to go to Packford. Be all right if I pick you up at the National Gallery at ten?"

I was there on time. At the green light we turned right, and down Whitehall to Westminster Bridge. I didn't expect a straight answer but I had to ask why Packford. What was going on down there?

"Might as well tell you," he said. "You'll find out quickly enough when we get there. What we think is that *if* anything happened in the murder line, there ought to be a body, so we're having a look-see. There's going to be the devil of a lot of local talk, though, if nothing turns up."

There's a lot of traffic at any time till it splits up a bit near the Oval, and it wasn't till we swung right again into the long straight that I was at him again.

"A lot of men on the job?"

"Not all that many." He laughed. "But you can't just go wandering all over people's property without a by-your-leave, so we let it out that there'd been a robbery. The former tenant, Mrs. Carter, had lost some valuable jewellery, and we'd had the tip the thief had been surprised and had had to park it somewhere near."

"How far are you going to search?"

"The garden's been done already. That top meadow ought to be done by now, too. They were on it as soon as it was light."

That probably left only the wood. That. I thought, was where a body would have to be: not that there's ever much undergrowth in those chestnut woods. When the wood's cut for hop-poles or stakes or fencing, most of the undergrowth is cleaned away, too. When you swing an axe you need a clear course. As for hiding or burying the body, that Saturday night had been bright moonlight. Whoever carried that body would have kept to the dark: a quick slip across the forty yards or so of meadow to the shadows of the wood.

Matthews slowed down just short of the farm and drew into the open yard. A couple of cars and a station-waggon were already there. We left our car and walked along a track that led down-hill past a field of winter wheat. It had rained the previous night and the rutted track was deep with mud. We turned along the west side of the field and in another hundred yards were at the gate of the meadow. In a moment or two one could see a something that moved in the wood.

The layout was like an "L" with its foot the wrong way. The foot was the meadow in front of us; narrow, as I've said. Then it turned at right angles to enclose the wood on the other side, and everything was still sloping fairly sharply down. Only the very tops of the trees would be visible from the main road.

"How big is the wood?"

"Not all that big," he said. "A bit over an acre. When you get close up you can almost see through it."

We climbed over the field gale and out across to another gate in the gapped hedge of the wood. A rough bridge of chestnut butt-ends and turf led across the ditch, and the ditch itself hadn't been cleaned out for years. The gate-posts had sagged and the gate itself was tottery.

"They used to bring the poles out this way donkey's years ago," Matthews told me. "Now they get them out the other side."

Ten yards into the wood and we could see a nearer man or two, moving methodically along his set course, scuffling now and again with his feet or pushing down the probe. We moved along to the right and there was Jewle, coat collar round his ears against the raw damp of the morning. The local C.I.D. man was with him—an inspector of the name of Venables. We shook hands.

"So you're the one who started all this," he told me. "But for you, I might have been in a nice warm office."

He wasn't all that serious. For that matter. I wasn't all that happy. Theories aren't always that good when you come to the point of trying out, and I don't mind saying that on that raw morning in the cold of a damp wood I was doubting the very things of which I'd been most sure. It wasn't any great consolation to remember that it hadn't been I who'd initiated that search.

"What about some coffee?" Jewle said.

We backed to a holly clump where the men had left some gear and had some hot coffee from one of the giant flasks. In the air was always the heavy smell of decaying leaves. In my youth that scent had been something hauntingly romantic: now it was only a depression and the premonition of a wasted morning.

"Nothing unusual anywhere?" Matthews asked.

"No disturbance at all," Venables said. "A few old rabbit burrows, that's all. And an old badger set. No one ever comes in here till the chestnut's about ready for felling. Shouldn't take long now to get through."

We moved to the right again. The wood was narrowish everywhere and the six men could easily have kept in touch. Midday came after a long half-hour, and the line of men moved along the final stretch of boundary hedge.

"Well, that's that," Jewle said. "Let's have a look round."

That hedge lay along the upright of the "L". A few yards along it was a field gate, and leading into the wood were the clearly visible ruts from the drays on which, ten or twelve years before, the heavier poles had been loaded. The ditch itself was in much the same shape but the bridge across it was very different This one was far more stoutly made and about ten feet wide and at its bottom, to leave a passage for water that had once come through, were twenty-inch concrete pipes, now sunk a few inches below the ditch soil.

Venables opened the gate and we went through. We stood for a minute on the weedy turf of the low bridge and looked around. To the left, skirting the last yards of the wood, was a rough track that led through another gate at the meadow end.

"Let me see," Jewle said. "The track joins a lane and comes out in the village."

"That's right," Venables said. "At Denny's little timber yard."

Jewle grunted. He had another look round. "Better try this ditch and then we'll see."

He moved forward. He stopped and sniffed. "Damn peculiar smell here."

He sniffed again. I didn't need to sniff. It was the sort of smell you get in an old cottage when there's a dead mouse just under the flow.

"Something's here! Something rotting."

He moved out, still sniffing. He turned towards the ditch and reached back a hand for a probe. He didn't use it.

"Try under the entry here. Get something to push through these pipes."

They'd lashed some thin chestnut poles together, and what was left of Moira Matching lay on that improvised stretcher. She hadn't been a pretty sight, and after the one look I'd moved a bit away. When she'd been pushed along the channel of the piping she'd had no coat: just a dark blue skin and a paler blue jumper, both now badly stained. One of the nylon stockings was torn and one of the shoes seemed to have been pushed in after her.

As Jewle had said, the ditches and that rough bridge were the first things that should have been tried. From where the body had been found, it was less than a hundred yards to the small gate of Little Meadows. Whoever had carried that body through that gate had had a quick look round in the moonlight and had made for the nearest shadow, and that could only have been that far end of the wood. He'd moved forward, looking for somewhere to hide the body, and then he'd seen the darker space beneath that bridge.

There'd been a brief conference and Venables had agreed that the body had better be taken to town. He'd gone off to arrange for transport. The body would be carried at the right moment to the front gate of the house.

"You see to that," Jewle told Matthews. "Mr. Travers can take your car and I'll get back to the Yard. And make sure there's no talking. Nothing of this is to get out till the word go."

So Jewle and I walked back along that mired track that led to the farm. He wasn't particularly cock-a-hoop. There'd been a theory— that was all—and it had turned out right.

"It's going to make a hell of a stir when it gets out," I said. "Carlisle'll be big news. When're you grabbing him?"

"No hurry for that," he said. "He may be a bit edgy but he'll be pretty sure he handled us all right yesterday morning. Plenty of time after the post-mortem."

"Any objection to my being there when you put him under the grill?"

"Mightn't be. There'll have to be a conference first. It might be thought expedient to have you there. You know how it is. They make the decisions."

We weren't in all that hurry and we pulled up at Bromley and had a quick lunch.

"Bromley," I said. "If it hadn't been for that word Bromley, Moira might have been tucked away under that little bridge till there wasn't much left but clothes. Unless water started coming along that ditch again, she'd have been there for keeps."

"Yes," he said. "It just shows. It's the luck of the game. Wonder how many things have been under my nose and I haven't seen them. Far more than what I did see. You can bet your life on that."

We got back to the Yard soon after three and Matthews was in about half an hour later. I was left to myself for a few more minutes and when Jewle came back there was the first news.

"Manual strangulation," he told me. "Only took them a minute to show that. Must have been terrific compression."

The usual tea-tray came in. There wasn't much point in discussing the case, but it helped to pass the time and in our job you somehow never get far away from shop. The savagery of that strangulation, for instance; wouldn't it point to some sudden, tremendous rush of hate rather than premeditation? Then there was the question of that mink coat. It hadn't been in the Jaguar with her other belongings, and it hadn't been with the body, and something there was badly out of keeping. Everything connected with her should have been removed from the neighbourhood of Little Meadows: either with the body or else in the car. Where then was the coat? Surely Carlisle could never have been such a fool as to hang on to it. What was a couple of thousand pounds compared with his neck?

At last the buzzer went. Jewle reached for the receiver.

"Speaking. . . . I see. And any pregnancy? . . . Uh-huh. . . . Good. . . . Yes, I'll be along."

"No pregnancy," he told us. "Probably an illegal operation not too long ago. Time of death not too easy to pin down, but oughtn't to be too far away from January the 9th. The Big Man himself is due at any minute and then we'll know for sure."

There was no point in my waiting. Jewle would definitely be there till late and he said he'd ring me some time before ten, so I walked to Trafalgar Square and caught a bus.

Hallows was in and we and Norris had a bit of a talk and then I rang John Hill.

"This is in very strict confidence," I told him. "Not a word to a living soul, but the lady's no longer missing."

"Where was she?"

"Not what you think," I said. "She was dead. Been dead for days. Can't say more. I'll try to see you before the story breaks. Just thought you ought to know we've still got an interest in things, in spite of what's happened."

I spent a restless evening at home, waiting for Jewle to ring. It was as near ten o'clock as makes no difference when the telephone went.

"Nothing new," he said. "Time and everything confirmed. Mr. C's being hauled in soon after nine if you'd like to be here."

I wasn't taking any chances. It hadn't struck nine when I went into Jewle's room.

"You're strictly an observer," he told me. "If you're asked to confirm or deny anything, you'll do it, that's all."

I said that suited me fine. All I'd hoped to do was listen. When he went out, I had a look at a newspaper or two and, when he came back, Matthews was with him.

"You know how touchy the Higher-Ups are," Jewle told me, "so just sit back there and look inscrutable. He's going to be allowed to do quite a lot of lying before we begin pulling him up."

"He's here?"

"Nicely parked," Jewle said. "Get the stenographer in and we might as well make a start."

Carlisle wasn't looking pleased. Before he could open his mouth he was having to listen to Jewle.

"Sorry to drag you out at this hour, Mr. Carlisle, but it's rather important and we still think you can help us. Sit down, will you.

Smoke if you want to. And you might like to take your overcoat off. You might be here some time."

He said he'd keep it on. Matthews moved a chair forward and he sat down. He gave me a look. The look switched to the stenographer.

"What's *he* doing?"

"Purely routine," Jewle told him. "Every interview has to be recorded. You'll be shown a copy later. Which reminds me. Your real name is Rockwell Carter?"

"That's right," he said. "But anyone's got the right to change their name."

"True enough. But unless Carlisle is your legal name, we'd better stick to the one on your birth certificate. But to get on to that business of helping us, Mr. Carter. You said the morning before yesterday that you'd never met Moira Matching in your life. You still stick to that?"

He shuffled slightly on the chair. "Well, yes. I mean I might have met her and not known who she was."

Jewle smiled. "You've forgotten that we showed you a photograph? Think again, Mr. Carter. Are you positive you never knew Moira Matching?"

"I told you, didn't I? I never knew her."

"You never knew her." He leaned forward across the desk, pointing a linger. "Then perhaps you'll tell us this. Who was the woman with whom you used to spend Saturday nights and Sundays at Little Meadows?"

It shook him but only for a moment. "Oh, that. That was just anybody. You know what women are like. You'd only to give 'em the chance."

"But Moira was never offered the chance?"

"I told you, didn't I?" He looked round at me for confirmation. "How could she when I never even knew her!"

Jewle got up.

"All right, Inspector. Take him away."

"You can't do this. I'm a busy man." He shook off Matthews' arm. "I've got my rights, you know."

"Take him away," Jewle said. "When he wants to tell me the truth he can come back."

The door closed on him. Jewle sat down and pulled out his pipe.

"Just what I anticipated. But he'll talk. Might have to cool his heels again, but he'll talk."

We didn't have more than two minutes to wait. He must have changed his mind on the way down, for Matthews was bringing him back.

"All right," he said. "So I knew her. All I was doing was protecting her name. You can't blame me for that."

"Very laudable. You say now that you did know Moira Matching. In a moment you'll be telling me that there weren't various women at that Packford place of yours: there was only the one. Isn't that so?"

Carter guessed it was. He owned up to a few more things: that she was married, for instance, and was thinking of leaving her husband.

"Let's start at the very beginning," Jewle said. "Tell us how you met her and go on from there."

He didn't deviate too much from the truth in things of which we had proof and yet you could sense a kind of unreality. From what I knew of him, the emphases were wrongly placed.

He said he'd met Moira at a palais de danse where he was appearing, and after the first show she'd introduced herself to him and he'd remembered her as a kid with whom he'd been at school. They'd had tea together and arranged another meeting in town. And that was how it all started. The next real thing was when she saw an advertisement about Little Meadows. His flat or a hotel was too dangerous for someone as well known as he was.

Jewle glanced at me; just a gesture to show we'd followed what had been said.

"We know all that, Mr. Carter. The agents were Sands and Harmon and the people who handled things for you were Mycrofts of Suffolk Street." He smiled reprovingly. "You see how foolish it was of you to tell us lies. But do go on. You used Little Meadows regularly. You took care not to be seen yourself, but Mrs. Matching had to be seen once by your daily help, Mrs. Polster. But go on with your story. Tell us how you and Mrs. Matching got along together."

After that revelation of how much we knew. Carter chose his words more carefully. You could virtually see his brain working. Everything had been fine at first, he said, and then she became a bit of a pest. She was set on getting back into show business and hinting at a double act or a double-double one: getting married, for instance, after a divorce from her husband. He'd done his best to put her off. The whole thing had been unreasonable. Professionally she was just nobody and he was—well, he was Rocky Carlisle.

"Right," Jewle said. "Now let's get to Saturday. January the 9th, the night when she did leave her husband. Tell us about that."

"Well," he said. "I was working till half-past eight: doing a live show on television with Dave Youngman—"

"Just a minute. You're sure of that?"

"Of course I'm sure. You can check it. I didn't get away from the studio till a quarter to nine and that made it about a quarter to ten when I got to Packford. And she was there and a whole lot of suitcases and she said she'd left her husband for good and she'd told him she was divorcing him for me—well, not me: she couldn't say that. What she said was another man. So then we had to have a show-down. As a matter of fact it was a hell of a row, and what happened was, she bundled all the cases back in her car and off she went. And I haven't heard a word from her since."

"You've no idea where she was going?"

He shrugged his shoulders. "Well, she couldn't very well go back to her husband. What I thought was, she'd be going to a friend of hers."

"Hulda Bland?"

That jolted him again. "Well, yes. I didn't see where else she could go, unless it was a hotel, and it was a bit late for that."

"I see." Jewle looked at me again as if for confirmation. "That may explain something that's been worrying us, why you turned down an American tour very shortly before, and then made your agent open negotiations again immediately after."

"That's right!" He actually smiled. "I thought I'd get right away, and then when I got back it'd be all over."

"No more pestering, eh?"

"That's right, Superintendent. That's just how it was."

"I see."

Jewle leaned back and you could almost feel the silence in the room. He leaned forward again.

"But you knew she'd never pester you again."

"I did?"

"Yes, Mr. Carter, you did. You knew she never even left Little Meadows that night. No, don't look down. Look at me, Mr. Carter. I say you knew she was dead."

"No! No!"

"She was *dead*. We found her yesterday morning. In those big drain pipes where you pushed her body that very night!"

"But I *couldn't* have!"

I never saw such a look on a man's face: the sudden horror, the incredulity. He couldn't have been acting. And then in a moment I might have been back in Julian Matching's office that day when I'd told him about the grave, except that Carter had no desk on which to lean as he sobbed his heart out.

Jewle motioned to Matthews. Matthews took Carter gently by the arm and led him from the room.

"Something's gone wrong," I told Jewle. "He couldn't have been all that shocked if he'd killed her."

"Who else do you suggest?" He grunted. "He's been under a pretty big strain these last few days. No emotional control. What else do you expect from a man like him?"

I think, for all that, he'd found it something of a shock himself: at any rate he said some coffee wouldn't do us any harm. I was half-way through mine and was stoking my pipe when Matthews buzzed through.

"He's feeling a bit better. Swears to God, though, he didn't kill her."

"Right," Jewle said. "See he has some coffee and then caution him. Tell him he'll be held unless he comes absolutely clean."

"He'll be held in any case."

"Let him work that out for himself. He can swear what he likes, but he's not coming back here till he tells the truth, the whole truth, and nothing else but."

14
FANTASTIC STORY

A FEW minutes later. Matthews rang again. Carter was ready to talk.

"Let him cool his heels for another half-hour," Jewle told him. "This time he's got to have the fear of God put into him."

"You don't think that'll give him time to cook up some other yarn?"

"That's up to him," Jewle said, and rang off.

It was eleven o'clock to the dot when Carter was brought in again. Jewle warned him and told him to sit. Carter looked to me to be a badly scared man.

"Right," Jewle said. "Let's get back to the night of January the 9th. It's ten o'clock and you've just arrived at Little Meadows. Go on from there."

"Well," he said, "I knew something was different when I drove in. She always used to drive her car straight into the garage and close the door, only this time it was standing just in front of the garage, see? Then when I went in, there weren't any lights on, so I turned on the light in the lounge and I saw her. She was lying back in a chair and I thought she was asleep. Then I saw her suitcases just inside the door and I knew she'd left her husband for good, just as we'd arranged. I said, 'Hi, there! wake up!' only she didn't, so I went across to give her a shake." He moistened his lips. "Then I saw she was dead. I saw the marks on her neck."

"Take your time," Jewle said quietly. "And what did you do then?"

"I don't know," be said. "I was struck all of a heap. I know I cried. You won't believe it but she was the only woman in the world for me and I knew she couldn't be dead, not after what we'd planned. Then I was scared. I thought about the police and what'd happen to me if anything got out, and that's when I thought I'd hide her somewhere till I'd got time to think. Then I had a drink to steady my nerves and then I got the keys out of her bag and undid all the cases in case there was anything inside to do with me, and then I put them back in the boot of the car. What I was thinking was I'd take the car somewhere and leave it, so I backed it out round mine and then I was afraid to go and leave her in the house so I went back again."

So far, and maybe curiously enough, I was inclined to believe him. What came next put more than a strain on credulity. He'd returned to the lounge, as he'd said, and had made up his mind to hide the body temporarily in a shed and then leave the car at Sevenoaks station. He had picked her up and gone out through the back door into the bright moonlight.

"Hallo, Mr. Carter. Something wrong?" a voice said.

It was a man. Carter stammered something about an accident. From somewhere he got the presence of mind to say she'd fainted and he was bringing her out to revive her, but he couldn't put the man off.

"I suppose you know she's dead? Your wife, isn't it? Hadn't we better go back inside and talk this over?"

The man said he'd been out with his dog and the dog had run into Little Meadows garden and he'd been looking for it. His wife's dog—a Peke. That's how he'd come to be round at the back. In the lounge he wormed practically the whole story out of Carter and surprisingly said he believed him.

"Someone's trying to frame you," he said. "You know what you'd better do? Get that car of hers out of the way as soon as you can. I'll stay here till you get back."

"How do I know you won't ring the police?"

"Look," the man said. "Here's my wallet. There's fifty or sixty quid in it. Take it with you and hand it over when you get back. Then we'll decide what's to be done with her. I'll keep the lights off and if anyone comes, I won't answer."

Carter took the wallet, drove the car to Sevenoaks and walked the best part of six miles back. When he let himself into the lounge again, both man and body had gone. He searched everywhere, indoors and out, and saw neither. He didn't even see that dog.

Jewle let out a deep breath. "And you still have that wallet?" he asked.

Carter hadn't. But to get back to that night. He removed every possible trace of Moira from the house, left a note for Mrs. Polster saying they wouldn't be coming the following Saturday, and drove his car back to that all-night garage. He had a few wretched hours of sleep and a nightmare Sunday and then, on the Monday morning at about half-past nine, there was a telephone call.

The substance of what he was told was this.

"Mr. Carter, I've only just found out you're Rocky Carlisle. Thought I knew you when I saw you. But don't worry about you know what. It's been taken care of. No chance of ever connecting anything with you. Only one other thing, though. You might give me back my wallet. Also, all this has cost money, so this is what you have to do. Go to your bank today and draw out five hundred pounds in old notes and meet me tomorrow morning at Mendel's Cafe in Fleet Street at half-past ten. No, not blackmail. It just happens that I'm in a bit of a jam. I shan't make demands on you again."

Carter was there on time. He ordered coffee for himself and a minute or two later the man sat down at his table. Carter hadn't seen him any too well, but now he had a good look at him. He was a man of about fifty, six feet tall, strongly built, black-haired and with a bushy moustache and glasses. His complexion was rather pale, the nose was rather large and the eyes brown. Carter hadn't been able to place the voice, but he definitely wasn't what you'd call a gentleman. He said his name was Fraser.

He ordered his own coffee, then asked for the wallet, and he didn't even bother to check the contents. Carter gave him the packet of notes and he merely slit the end, had a quick look and put the packet into his overcoat pocket. "Best investment you ever made," he said. "We've got each other out of a jam. And don't you worry. When I hide anything, it won't get found, not till Doomsday."

He gulped down his coffee, held out his band and left. And from that moment Carter had heard nothing whatever from him. All that remained of him was a nightmare memory.

That was all. Jewle let out another deep breath. "The man's moustache. Was it real?"

Carter didn't know. It had never occurred to him. "Anyone can put on glasses," Jewle said, "but do I gather he told you he was actually a local resident?"

He hadn't. Carter had only inferred it.

"Well, I don't say I believe your story or that I disbelieve it. You've previously told us a lot of lies, and let's say it's just something you've now told us and leave it for the moment like that."

"It's true! I swear to God it's true! My bank will tell you I drew the money out And you can ask at that café."

"All in good time," Jewle said. "But if that man as good as told you he was a local resident, he was a fool. You'd know him just as he knew you. You'd have a hold over him. Admitted the two holds would cancel each other out. But something else. Did Mrs. Matching bring that mink coat of hers to the house?"

Carter swore he'd never seen it that night. "One other thing. When Mrs. Matching left Grange House that Saturday night she look with her some valuable jewellery from her husband's safe. You know anything about that?"

Carter stared. He swore he knew nothing about any jewellery.

"What jewellery was she actually wearing that night when you found her?"

He couldn't remember. He was almost sure she'd only been wearing her pearl necklace. She never troubled about jewellery at Little Meadows. The only other thing she did sometimes wear was a valuable cross-over diamond ring, and he was positive she hadn't been wearing that. It was something you couldn't miss.

"Something else," Jewle said. "To get the missing jewellery from her husband's safe, she gave him a sleeping draught in some wine he always took after dinner. Did she ever give you even a hint of that?"

He looked horrified.

"Never," he said. "Never. I'd have stopped her. Whatever I am, Superintendent, I wouldn't have stood for anything like that."

Jewle leaned back for a moment, then got to his feet. He looked round at us. "Any other questions?"

We had none.

"Very well, Mr. Carter, this is what happens now. You'll be taken down again and wait till I've made my report. An hour, two hours. I don't know. You can ring your office if you so wish, saying only that you're detained on urgent business. A copy of your statement will be given you and if you find it in order, you'll sign it. If you wish it, you can also have lunch."

A very subdued Carter went out with Matthews. Jewle sat down again and got out his pipe.

"Can't do much till that report's typed out. A curious morning, don't you think?"

"Fantastic," I said. "I mean that story of his. It's like as they say, so extraordinary it has to be true."

"Yes," he said. "Also it fits in with a whole lot of things. That jewellery, for instance. I never quite saw him mixed up in that."

"That mysterious man," I said. "Could he have been the third man? I mean, could she have been playing around with him as well as with Carter?"

"All in good time," he said. "Every single detail'll have to be double-checked." He gave a slow shake or two of the head. "Somehow I feel sorry for that poor devil, whether he lulled her or not. She was a lying, treacherous bitch. Messed up Matching's life, and now his."

The time was getting on and I said I'd be moving.

"Soon as we know anything, I'll see you have a ring," he told me. "And meanwhile, you might keep out of things. This is our job from now on. You agree?"

You can't argue when it's put to you like that.

Whoever was paying for that job—John Hill, Matching, Haddowe or all three—was going to be in for a pretty big bill and it was up to us to drop out at once when the assignment was completed. That it wasn't completed because we hadn't found the jewellery was a very debatable point: it wasn't something we could arbitrarily settle for ourselves. As soon as I was back at the Agency, I put it up to Hill. He suggested a kind of compromise. The jewellery was almost certainly gone for good, but he'd like us to keep a watching brief. I said we would. Since our own interests were concerned when the murder story broke, the charges would be strictly nominal.

What that watching brief really meant, of course, was protecting the clients' interests against undue publicity, and that boiled down to a tactful handling of Jewle. But that wasn't quite the overall picture. How, for instance, would things develop if Carter's story were absolutely true? That was certainly the way we wanted it. Just a little delicate handling on Jewle's part and Julian Matching would scarcely need to be brought in at all.

Was the story true? I now thought it was, and I'd been in a good position to judge since my eyes had never left Carter's face. As I saw it, there'd been three distinct phases. When he had first entered Jewle's room he'd naturally been a bit uneasy, but Matthews had doubtless been stringing him along on the matter of help and he'd still have in mind the apparent satisfaction with which Jewle and I had left his office after that very brief interview. That was why he'd soon begun to throw his weight about, even when Jewle had had him taken out.

The second phase was the return. The speed with which he'd changed his mind showed that he'd had a really convincing story ready—one that he'd almost certainly concocted as soon as he'd got back to town in the small hours of the Sunday morning. Jewle had let him run smoothly on, and then he'd suddenly pricked the bubble with the news of Moira's death.

The third phase—the vital one—came after Carter had recovered from that emotional outburst. He was a different man when he entered the room for that last time. He wanted to get things once and for all off his mind, and what he then said—and in far greater detail than I've actually given it—couldn't have been thought up during that hour downstairs.

"One thing I can't understand," Hallows told me. "Why did he contradict Jewle when Jewle told him she was dead?"

"He didn't," I said. "Perhaps I didn't put it clearly enough, but when Jewle said Carter knew she was dead, Carter immediately thought of the moment when he went into the lounge that night and saw her apparently asleep. It ties in with another remark he made. Jewle accused him of putting the body under that bridge, and what happened? He didn't have time to think, mind you. What he said came out spontaneously. He said he *couldn't* have put her there. And he couldn't—if what he said later was true. And that took place, mind you, at the end of the second phase: before he actually told the full story. I didn't realise that till afterwards. Carter said, 'I couldn't have!' and we took that to mean he wasn't the kind of man who could possibly have done such a thing. What he really meant was, that he was just as ignorant of everything as we were. Since the body had disappeared while he was trudging back from Sevenoaks, that was perfectly true."

"Sounds more logical when you look at it that way. But one other thing. He definitely knew she was dead, so why did he burst into tears?"

I said I was no psycho-analyst but my guess was those tears came from a whole lot of things: the misery of his last few days, for instance, plus that forced recalling of what had happened on that Saturday night, and the knowledge of what must happen to his own future.

"Right," he said. "So his story's true and, if so, she was killed by that mysterious man. He was waiting for her at Little Meadows that night and killed her as soon as she stepped out of the car to open the garage door. He got the house key from her bag and carried her into the lounge and then waited for Carter to arrive and be framed."

It was that last word that seemed to throw a whole flood of light on things. The *framing*—that was the dominating thing. Whether the murder was planned or not was no great matter, but it couldn't have been wholly for the sake of robbery. "X"—the new "X"—must already have found the jewellery and he had a mink coat, so all he bad to do was to take the body and the cases to the lounge and then make for a public telephone and warn the police that suspicious things were happening at Little Meadows. That would have been the perfect frame—the story-book frame—but it hadn't been what he'd done. For the sake of five hundred pounds, he'd even dared to show himself and he'd done it again at that Fleet Street café. He'd even so collaborated that he'd made himself an accessory after the fact.

Something was badly wrong. The more logical you became, the more things became a circle. If "X" killed her, then he should have bolted. He had the jewellery and the coat and he could have framed Carter from a distance. If he didn't kill her, then Carter did, and we'd just spend time in proving to our own satisfaction that Carter didn't. The only thing to do was to wash out speculation and get down to one solid fact—*that "X" existed*. And the two simple questions that followed were, who was he, and where?

It was tough to sit still and not try to find the answers, in spite of that embargo by Jewle. We'd already found one "X", starting with hardly a single clue. To find the second ought to be far less hard.

"What'll Jewle do?" I said.

"Hell have men on the job already," Hallows said. "Enquiries about any local resident named Fraser who fits the description or whose wife keeps a Peke. That yarn about a stray dog's a bit far-fetched but it'll have to be tested. Also he'll be trying that café just in case anyone there's seen 'X' before."

We didn't want duplication. Someone or other was bound to spot either Hallows or myself, so over our coffee and sandwiches we did some more thinking and, of course, it led us back to that Saturday night.

I said, for instance, that I'd never believed that Peke story myself. People just don't go taking pet dogs for walks at eleven o'clock even on a moonlight night.

"Eleven o'clock," I said. "That's about the right time when 'X' ran into Carter at the back of the house. It just about allows for all Carter had had to do before he finally decided to hide the body—except that it doesn't fit some other things."

"Such as what?"

Let me insist straight away that we were merely looking for ideas that might lead us to "X". If we'd only gone just a bit further I could have picked up the telephone and told Jewle how he could lay his hands on "X" within a few hours. What was to happen was that we couldn't see the tree because of the wood.

"Think back," I said. "Dinner at Grange House that night was at about seven and it wouldn't be later than half-past when Julian was stacking the dishes in the kitchen and then having that doped glass of port. He was out for an hour, and by then Moira was gone. I'd say she didn't leave a minute later than eight, and in under half an hour she'd be at Little Meadows. If Carter killed her, then it wouldn't be till half-past ten. If 'X' killed her, it'd be on arrival, which means he was hanging around from then till Carter emerged with the body at about eleven. That's two and a half hours."

He didn't see where it got us, except that it exploded that yarn about a lost Peke. To tell the truth. I'd got a bit muddled and what had been behind those timings had suddenly disappeared. All I felt in my bones was that somewhere in those timings lay a clue. And just then Hallows thought of something.

"'X' was after money, that's a cert, so what would he have done with that mink coat?"

"Tried to sell it," I said. "Or pawn it. It wouldn't have brought in much but it'd have been safe. It's possible, of course, he knew a fence."

He didn't like it. "X" was out for money as that five hundred that he'd got from Carter showed. A coat might have cost two thousand guineas, but a fence wouldn't be likely to offer more than two hundred pounds.

"My guess is he'd have advertised in a high-class paper or magazine," he said. "If he did, it would probably be on the Monday. That doesn't say it appeared next day."

It seemed worth trying. A quarter of an hour later we were on our separate ways to try out a couple of dailies.

You can usually get back copies up to at least a fortnight without having to go to the morgue, and that saved us time. I began at the Personal column for the first likely day. Wednesday, January the 13th. The very next issue produced what was almost certainly what we wanted.

> Canadian wild mink coat, superb quality, almost new. Cost two thousand guineas. Owner, going to tropics, will sacrifice at £1,000. Any inspection. ZN2811 *Daily Record*, E.C.4.

That advertisement hadn't been repeated, which was something I didn't quite like. It could mean that the coat had been sold and, if I wrote to that box number, "X" wouldn't even bother to reply. It was when I was almost back at the Agency that I thought of something else: something that almost pulled me up with a jerk. Hallows was back. He'd found the same advertisement in the *Globe*, though his hadn't appeared till Saturday the 16th.

"What do you make of that mention of two thousand guineas?" I asked him. "That's the very figure we were given, but how did 'X' know it? If he had it valued, surely it wouldn't have been at exactly that?"

There seemed just the one answer—Moira must have told him herself. And if he and Moira had been acquainted, then he was the one who killed her. My idea was that he was someone connected with show business. Moira had been about to make a come-back and that meant making contacts. "X" had learned that she'd be going to Little Meadows that night and he'd been waiting.

That was speculation, and could wait. I rang the advertising department of the *Record*. To the youngish lady who replied, I said I'd only just had that advertisement brought to my notice, and, as I was due to leave for America in the morning, there wouldn't be time to answer it by post, so could she possibly let me have the address. She said she couldn't. She pointed out reprovingly that an advertiser asked for a box number because he wished for anonymity. I asked if that applied to every paper and she said it did.

The problem was, what next? I could write to the box number but that might mean a delay of days, even if "X" bothered to reply at all.

"What about you?" I asked Hallows. "You've plenty of friends in Fleet Street. Surely someone could get round someone who could think of a short cut? It wouldn't be asking for anything criminally wrong."

"Don't know," he said, "but I can try. No use going till the Street starts warming up. It might mean a little judicious baksheesh."

I left it to him. It was still only five o'clock, so he was going home for an hour or two. There was nothing to keep me either and I went home, too.

We were just sitting down to the evening meal when Jewle rang.

"Thought you'd like to knew that our friend left us this afternoon. We have his passport and he knows he'll be kept under surveillance. Not that I think he's at all likely to bolt."

"He stuck to his story?"

"Yes," he said, "and we're inclined to believe it Everything we've tried has turned out true. He *was* doing a show that Saturday evening and he'd had his garage bring his car along and he went off just before nine. That wouldn't get him down there till pretty near ten. Also he did draw a certain sum as requested from his bank. Also someone remembered him as in that Fleet Street café on that Tuesday morning. Someone who thought at the time he had a remarkable resemblance to a certain singer."

"You didn't get a lead at the café on the one who met him?"

"No," he said. "Nor anything yet out in the country. But we're hoping. One thing *is* being done. We're releasing just so much of the story. Can't hold it up any longer. Also we want publicity for the same gentleman. I've seen the husband, by the way."

"How'd he take it?"

"Well, he seemed fairly resigned. Shocked at the circumstances, of course. Still, if he's had any sense he's probably been expecting something of the kind. That's about all. If anything else breaks, I'll let you know."

15

THE FINDING OF "X"

I'D JUST taken Bernice her early cup of tea when the telephone went. It was Hallows. He said he mightn't be in the office till after ten. Had to wait for a telephone call.

"Any luck?"

"Can't say till I get the call."

"How'd you work it?"

"The less you know, the better," he told me. "This is a private matter between me and a couple of friends. Neither belongs to those two papers we tried, by the way. That ad. was in another one, too."

By the time I'd dressed, my two papers had arrived. Jewle had released the story far too late for photographs and banner headlines. The staider paper had it on an inside page, and the other front-page-right, and only a couple of paragraphs at that. The body of a woman, now known to be a Mrs. Moira Matching, had been found partly buried near a wood at Packford, Kent. She had left her husband some days before, and almost certainly for another man. The police were anxious to interview that man. A description followed.

There was no point in my getting to the Agency so I took it easy after breakfast and kept my mind off things with a crossword. A few minutes after nine, when I was thinking at last of making a move, the telephone went again. I knew it'd be Hallows, but it wasn't. It was Jean Lindman.

"I took a chance you'd still be home," she said. "You've seen the papers?"

I didn't say so, but considering I'd been in the thick of everything, I thought she was being a bit naive.

"It bad to come out," I said. "You can't hold up things like that. But oughtn't you to be pleased?"

"That wasn't nice of you," she told me, and the voice seemed uncommonly hard. "Can't you tell me now who did it?"

"You tell me," I said. "Why do you think we're still working on the case? Or didn't you know that?"

She didn't answer. I cut in again. "You tell me something. Why're you so anxious to know?"

There was another pause. I caught the sound of a little laugh.

"Well, perhaps you were right. I am a horrible person. Maybe I feel sorry for him. Now you know."

"Well, we're not all made alike," I told her sententiously. "Julian in yet, by the way?"

"He should be in at about eleven. Thank you for letting me bother you."

Before I could say a goodbye, she rang off. Women, I told myself. Byron was right. Love was their whole existence. It was Julian she ought to be working on, not me. Who did she think I was? Some sort of marriage broker?

That was Travers, the misogynist: just another facet of a many-sided—or should it be lop-sided—character. I treated myself to a smile as I put on my overcoat. By the time I'd caught a bus I'd forgotten all about her.

Hallows practically followed me in. He didn't say a word. Just handed me a slip of paper.

H. Fraser, 36 Coventry Terrace, Wood Green.

"Fraser! That's the name he gave Carter. How'd you get it?"

"I'd rather not tell you, except that someone wanted to do me a good turn: someone who knew who I was. Told him I was working on a fur robbery and wanted to bring off a coup independent of the boss. A big bonus and all that."

The Underground would involve a change, but it got us there quicker than anything else. We made enquiries at the station, and ten minutes later were having a first look at Coventry Terrace. It was a typical yellowish-grey Victorian terrace but a better class than most. The little gardens were cared-for and its front hedges trim. Another few years, maybe, and the march of time might make it a slum, but it wasn't that yet.

Number 36 was one of the few that needed a coat of paint. Its little front garden was a decrepit lawn with a central flowerbed in which were a few wallflowers, so small that they might have been weeds. There was no bell-push, only a knocker.

A woman who must have been nearly seventy opened the door. She was short and dumpy, wearing an apron over an old brown blouse and a black skirt. She looked startled. Maybe she'd been expecting someone else.

"Mr. Fraser in?" I'd lifted my hat and made the question pleasant.

"Fraser?" she stared again. "That's funny. Are you the gentleman who wrote him the letters?"

I took a chance. "That's right. Only we don't seem to be able to get hold of him."

"I know," she said. "He's never been so long away before."

"Look," I said. "Might we come in just for a minute? Perhaps you can tell us something. It's to do with his insurance policy."

The door opened on a passage-way. A yard or two along, a door opened into the room with the front bay window.

"This is his room," she told us, "but I'm sure he wouldn't mind."

The room was like the house—a survival: plush-covered furniture, central table, whatnot with ornaments, two or three spotted engravings, a worn green carpet and a fireplace with green tiles and a mantelpiece thick with various vases. If the fire had been alight it might have been reasonably cheerful. At the moment it was only laid.

Hallows and I sat down. "You were saying he'd been away?"

"That's right," she said. "His business often took him away for a day or two, but he never was away as long as this. Ever since last Thursday week."

I sympathetically clicked my tongue. I said that made it awkward. His insurance had expired and we thought we ought to see him about it. A personal talk might clear the whole thing up.

"Where does he actually work?"

"Up in London," she said. "That's all I know. I'm not one to poke my nose into other people's business. He never told me so I never asked him. He did say once he was some sort of inventor, whatever that is. I reckoned he invented things. Whatever it was, it never brought him in very much. Real hard-up he was at one time. Still, he always managed to pay his rent, even if it wasn't regular." She shook her head with some inner disapproval. "Still, he needn't have let his insurance lapse. That's one thing I'd never do, and he did have the money."

"You mean within the last month?"

"Well, no harm in saying he did, so long as you don't tell him I said so. He told me just before he went away he'd sold one of his inventions. Paid me up a month ahead and gave me a pound note to buy something for myself. And he'd bought himself a whole lot of new clothes. And about time, too. I used to tell him he was letting himself get too shabby, if you know what I mean."

"He's been with you quite a fair time, hasn't he?"

"Just about two years," she said. "Two years come Easter. He was never no trouble, right from the first. Just used to have his breakfast in and all the other meals out, except, of course, Sundays."

"You said there was something funny about the letters," I reminded her.

"Oh, them," she said. "I thought there was something funny at the time. 'Mrs. Price,' he said, and that'd be a day or two before he went away, 'Mrs. Price, if any letters come addressed to a Mr. Fraser they'll be for me, so don't turn them away.' I didn't say anything but seeing his name was Rodes I did think about it. Wouldn't you have?"

I looked at Hallows. "This is amazing! His insurance policy is in the name of Fraser and you say his name's Rodes?"

"That's right," she said. "I ought to know. Rodes—spelt R-o-d-e-s: Harry Rodes. What letters he had always came like that."

I clicked my tongue again. "I don't like the sound of it, Mrs. Price. Did any letters come?"

"Five or six," she said. "I've got them in the back. Been keeping 'em for him."

Hallows looked round as soon as she was out of the door. "Leave it to me and I'll get one of those letters."

She was back almost at once. Two had the names of firms on the envelopes. Hallows asked to have a look.

"This is the one we wrote," he told me. "I know. I addressed it myself. Under the circumstances we ought to have it back. Don't you agree, Mrs. Price?"

She shrugged her shoulders. "If you two gentlemen thick it's right. I'll have to tell him, of course, when he comes back." The look changed. "You don't think he's got himself in any trouble?"

"Let's hope not." I got to my feet. "I wouldn't have put him down as that sort of man. Hell be back. I suppose he left all his things here?"

"Everything, far as I could see. His shaving things and everything."

She showed us to the front door. Hallows put a last question. "He did have a car, didn't he?"

"That's right. The one he had when he came. Just before he left he said he was going to get a new one."

"You know where he kept it?"

"At one of them garages. The second on the left and then straight on, if you want to enquire."

I thanked her again. "And when he does get back just tell him we called. He'll know what it's about. I'm Mr. Harris and this is Mr. Brown."

We didn't like the look of things: a man named Harry Rodes and calling himself Fraser who'd been away from his lodgings for a week, and had left behind him his toilet things and hadn't sent a word of any kind to his landlady. Either Rodes had bolted for good or something had happened. But he surely wouldn't have bolted before the receipt of answers to that advertisement. Too much money was at stake. And no one, as far as our knowledge went, could have scared him.

We took that second turning and stopped and opened that letter. It was from a Kensington firm calling itself the Fine Furs Company Limited. It seemed pretty important: branches in Paris, New York, Chicago, Montreal and Quebec: head-quarters in Winnipeg.

Dear Sir or Madam,

Re your advertisement in the Daily Record of the 14th inst., we would like to inspect the coat in question.

We shall be glad of a reply at your earliest convenience, by telephone if possible, so that an appointment may be made with our Mr. Duchesne.

Assuring you of our interest, we are, for Fine Furs Co. Ltd.,

Retail Manager.

The name was an indecipherable scrawl, not that it mattered. My own view was that Rodes-Fraser would have had a hard time in convincing any company of his lawful ownership of that coat. Maybe he'd have taken a room at a big hotel and tried to conduct the interview there. Not, again, that it mattered.

A couple of hundred yards on we came to the garage: a fairly big place with a double row of pumps. We went through to the office. The manager was there. I told him we'd been trying to get in touch with one of his customers, a Mr. Rodes. Was his car in?

He smiled. "It was—a minute or two ago."

He pointed it out to us: an ancient Standard that looked as if it had come home to die.

"It actually went?" I said.

"He uses it quite a lot. Must get him somewhere."

"The last time I saw him he said he might be getting another."

"He did speak about it," he said. "As a matter of fact he had a look at that Wolseley there. A nice job. Only done seven thousand. He a friend of yours?"

"In the way of business—yes. How long since you saw him?"

He called to a mechanic. "Arthur, how long since Mr. Rodes was in?"

"Wednesday week. You was showing him that Wolseley."

"That's right," he told us. "I remember now. Wednesday week."

We moved on and round into the High Street and back to the Underground. At a telephone booth I had a look at the directory. I didn't expect to find Rodes there but I did. And my eyes popped a bit at what I read.

RODES, H. Enquiry Agent. 5 Willow St., E.C.4.

"An enquiry agent," Hallows said. "Dammit, I ought to have known. He has an occasional advertisement in the Sunday papers."

You can't do much talking in a Tube train. We got off at Holborn and walked to the lower end of Fleet Street.

"How the devil could a man like Rodes get mixed up in all this?" Hallows wanted to know. "It couldn't have been by accident. Someone must have employed him."

"Let's have a look at where he hangs out," I said. "It might tell us a bit more."

Willow Street turned out to be in that maze of narrow streets to the left as you go up to Chancery Lane. Even when we'd been directed to it, it took a bit of finding. The frontage of that short street was like a gapped saw. Rodes was above a two-storey building wedged between two taller ones. The ground floor was a second-hand bookshop, and a side door with a short flight of stairs led up to a landing.

"You'd better go," I told Hallows. "Think out some yarn or other to use on him. If he's in."

I looked at the selection of books in the boxes in front of the shop. A couple of minutes of that and Hallows joined me.

"Nobody in. If he'd been in, he must have heard me."

"Right," I said. "You move on and I'll have a word in the shop."

It was quite a small place, walls shelved and a double row of shelving down the middle. In the little clearance at the far end, a hook-nosed elderly man with a straggling beard was reading a book. The bell above the door had hardly tinkled when I went in and I was almost up to him when the shadow case by the window made him aware of me. He pushed the chair bade from the table as he rose.

"Pardon me, but I'm enquiring about your neighbour upstairs—Mr. Rodes."

He smiled. "Would you mind speaking a little louder, sir? I'm a bit deaf."

"Mr. Rodes," I said, and pointed up. "I've been trying to get hold of him these last few days. Have you seen him?"

"No," he said. "I very rarely see him, unless he happens to pass the window. If he arrives from that end of the street he wouldn't have to do that."

"Have you heard him moving about?"

He shook his head. "Not recently. These old premises are strongly built, you know. There isn't much sound comes through."

I thanked him. He followed me courteously to the door; a quiet, unhurried, gentle old man who'd be back at his book before I joined Hallows the few yards along the street.

It was one o'clock and the lunch-hour rush. We went back to the Agency for a scratch meal and then I rang Jewle. He was out, so I asked to be rung back. I wouldn't leave a message: it was something important and personal. We went on waiting and at two o'clock Jewle rang.

"Think I've got some news for you," I said. "We may have found a certain man you want."

"Where?"

"In the neighbourhood of Fleet Street. Hallows is on the grape-vine now. He ought to be ringing at any moment. He was pretty sanguine when he rang just now. Just a question of baksheesh and he thinks he'll have the address. What about coming along?"

"To where?"

"Well, *The Daily Telegraph* building?"

"Right," he said. "I'll be there right away."

We grabbed a taxi at the end of the street. Hallows was to keep out of the way and make an appearance with the vital news a few minutes after Jewle joined me. I kept out of the way, too, till I saw Jewle. I let him wait for a bit.

"Sorry I'm late," I told him, "but I had to wait till Hallows rang. He ought to be here by now."

"He's got the address?"

"So he says."

He grunted. "How'd he get on to all this?"

"You know Hallows," I said. "He knows everybody. I didn't see any harm in his nosing around. Looks like him now."

He shook hands with Jewle before turning to me. "Cost me twenty-five quid. Hope you don't mind."

I shrugged my shoulders. "Depends what you got for it."

"Don't think you'll grumble. His real name's Harry Rodes and he hangs out in Willow Street. About a couple of hundred yards away."

"Right," Jewle said. "Let's get going."

We crossed the road and turned left at the tavern. We came into Willow Street at the Chancery Lane end.

"How do we find him?" Jewle wanted to know. "What's his line of business?"

"Can't be sure," Hallows said. "My informant said he was some sort of detective. A cheap private eye."

"A what?"

The glare went.

"Wait a minute, though. Rodes. Harry Rodes. Think I've seen the name somewhere. All right, then. Let's find him. You take that side of the road, Mr. Travers, and we'll take this."

They found him. Just inside on the wall of the side entrance was a notice—HARRY RODES, and an arrow pointing upwards. We went up the stairs to the landing. There was just enough room for us. The one door was half-glazed with frosted glass, and on it:

HARRY RODES
PRIVATE ENQUIRIES

Jewle pushed the bell and we waited. He pushed it again. He rapped at the door and then put an ear to it. He didn't look happy.

"What's happened? Think he's flown the coop?"

"Why should he?" I said. "Hallows only made contact with his man an hour ago. And he's only just paid him. You people haven't done anything to alarm him?"

"How could we? We hadn't the faintest idea who he was. Think I'll ask that book-shop downstairs."

Nothing's easier to open than a Yale lock once you've mastered the trick. I think Hallows had the two gadgets ready in his hand. Jewle's just a bit ponderous in his movements and the stairs were badly lighted, and Hallows was calling down before he reached the door.

The door in front of us was now slightly ajar.

"What's been going on? It wasn't like that just now."

"Just gave it a firm push," Hallows told him blandly, "and there it was."

The smallish room was probably intended as a waiting room: four chairs by the walls, a central table with some old magazines, a worn carpet on the floor and a very old filing cabinet in the corner. An unlighted electric fire was plugged into a socket. You saw all that in the first quick look. There wasn't a second.

Jewle was sniffing. I was sniffing, too: back for a moment at a little turved bridge over a ditch. Jewle moved forward and opened the door that led through.

The room was the size of the outer one. To the left was a biggish window with its light falling left across a flat-topped desk behind which was an old swivel chair. There was a small fireplace with an electric fire plugged to a point by the floor. There were two other chairs and a couple of green filing cabinets. In the corner to the right was a safe. The body of Harry Rodes lay with feet towards that safe, head towards the desk. He was wearing his overcoat, and his hat lay a yard away by the fire. He was on his back, head turned slightly to the left.

Jewle whipped a handkerchief across his mouth and nose and motioned us back to the other room. A minute and he was calling us in. He tilted the head our way.

"You knew him?"

I shook my head. The stench was bad and I didn't feel like opening my mouth. Hallows didn't know him either. Jewle let the head fall sideways again. He followed us back to the room.

"Shot through the back of the head. Days ago."

He brought out some small change and gave Hallows half-a-crown.

"Think you can get some strong disinfectant? I'll have some telephoning to do."

We got our pipes going but that smell still seeped through.

"Looks pretty bad for Carter," he told me. "I don't know who else would want him dead. Or would he? This man Rodes wouldn't have incriminated himself by confirming Carter's story. That's a certainty. He'd have sworn he'd never seen Carter in his life."

"You're getting Carter to identify him?"

"That's right."

"And if he does?"

He shrugged his shoulders.

"On the face of it, it'll clear him. But that isn't the main point Rodes was a private detective. Go on from there."

"Yes," I said. "Someone had to employ him. He couldn't have got mixed up in this business by sheer chance."

"Maybe Carter did, just to keep an eye on the husband on Moira's behalf. Maybe that story he told us was made to fit it—if he knew he was dead."

Hallows came back. Jewle said we should wait where we were.

Another minute and a strong smell of carbolic was seeping through to our room. There'd been a telephone on Rodes's desk and we could hear Jewle using it Hallows moved his chair close to mine. That room was deadly cold and he'd switched on the fire.

"Why did you say you didn't know Rodes?"

"Because I doubt if he'd have believed us," I said. "You ever know anybody who really believed other people's coincidences? Also he's still suspicious about that supposed informant you got the information from."

"You're right," he said. "Far better play it dumb. Any ideas yet about him in there?"

I shook my head. Plenty of ideas but far too early yet to put them on a drawing-board.

"The whole thing's too involved," I said, and cocked an ear. Jewle had finished telephoning and we could hear him moving about the room. A minute or two and he came through.

"What about you two getting yourselves a cup of tea? A few minutes and we'll be cluttered up here. No need to get back for an hour."

"You've got hold of Carter?"

"At a recording studio. He'll be free about five."

We found a cafeteria. Hallows bought a couple of evening papers. The Press had been at work. There was nothing about Julian Matching, which meant that he hadn't been reached. There were photographs—Grange House, Little Meadows and that bridge across the ditch. Both papers carried pictures of Moira, and my guess was they'd come from Joe Wintle. No connection yet with Rocky Carlisle. But the news hounds were still on the job and I didn't see how the morning's papers would miss the full story. Not the story Carter himself had told us, but just enough to titillate the readers and steer clear of libel. If Jewle released the Rodes story, he'd be pretty hard put to it to prove there'd been no connection.

"That Monday morning when we saw Rodes," I said. "You said you ought to know him. Anything come back to you when you saw him just now?"

"No," he said. "I've been trying to think. All I've got at the back of my mind is something to do with the police. Must have been quite a time ago. Maybe if I don't do any thinking at all, it'll come back."

We'd spun out the time and drunk more tea. By walking slowly back we just about made it on time. A uniformed constable was in the passage-way by the stairs, but Jewle must have given instructions. When we told him our names he waved us up. Only one car was standing outside.

The circus had gone and nothing was left of Rodes but the chalk marks on the floor. The room reeked of disinfectant.

"You learnt anything much?" I said.

"Mostly negative," Jewle told me. "He's been dead for anything from seven to ten days. We may tie it down a bit later."

"Anything in the files?"

"Not a damn. Probably there for show in any case. Nothing whatever in the safe. No prints on the safe if that means anything to you. Not a single print but his in the room. No gun, of course. We might learn something about that from the bullet."

He looked at his watch. There was a cheap alarm-clock on the mantelpiece but it had stopped.

"Matthews is taking Carter to the morgue. The call ought to be coming through." He looked at Hallows. "While we're waiting, would you like to tell me the name of that friend of yours who coughed up the information?"

"Sorry," Hallows said. "I just can't. I had to give my word. Also I might get some more from the same source once he knows Rodes is dead. He'll talk to me if we pay for it, but I'm damn-sure he wouldn't to you."

"Maybe something in that," Jewle said, and then the telephone went. He picked up the receiver.

16

JEWLE IS SATISFIED

CARTER had definitely identified Rodes but Jewle had wanted a word with him, which was why we were on our way to the Yard. He was in Jewle's room with Matthews. He didn't say a word when we came in, but from the way he looked at Jewle, he had plenty of questions on his mind. First there had to be answers.

"You knew who this man Rodes was?"

Carter looked surprised. "No, sir. Only what I told you. What he told me."

"Well, he was a private detective, one of the shabby kind," Jewle said. "That convey anything to you?"

It didn't convey a thing.

"You didn't employ him?"

"Me?" He tried to smile. "What should I want a detective for?"

"That's what I'm asking you," Jewle told him. "Did Mrs. Matching employ him?"

"But why should she?"

"Just asking," Jewle said mildly. "No use asking you, of course, whether it was you who killed him?"

Carter cringed. I knew what he was feeling—that he was being drawn into the toils again.

"All right," Jewle told him resignedly. "You can go. But on the same conditions. And if we happen to want you, you come at the double. You want to say something?"

Carter fidgeted. "It's about me. If any of this gets out."

Jewle looked round at us as if he couldn't believe his ears. He leaned forward, wagging a finger.

"*You?* You carry on for months with another man's wife. Two people have been killed because of it and you sit there and ask me to start worrying about you?" He let out a breath. "I've got enough on you. Carter, to take you into custody straight away. Get him out of here before I lose my temper."

Carter went out.

"Sorry about that," Jewle said. "But slimy characters like him make me sick. Give me the old-fashioned crook every time."

"Nothing else developed?" I said.

Nothing had, so he was likely to be busy. He hoped the post-mortem might narrow the time of Rodes's death, and there was a whole lot more he wanted to know about him. There'd be a photograph in the morning papers.

"You've been a great help," he told Hallows. "If Mr. Travers can let you do a bit more eavesdropping, you might come up with a bit more still. Every little's going to help."

A police car took us back to the Agency, so we couldn't do any talking till we got there and I'd switched on the fire in my room. I remember I started off with that old quotation about the tangled web we weave when first we get into the deception business.

"Looks as if we've landed ourselves in a pretty bad mess," I said. "Someone in Wood Green will spot that photograph or recognise the name, and this time tomorrow Jewle'll know all about our call on that landlady and the garage, so what becomes of that yarn of ours about an informant?"

"I know," Hallows said. "It looks bad but we've always had the luck to wriggle out of things. All we can do is keep our fingers crossed. The trouble is, we've got to use that informant gag to find out why Rodes was paying a call on the City Trust Company that Monday morning."

All that afternoon that queer meeting with Rodes had been on our minds, and it was only now that we were bringing things into the open. There was no longer any mystery. What Rodes had been about to deposit was almost certainly that jewellery, and the box, from what Jean Lindman had told me, had been the kind of thing he must have been carrying—too large for an inside pocket. There'd been the whole attitude of the man: the mention of coshing, the wonder if we'd been attacking him, the effective way he'd got rid of Hallows at the foot of Ludgate Hill.

"No hurry," I said. "Rodes won't collect it now. And if anyone there recognises him as a customer, they won't do anything about it. It's part of what they owe to a client. What I say is, we just lie doggo and wait for Jewle. He's ringing us tomorrow if anything comes in."

It's all very well to assure yourself that you're going home to forget about a case. That's a soporific to which, unfortunately, I've long become immune. I did manage to keep things strictly personal when I eased into my chair after supper and began wondering how I could explain to Jewle those subterfuges we'd thought it necessary to employ. Jewle and I were friends: we liked and trusted each other, and that's how I wanted it to stay: but when it came to a question of the Law v. Ludovic Travers, that was a different thing. I'd as good as told him we'd stop any enquiries, and in the morning he was more than likely to discover that we hadn't. That meant that from now on he couldn't trust either me or the Agency.

You see the subtle shift? Now I was thinking about the Agency, and from that it was natural to move on to the case itself. Something had been on my mind, but the events of that afternoon and early evening had kept it somewhere deep. Now bubbles of thought began to rise and soon I was shifting uneasily in my chair. This added itself to that till I thought I knew. *It was Jean Lindman who had employed Harry Rodes.*

She'd always been in love with Julian Matching and, as long as he was unmarried, there was always hope. When his mother died the last chance came, and then he'd suddenly got married, and to a woman whom she soon both hated and despised. After the first few months she'd probably tried to hate Julian himself and then had come the first signs of a breach at Grange House. Now it was her business to enlarge that breach, and the tales of weekends spent so frequently away from home gave her the chance. Julian had been a fool. He'd taken those absences at their face value: it was she who'd suspected what they really were. All she had to do was put the incontrovertible evidence before him.

Very well then. The Jean Lindman who'd later made private enquiries about the Broad Street Detective Agency, made her own enquiries and chose Harry Rodes. But not soon enough. Things began to happen too fast. All the evidence necessary for a divorce was in her possession and then—at maybe the vital weekend—Moira Matching left her husband. After that there was no need to humiliate Julian by giving him that evidence. Everything now would be brought out into the open and there'd ultimately be a divorce.

But Rodes hadn't been taken into account. Jean had informed him of Moira's intentions and he'd been on the watch. That night he'd followed Moira from Grange House to Little Meadows and, as soon as she'd taken her cases into the house, he'd followed her. She'd been wearing that mink coat and somehow he'd discovered the jewellery. So he'd killed her and framed Carter. Harry Rodes not only had the cash—so to speak—in hand: he was set up for life, and Carter would be his banker. He wasn't afraid of Jean Lindman. If necessary he could incriminate her, too.

Everything fitted. The joints weren't more neat on a Queen Anne bureau. Jean had asked me to her flat. And for what? To find out who'd killed Moira. She'd rung me a second time for the same reason. What she might be realising, in addition to any fears of being compromised by any revelations on the part of Rodes, was that she herself had done that killing, as surely as if her own fingers had held the throat.

I shifted uneasily in my chair again: then suddenly I got up and went to my room. I don't quite know why I did it, unless it was some sudden anger: the wish, perhaps, to make her suffer.

In a minute she was on the line.

"Travers here," I said. "I thought you'd like to hear the news before you read it in your morning paper."

I waited. Again I don't know why, unless the actual receiver in my hand made me realise I was about to take an enormous risk if I virtually accused her of complicity.

"News?" she said. "You mean something I ought to know?"

"Well, you seemed very interested in finding out who committed a certain murder. We do know a man who was involved in it. A shady detective named Harry Rodes. Sometimes called himself Fraser. I suppose that doesn't convey anything to you?"

She didn't answer.

"Are you there?"

"Yes," she said. "Yes. I was just thinking. I don't know anyone called Rodes."

"I thought you'd like to know," I said. "Don't think me rude but you were rather persistent."

"Persistent? About what?"

"Wanting to know who'd done that murder. You asked me on at least two occasions, so I rang to tell you somebody who was implicated. Oh! and something else. Rodes himself is dead, too."

"Killed?"

"Yes. That's what you'll see in your paper. All his files and so on are being gone over now. He's almost certain to have left enough information to build up the whole story. I'm pretty sure myself that another couple of days'll clear things up. There ought to be some dramatic surprises. Just thought I'd give you the tip."

"Thank you." Here voice was curiously quiet, as if what she said didn't matter. It was what she was thinking: the rest was only background. I waited a moment, but she didn't even say goodbye. All I suddenly knew was that the line was dead.

I went back to a warmer room and a comfortable chair and somehow I was glad I hadn't said even half the things I'd originally intended. What I'd said had been almost innocuous: it had been for her to make the interpretations. If she'd been the owner of the cap, then she'd know if it fitted.

There'd been something, too, at which I hadn't actually hinted—the murderer of Rodes. Surely it couldn't have been she who'd shot him? Women, I told myself, just didn't do such things. Nine times out of ten they kill by poison, and somehow I couldn't see Jean Lindman going to Willow Street and that shabby office. So that left only Carter. Maybe that look I'd seen on his face—half anguish, half despair—hadn't meant after all that the law, in the person of Jewle, was trying to trap him a second time. Maybe it had been the beginning of a new set of lies which Jewle laboriously would once more have to break down.

The morning's papers carried pictures of Rodes: one clean-shaven as we'd found him and the other with moustache and glasses, as he'd been at Little Meadows and the Fleet Street café. The letterpress merely said that Rodes, *alias* Fraser, had been the man whom the police had been anxious to interview in connection with the murder of Mrs. Moira Matching. Rodes, a private detective, had been found dead at his office at Willow Street, and the police were now trying to fill in various gaps in his history.

I felt a pretty worried man as I made my way to the Agency that morning. Information would be pouring in and some time that day Jewle would be having me on the carpet. I think Hallows was feeling much the same as we killed time till Jewle rang. I didn't say a word to him about Jean Lindman. That was something personal, at the moment, between her and myself.

At lunch-time we took turns to go out for a hot meal. The afternoon wore boringly away and we were actually thinking of tea when Jewle rang. I'd never known him so cheerful.

"Everything's gone well?"

"Unbelievably well," he told me. "The first time for days I've been able to sit back and relax. If you and Hallows are free, you might like to come along."

Unless he was being far more Machiavellian than I'd ever known him. Hallows and I were still in the clear. Even then I wouldn't say we were even remotely hilarious as the bus took us towards the Yard.

"If everything really is okay, why not let me spring something else on him," Hallows said. "That bit about the Trust Company."

It seemed a good idea. The place would be closed to business but Jewle could get to work in the morning. And it still looked a good idea when we walked into Jewle's room. He laid his pipe aside and was smiling.

"Glad you could make it."

Hallows was nudging me to look round. Draped across a side table was a mink coat.

"That *the* coat?"

"That's right. Rather a long story. What about some tea? Just about to have some myself."

It was one of the cosiest talks I ever had in that room. A few bad moments, mind you, but they didn't matter.

"About the coat," Jewle began. "Rodes took it to a firm of furriers the first thing on the Monday morning after the murder. Wanted it overhauled. The firm told us it was in need of a clean. At any rate, Rodes said it was a rush job. An American niece who owned it was due to go back on the Thursday night plane so he'd call for it on the Thursday morning. He didn't. They saw the papers this morning and gave us a ring. You see the point? He wouldn't have missed collecting that coat, and that makes him dead on the Thursday morning.

"Another thing that ties it in. A garage proprietor at Wood Green got into touch with the local police. I sent a couple of men down there. Rodes's old jalopy was there, and he'd been thinking of buying a new car. That's incidental. What we got was Rodes's lodgings and his landlady said she hadn't clapped eyes on him since he'd left early on the morning of the fourteenth. I needn't tell you that was a Thursday. She also gave permission for us to go over his two rooms. Didn't find anything, though, except the usual. And all the time up here we were getting a line on Rodes himself."

He turned to Hallows.

"Mr. Travers mightn't remember it. Bob, but you ought to. One of the first police scandals. About the biggest before Brighton. A C.I.D. sergeant and one of his men were running their own burglary racket. The sergeant's name was Harold Redway."

Hallows clicked his tongue exasperatedly. "Of course. I ought to've spotted Rodes as soon as I saw him."

"Well, that's it," Jewle said. "He got five years. When he came out he was lost track of for a year or two and then he turned up in Birmingham as a private enquiry agent, operating under the name of Roberts. That came out because they nabbed him for blackmailing a client. He got three years. When he came out again he put the touch on another client. It couldn't be proved, because the victim lost his nerve at the last moment, but Roberts is thought to have got about a hundred pounds. With that he shifted to London and bought an old car and changed to Harry Rodes.

"A leopard can't change its spots, so he began the same old game. Remember that all that stuff in his office was merely for show—except possibly the safe. He didn't need any case files. I'd say he did little peep-hole jobs, just enough to keep his head above water and pay for an occasional advertisement, and all the time he'd be waiting for another big job. That doesn't say he didn't put the screw on now and again, but it couldn't have been for much."

"Yes," I said. "And then he had the luck to get into the Matching affair."

"That's right," Jewle said. "The gun, by the way, was probably French or Italian—a six-point-three-five millimetre. It wouldn't have made all that noise. Also the old boy who keeps the shop underneath is a bit deaf."

"Would that be rare? I mean, the gun?"

"Good lord, no," he said. "That kind of gun can be picked up far more easily than English or American. We tried a reconstruction late last night, by the way. What we think is that Rodes was bending down and getting something out of the safe when the bullet hit him. His back, of course, to whoever fired."

That seemed to be about all. Hallows took advantage of the pause.

"Well, it mayn't seem all that important now—to you, I mean—but I've been doing some more digging myself. Rodes was also known in certain circles as Fraser, as you knew. What's important to us is that he had an engagement—on the Monday morning, the eleventh. I'm told it was—with another informant, and while this informant was waiting near the rendezvous, he saw Rodes go into the City

Trust Company. He was there about a quarter of an hour and when he turned up he apologised for being late. Said he'd had a bit of an accident. Slipped up on some ice and cut his head."

"That's right," Jewle said. "There was a scar. Hadn't even begun to heal up. Almost as if he'd been coshed or something a day or two before."

He suddenly looked even more interested.

"Depositing that jewellery. You think that's what he went there for?"

"Worth verifying," I said. "We can't handle it but you can. It might be worth quite a lot of money to us."

"Right," he said. "First thing in the morning I'll get in touch. The City Trust Company, you said?"

He made a note. The tea tray had long been a wreck and we got up to go. At the door he said something a bit startling.

"Would you mind waiting downstairs. Bob? There's something I'd like to mention to Mr. Travers."

This is it, I thought, but it wasn't.

"I think I'm beginning to see my way clear through all this maze," he told me. "I don't say it's final but I'd like to put something up to you. You know what I think?"

He opened a drawer and took out that report Hallows and I had made. A page corner was turned down.

"Don't be afraid of making objections," he told me, "but I'm pretty sure Moira Matching as good as killed herself." He smiled. "No, not what you think. The way I see it is that she employed Rodes in that jewellery business. She wanted someone to be that Martin J. Hamstall who was to get Matching to bring that jewellery home. It'd take a man like Rodes to think all that out, once he'd been approached. All he'd have to do was be on hand that Saturday evening and follow her in that jalopy of his. He did have it out that night and he didn't bring it in till the Sunday morning. It was probably he who gave her the dope to put in that glass of port."

"Sounds feasible to me," I said, "except for one thing Who shot Rodes?"

"Look," he said. "You've heard about Rodes. Hallows knows the kind of circles he was moving in. Someone thought he was being double-crossed. Or it might have been someone Rodes was putting the bite on, or both." He smiled. "Other people can slip Yale locks beside Bob Hallows."

"Well, it's your job," I said. "From now on, then, you'll be trying to find who that someone was. Shall we say, just for the files?"

He shrugged his shoulders. "If you like. But whoever shot Rodes has got to pay for it. He can talk to the judge about the motive."

That was all, except that be said he'd get in touch first thing in the morning with the City Trust Company, then give me a ring. There wasn't any need to keep Hallows, and I went home, too. If you go up Northumberland Avenue it isn't far to walk, and I wanted to think. By the lime I reached the flat, everything seemed about as good as it could be.

Jewle could have his theory as to who employed Rodes, and I could have mine. As to who'd killed Rodes, Jewle might be right I was prepared to cede the point, not that it seemed to matter. If anything it bolstered my theory. I hadn't been able to place Jean Lindman for that killing.

And what now? I asked myself. If that jewellery was really in a deposit box, then I could gratefully wipe my hands of the whole business. We'd have found both Moira Matching and the jewellery, and all that would remain would be to send John Hill an account. Jean would probably get her man, but what was that to me? The chances were that I'd never set eyes on her again. Unless, and I smiled wryly at the thought, they sent me an invitation to the wedding.

17

FIND THE LADY

By ELEVEN the next morning that business of retrieving the stolen jewellery was all over. John Hill had been there but not Matching. Jean Lindman had rung to say he wasn't feeling too well. She had a blinding headache and was sending their senior assistant, the one I was to know as Mr. Whiterod. Jewle and I made up the quartette. If the Agency had had to handle things alone, it might have taken days. That morning it took precisely half an hour from the time we entered the building to when we left.

I'd have thought that Whiterod would have taken the jewellery back to Walton Street, but he didn't. There's as much red-tape in the insurance business as anywhere else, and Hill look temporary charge of it. It was only a short distance to Lombard Street and I walked with him. As I told him, I wasn't going to have him coshed even if it meant starting recovering it all over again.

"Who's going to be happiest about all this?" I asked him.

"Everybody," he said. "Me, you, C.T., everybody."

"Your uncle?" I said. "Does he still have an interest in the business?"

He laughed.

"He *is* the business. Julian's only in charge. I suppose he's actually a paid employee. After that, the balance is controlled by C.T. Mind you, there's a pretty fair amount paid to his son's widow."

"Funny," I said. "I'd always regarded Matching as a reasonably wealthy man."

"He shouldn't be poor," he said. "As far as I know he has about three thousand a year, subject to tax, and an expense account of about two-fifty. He ought to get by on that."

He wanted me to have some coffee in his office but I said I was busy, so we shook hands at the swing doors. I watched him, and our bonus, safely through and began walking back to the Agency. A minute or two and I went into a milk bar instead and ordered coffee.

That business of Matching was on my mind. I don't like having a false impression of things, and mine has to be a suspicious nature. What I couldn't help wondering was how I'd have looked at the case if every conceivable circumstance connected with it had been in my mind. One thing, very definitely, would have had to be considered, the sort of thing with which we'd been concerned over and over again. If Matching had somehow faked that theft by his wife, then he'd have stood to gain. The insured value of the jewellery would have been paid to C.T. Haddowe and he'd have been in possession of the jewellery itself. The mounts wouldn't matter: the stones would have brought a handsome sum, and who in a better position to dispose of them privately than Matching himself.

Mind you, I knew I was chasing shadows, but there's a fascination at looking at things in retrospect, even if it means a recognition of the gross mistakes one might have made. I knew that it was Rodes who'd stolen that jewellery, and it couldn't have been from anyone else but Moira, and yet I kept on thinking. Matching's father had left nothing and it had been Julian who'd had to look after the house and the widow. And he must have been far from a three thousand a year man then.

What had he had when his mother died? I didn't know. Possibly a very, very few thousands. And that at the most. And only for a very short time. As soon as he'd married, there'd been the lavish improvements to Grange House. There'd followed the gift of a Jaguar and a mink coat—and what had been described as valuable jewellery: the jewellery, by the way, which hadn't been found. If my economics were right, all that expenditure would have virtually eliminated his capital. And it must have been costing a lot for mere living, what with Moira's expensive tastes and the salary of the Gambets.

Mine's a flibberty-gibberty sort of mind that's always darting off at angles, and I began thinking about that Saturday night at Grange House. Then something else emerged: something that had worried me a day or two back. Something to do with times, and why Moira should have waited by rights for two hours at Little Meadows till Carter came. A minute and I still saw no clue. Moira was in the habit of ringing Carter on a Saturday and she knew he couldn't arrive till ten. And why shouldn't she be there early? Nothing to do but stir up the fire in the lounge, pour herself a drink, put on a record and wait Also, when you looked at it fairly and squarely, it was Rodes who'd done the waiting—after he'd killed Moira.

All the same, I couldn't get rid of the idea that somewhere was something I was missing. Among the other things that I hate are untidy ends, and as soon as I was back at the Agency I tried to get hold of Carter. I was lucky. He said he wouldn't be going out for best part of an hour.

A taxi got me to his flat in twenty minutes, and his secretary showed me into his room. He looked a bit apprehensive.

"It's possible I may be able to do you a good turn," I told him. "Even clear you of all this business. On your part, you'll have to tell me the absolute truth. Don't tell me what you think I'd like to know. That's no good. Even if it seems to incriminate you in some way, I want the truth."

I began by asking him about those Saturday telephone calls to verify the times when he could get away.

"That's right," he said. "He was in on a Saturday so she used to ring me from upstairs."

"What'd she tell you that particular morning?"

He thought. "Well. I know she said she'd packed almost everything the previous day and had it in the car. And she wanted to know when I'd be along. The next time she called me—"

"Wait a minute. You mean she rang you twice?"

"That's right I'd told her to ring me again at the studio. Didn't know what time I'd actually be on, see? I might have got away earlier. It all depended. And that's why she rang. It had to be about half-past six because we were doing a quick rehearsal."

"And what did she say at half-past six?"

"Well, she wanted to know about me getting away, and I told her not much before nine." He thought for a moment. "I asked her if everything was all right and she said it was. I remember she said he'd gone out and she was all alone in the house and she was ringing from downstairs. That was a laugh."

"You mean it amused her because she had to ring from upstairs as a rule?"

"That's right."

"I see. And the married couple—the Gambets—weren't there either. She'd managed to get rid of them."

"As much him as her," he said. "I admit she'd mentioned it, but from what she'd told me she hadn't expected him to fall for it. It sort of dropped right into her lap, if you know what I mean. She'd been worrying about getting her things away and so on and then it went and turned out like that."

"And did she tell you anything about herself? When she'd be able to get away altogether?"

"Yes," he said slowly. "I remember she did. She was going to turn the gramophone on loud after they'd had their meal, and then he'd go into that room of his like he always did and then she'd start off a long-playing record and slip out. By the time it stopped she'd be well away."

"But he knew she was going away?"

"Yes, but not when. Not the actual day. She was keeping him on a string, see? If he'd known when, he might have tried to stop her."

That was all I virtually learned. The trouble with that case bad been that everything had been so apparently cut and dried that we hadn't bothered to dig deep and still more deep. I didn't do any stringing along. All I told Carter was that what he'd told me would almost certainly help, and what I chiefly remember is the kind of spaniel look in his eyes when he held out his hand at the door. And while I was having lunch at a near-by restaurant, I couldn't help wondering if Jewle's scathing accusations had been strictly just. It was Moira who'd thrust herself on Carter, and he'd done no more than most other men would have done in his case. Love and ethics are vastly different things.

My mind was so full of what I'd learned that morning that I felt the urge to be somewhere alone, and to think, so I rang the Agency and made my way to my club. In the afternoon the reading room is usually dead and, in any case. I'd only to close my eyes and pretend to be asleep. The upshot was that, after I'd been trying to concentrate for best part of an hour, I did fall asleep and it was after four o'clock when I woke. But for a member reading by the fire, I was alone.

I went to the cloak-room and dowsed my head in cold water. I had tea, and then I did what I've very rarely done—let chance decide. Mind you, I don't say I mightn't have cheated if the test had turned out differently, but I took the small change from my pocket and counted the heads and tails. The tails had it. That meant I ought to see Jewle. Before I could change my mind, I rang him on the club telephone. Matthews was there but Jewle mightn't be in till six. I took an irrevocable sort of header and said I wanted to see him urgently.

"Why not see me?"

"No disrespect," I said. "but it'd save time to start at the top. Be all right if I'm with you at six?"

He said he thought he could ensure Jewle's being there, so that was that. I hated the waiting. When a tooth aches, it's best to cut out hope and get along to the dentist in double-quick time. And it seemed an awful long time till at last I was in Jewle's room.

"What's all this about?" he said as he held out his hand. "Matthews here thinks you've got something to tell us."

I took off my hat and overcoat. It might be a longish session.

"Just something I'd like to put up to you," I said. "Don't think I'm being clever. It's only that I've had the chance to see things in a different light from you people here."

He smiled. "Why the apologies?"

"Just wanted to make my own position clear," I said. "You, for instance, were telling me a theory just about this time yesterday, so I'd like you to listen to one of mine."

"That's great," he said. He passed me his tobacco tin. "Make yourself comfortable and get it off your chest."

I stoked my pipe and got out the rough notes I'd made. "As I see it, we have to go a long way back," I said. Then I stopped. I put the notes back in my pocket.

"No," I said. "I think I'd rather go straight to the end. We can always go back. So what I'm going to try to prove to you is that it was Matching who killed his wife."

He stared. "That's a pretty big statement. And you say you can prove it?"

"I didn't say that," I told him. "I said I was going to try."

"Mind if what you say is taken down?"

"That's just the way I'd like it."

There was a queer sort of frigidity in the room till the stenographer came in. I got out my notes again and waited till he was ready.

"Check with John Hill for this, but when Matching's mother died, he couldn't have had much money. His actual financial position can be investigated through his bank. C.T. Haddowe was stiff the owner of the Walton Street business and all Matching got was three thousand a year plus an expense account. I think if you work it out, or get the facts from the Commissioners of Inland Revenue, you'll find that even after marriage he couldn't dispose of much more than two thousand a year.

"If that's so, then think of running expenses at Grange House. The Gambets couldn't cost under five hundred and they had to be fed. Moira had to have a private allowance, so add the lot together and I doubt if Matching came out even at the year's end. So where did the money come from to buy that mink coat, the Jaguar and the jewellery he gave her? I can't see how all that cost much under five thousand."

"You think he was robbing the till?" Matthews said.

"Let Mr. Travers finish," Jewle told him sharply. "This is beginning to be interesting."

"All that is for you people to test," I went on, "but I'm prepared to go as far as this, that Matching was in need of money. Remember there wasn't only what he'd already spent, but what he might need to go on bribing his wife, as it were, to stay with him. Then think of the kind of life he was leading at Grange House: the humiliations, the nagging, the fact that she'd insisted on a separate bedroom. Then go on as far as the early autumn when she began spending practically every weekend away. And almost daring him to do anything about it.

"What she didn't suspect, of course, was that he did do something about it. He employed Harry Rodes. Mind you," I told him quickly, "there's no proof. The evidence is largely circumstantial. Wait till you hear it all the same. All you have to accept for the moment is that Matching knew before very long just where Moira spent those weekends and with whom. You know how besotted he was, so you can guess the effect the information had on him. What I have to try to prove is that it made him ultimately murder her.

"Check with Carter and maybe the Gambets for most of what comes next. When Matching had worked himself up to the murder pitch—say in that last week when she'd told him she was going to leave him, and in her own time—then he started planning. In case you don't know it, he was a great reader of mystery stories, hence some of his ideas. In the first place he knew of her hostility to the Gambets so he suddenly acquiesced in the dismissal with salary in lieu of notice. That just suited Moira, too. It cleared the decks for packing up and getting the suitcases into the car. The irony was that it suited Matching far more. Check, as I said, and you'll piece together what actually happened on that Saturday night.

"Moira always rang Carter from her bedroom on a Saturday morning to find out what time he'd be at Little Meadows. On that particular morning, Carter wasn't dead sure, so he arranged to be rung at six-thirty at the studio where he was performing, and then he'd know. She told him her husband bad gone out and she was alone in the house, and she made a joke of being able for once to ring from the hall telephone. She also told him her plan for being able to get away for good after the evening meal and without her husband knowing till too late."

"That included the jewellery?"

I think I smiled.

"In the sense you mean there never *was* any jewellery. There never *was* any Martin J. Hamstall. There never *was* any dope in port. But to go on. Moira's plan after dinner was to play the gramophone so loud that it'd drive Matching as usual to his study. Then she'd put on a long-playing record and if he happened to become aware it had run down, by then she'd be gone for good. But what I say is this. Check with Lucy Milford and John Hill.

"Lucy Milford was the old family cook and she was induced to come and cook the dinner that evening. She left at about half-past six when there was nothing to do but put the meal on, and Matching was taking her back in his Humber. I say be drove out of earshot—just out of the gate—said he'd forgotten something and then went back in time to hear his wife telephoning to Carter. In other words, he was ready for her when she did that gramophone act after the meal. And he wasn't in bis study when the long-playing record went on. He was in the garage, waiting. And that's where he strangled her."

Jewle didn't interrupt: he just let out his usual deep breath.

"The next thing to do," I said, "was to bury her: in that hole he'd dug well out of sight in that top shrubbery. What happened is almost like a flash forward to Little Meadows. Rodes, as you told me, was waiting for the big bite, and he had an idea Matching was it. So he saw Matching with Moira in his arms making his way towards that shrubbery.

"'Anything wrong, Mr. Matching?'

"That would be Rodes.

"'You'd be a fool to bury her, Mr. Matching. Why not plant her on Carter? I'll fill the hole in and we'll see.'

"I think Rodes came back to the study after he'd cleaned the spade, and in time to see Matching taking the jewellery out of the safe. Don't ask me why, unless it was that it had to be taken out in any case. At any rate, Matching wasn't in any position to argue. Rodes pocketed the jewellery and then he put the body in the Jaguar after hiding the mink coat, and drove off to Little Meadows. He had quite a time to wait till Carter turned up. Much later he had to walk all the way back to near Grange House and collect his own car, and the coat."

"And that's all?"

"The rest you know," I told him. "Still, I'm ready to answer questions."

"Why did Matching break down in his office when you told him about discovering that hole?"

That was Matthews.

"Because his nerves were in shreds," I said. "Rodes had double-crossed him and there wasn't a thing Matching could do about it. That car should never have been found at Sevenoaks, for one thing: also Rodes was probably now swearing he didn't know what had happened to the body. Carter hadn't been framed and Matching didn't dare to take the risk of doing anything about that behind Rodes's back What it ultimately came to was that Rodes just had to be killed Matching killed him on the Thursday morning before he turned up for that meeting in Lombard Street. Check, and I think you'll find a gap between the time he should have reached London and the time of that meeting. I doubt if he even went to his office. And just one other thing that might have a bearing. Carter wanted an American tour. Matching was selling Grange House. For the same reasons?"

There didn't seem to be any more questions. Jewle took a turn about the room.

"No need to sign all that." He nodded back at the stenographer. "It's purely informative. If you like to wait, you can have a copy to check on."

He went out. The room seemed very quiet as I stoked my pipe again.

"That was a hell of a story you told us," Matthews suddenly said. "I will say this for it. It doesn't leave any loose ends."

"That's why I brought it to you," I told him.

Maybe he sensed that I didn't feel like doing any more talking, for he went out, too. When he came back, the stenographer was with him. I said I'd take my copy as spoken, and put it in my pocket. Then at last Jewle came back. He was looking pretty serious.

"I don't like it," he said. "I thought I'd shoot an arrow at a venture and I tried to get hold of Matching for a sort of general chat, just to do some sizing up, but he wasn't there. Gambet said he'd had a telephone message last night and had gone out somewhere. It wasn't with the car. And he didn't come in till well after midnight. Then this morning he went to town earlier than usual and he took a bag with him. Gambet didn't see it, but his pyjamas and toilet things are missing. Where he is we don't know. Gambet had tried the office when he didn't turn up at his usual time and there wasn't an answer. The place'd be shut."

He turned to me. "Suppose you've no idea where he might be?"

"No," I said. "You could try his uncle—C.T. Haddowe." I looked in my notebook and found the address but no telephone number.

There was nothing else for me to wait for. Matthews helped me on with my overcoat. Jewle patted me gently on the back as we went to the door.

"You may be right or you may be wrong but—well, thanks for coming."

As I walked slowly home I wondered about that other thing I ought to have told him—that Jean Lindman might know where Matching was. I also was almost certain that he'd bolted. That stupidly impulsive call I'd made the previous night had been a kind of match to set the explosive off: in other words, as soon as I'd finished ringing, she'd got into touch with him. I told her we knew about Rodes. I'd thought I was being clever—very clever—when asking what that name conveyed to her. I'd said the police were closing in. Give them a day or two and they'd have the whole thing tied up.

It was Matching, of course, who had asked her to ring me, even if the idea of getting me to her flat had been her own. Julian might have made the suggestion casually enough about obtaining that information, and, after all, a man should want to know the name of his wife's murderer. And there were plenty of reasons he could have given for not wanting to do the ringing himself.

There were, of course, two other points. Could Julian have told her the whole story? I thought not Whatever she thought of him, he'd no special regard for her. Hers wasn't the shoulder he'd want to weep on, So what about that other point—that she might have discovered things for herself. She was a pretty shrewd woman. She was also a woman in love: a woman to whom each of his gestures, words and looks would have conveyed infinitely more than they'd have done to me. In any case, there it all was. The morning ought to bring some definite news, and meanwhile I'd wipe the whole thing out. That was what I tried to do, and I never made a poorer hand of anything in all my life.

I was up early. At eight o'clock I rang Grange House Robert told me that the master hadn't been home, but late the previous night he'd rung to say he might be away for some days.

At a quarter to nine Jewle rang.

"No news yet," he told me. "No luck at Highgate last night either. He's probably lying up at a hotel."

"Probably," I said. "What's your next move?"

"Ports and airports. Any luck and we'll let you know."

I waited till a quarter past nine, then rang Walton Street. I recognised Whiterod's voice.

"No, sir. Mr. Julian isn't coming in today."

"Miss Lindman there?"

"Not at the moment, sir. She rang a few moments ago to say she mightn't be in till late. You'd like to leave a message?"

I said it wasn't all that important, thanked him and rang off. I grabbed my overcoat and hat and made for the nearest underground. It wasn't much after ten o'clock when I pushed the bell of Jean Lindman's flat.

She was wearing what might have been the same dark red jumper and black skirt. Her face was very pale and she might almost have been posing for me as she stood there rigidly for a moment.

"It's you," she said quietly. "I thought somehow you'd come."

"I'm here to help you. Jean. At any moment the police may be here."

She drew back to let me in. We went into the lounge. She didn't ask me to sit down.

"Look, Jean, if I'm going to help you, you've got to give me some straight answers. Is Julian here?"

"No," she said. "He's not here."

"But he's been here?"

She didn't answer for a moment: she had to think things out.

"Yes," she said. "But he's gone. Over an hour ago. I wanted him to stay but be wouldn't He slipped out when I'd left him for a moment."

"Mind if I sit down while you tell me about it? Why be was here all yesterday, for instance? And all night?"

Her cheeks flushed as she sat. I took the chair opposite. Two chairs. I thought, and two people talking long into the night before an electric fire.

"I'll tell you," she said. "There's a telephone extension at my bedside and I was woken up soon after midnight It was Julian. I said he was to try and get some sleep and then come here. And he did. He got here yesterday morning soon after nine and I made him stay."

"You knew what he'd done?"

"Yes," she said quietly. "But I didn't really know everything till he told me last night."

"But you'd suspected?"

"Yes. I'd suspected."

"You'd like to tell me why?"

"It doesn't matter much now," she said, "but there were little irregularities. Things I couldn't account for. Sales I hadn't been notified about."

"To put it bluntly, he had to get money because his wife was ruining him. Anything else?"

"Yes," she said. "There was a book."

"An account book?"

She shook her head.

"No. It was on the Thursday. He'd gone up to the workshop and I had to go into his room and I saw something green in his overcoat pocket. Just the end of it protruding. A book with a green cover. One of those paperbacks he used to read on the train."

Her lip drooped. On some faces it might have been a sneer.

"I wondered what kind of book it was. I'll never forget the title—not now. *Miles of Murder*. I opened it and looked at a page or two and put it back. The next afternoon—the Friday—he told me about the possible sale of that jewellery, and how he was seeing the customer at Brighton, an American called Martin J. Hamstall."

"And then?"

"Well, a Martin Hamstall was the man who employed the detective in that book."

I moistened my lips. Matching had wanted a name and he'd found one.

"I've got a good memory," she was saying. "That's partly what I'm employed for."

"Yes," I said. "And you've no idea where he is?"

"No. I wanted him to try and get out of the country but he wouldn't say yes or no. Then he just went out, as I said."

"You condoned that killing?"

Her head went back. Her eyes could have flashed but I didn't see them.

"You can't do anything to him for that. He was temporarily out of his mind. She'd driven him mad."

"Maybe," I told her quietly. "That'll be between him and his lawyers if and when he comes to trial. And what about you now?"

"I'm going to the office. Someone has to be there."

"Mind if I go with you some of the way?"

"That's nice of you. I'll be ready in a minute."

She disappeared through the door to the right. That would be her bedroom. A moment and I heard the flush of the toilet. I don't know why, but I slipped quickly across the room and gently opened the door. It was her bedroom, as I'd thought. In the second before I closed the door again, I saw the bed. It looked like a four-foot bed. The clothes had been drawn back and on the low bolster were two disordered pillows. I closed the door gently and slipped back almost shamefacedly to my chair. I'd caught a glimpse of something which was no business of mine. *Something that had come too late.*

It was a good five minutes before she appeared. We were almost at the door when the telephone bell went. She stared at me, then she ran. The bedroom door was open and I watched her as she held the receiver. I noticed that the bed had been made. Now there was just one pillow.

I drew back again. The few quick words were so vehement that I knew to whom she must be listening. A moment or two and she was back.

"Julian! He's gone to Walton Street. I've *got* to get him away."

"I'll go," I said. "You can follow me."

I heard her call something as I went along the corridor but she had no hope of catching me. All that interminable journey I was wondering if she'd found a quicker way, and would be there first. But she hadn't.

Whiterod looked mildly up from the counter.

"Ah, Mr. Travers! Mr. Julian is in now, sir, if you'd like to go straight through."

I closed the lobby door behind me. Faint sounds of hammering were coming from the workshop upstairs. They weren't distracting Julian Matching. He lay with his head and arms across his desk and still in bis hand was a black, ugly, snub-nosed thing. I'm no great authority, but it looked to me like a six-point-three-five. Not that it mattered. All that mattered was first to dial Whitehall 1212. And then to head off Jean Lindman so that, when Jewle came, she wasn't in that room.

THE END

9 781915 014665